SNAKES

AND

LADDERS

ALSO BY VICTORIA SELMAN

Ziba MacKenzie Series

Blood for Blood

Nothing to Lose

SNAKES
AND
LADDERS

VICTORIA
SELMAN

THOMAS & MERCER

Text copyright © 2019 by Victoria Selman
All rights reserved.

Published by Thomas & Mercer, Seattle

www.apub.com

Amazon, the Amazon logo, and Thomas & Mercer are trademarks of Amazon.com, Inc., or its affiliates.

ISBN-13: 9781542008792
ISBN-10: 1542008794

Cover design by Dominic Forbes

Printed in the United States of America

To my best boys, Max and Joey.
I love you to Heaven and back.
PS You can read this when you're bigger.
It's not a bedtime story . . .

CHAPTER 1

Dr Vernon Sange, killer of twelve, lies on his bunk. His hands are interlaced behind his head, his film-star face white as butcher's paper from being inside so long. On his chest, a portable CD player moves up and down in time with his measured breaths. The 'Queen of the Night' aria plays through his earbuds.

His eyes move around the room but his head stays still on its stalk. Every so often he flicks the tip of his tongue over his teeth, tapping the sharp point of his canine then drawing it back into his mouth.

He glances at the small table bolted to the floor. On it, a stack of Penguin Classics and fat history paperbacks are arranged alphabetically, each annotated with comments, quotes and corrections in Crayola felt-tip pen.

Dr Sange isn't allowed ballpoints or pencils. He's not allowed anything with a hard cover either.

The *Daily Telegraph* is on the table beside the books. It's been quartered precisely. Seven pages in, a man's name has been circled. The ink has bled through seven sheets.

There is no noise in here apart from Dr Sange's slow, rhythmic breathing. His cell is the only one in the corridor. Six by nine by twelve feet. Windowless. The walls grey up to head height.

As Dr Sange's thoughts coalesce, his pupils contract into pinhole points of black. His thumbs cruise his occipital bone.

'The husband!' he whispers, his voice hoarse from lack of use. His lips curl into a smile. He'll make the call tomorrow.

'My move,' he says.

CHAPTER 2

FBI Academy, Quantico, Virginia

'What makes a person murder someone they've never met? What makes them kill stranger after stranger until they're stopped? What makes a monster?'

I surveyed the packed auditorium. Hundreds of NATs, New Agent Trainees, all wearing blue polo shirts and khakis. All with the same bright-faced focus.

I'd been scheduled to give this lecture series two years ago, right after Duncan was shot.

We'd been approaching our first wedding anniversary. He'd been invited to run a set of FBI National Academy Associates classes at the same time as I'd be giving my talks. The plan was to travel up to Shenandoah afterwards, take some time out together. We'd been drooling over national park brochures for weeks: waterfalls, wooded hollows, mountain vistas. So damn beautiful you could hardly believe the place was real.

'I can't wait. Just you and me, hen,' he'd said, pulling me in for a kiss. 'A break from our lives.'

Though it turned out we didn't need a holiday for that. Not with an assassin aiming his rifle at my husband's head.

This was the first time I'd been back to Quantico since the shooting. And despite the intervening period, standing at the podium now, where I should have been then, I felt the familiar squeeze in my throat and tightening in my chest.

There's always a trigger involved before a serial killer hunts for the first time. My black dog, the spectre that haunts my days and nights, is a killer too. It doesn't take much to draw him out of the dark.

I swallowed hard and ploughed on. No way was I going to get all dewy-eyed in front of these guys.

'Why does it matter?' I said, looking at their expectant faces. 'Why do we care what makes murderers?'

A beefy bloke who looked like he'd have done well on the Yellow Brick Road run, the final part of the Academy's gruelling fitness challenge, raised an arm as thick as my thigh.

'The more we understand them, the more likely we are to catch them, ma'am.'

I smiled, and not just because of the military-style 'ma'am', which always reminds me of my army days.

No one appreciates the benefits of criminal profiling better than the FBI. Quantico's the birthplace of behavioural analysis. It's where the magic started.

I was just about to quote Robert Ressler at them – that line about how understanding one killer gives us the ammo we need to track the next one – when the door opened. An agent I recognised from Behavioral Analysis ushered in a man in a wrinkled suit, slept in by the looks of it.

I could tell the guy was a Brit before he even opened his mouth. Something about the way he carried himself.

'Mrs MacKenzie,' he said, his voice, all boarding-school plum, carrying across the lecture hall as he walked up the centre aisle. 'I'm sorry to interrupt. I've been sent by Scotland Yard. We need your help.'

CHAPTER 3

I was off the stage before he finished speaking. He'd come all the way from London to Quantico. That's over eight hours' flying time and a fifty-minute drive at the end of it. He hadn't pitched up to ask me to a wine and cheese party then.

'What's the sit-rep, DC Barnwell?' I said as we walked out of the theatre together.

He looked surprised. We hadn't gone through intros.

'Name's on your visitor badge. Want to tell me what's going on?'

A thick beige file stamped with the Scotland Yard logo was clamped to his chest, a cashmere-blend coat was draped over his arm and although his breath was minty, he was giving off a sour smell.

He must have come straight from the airport. And his demeanour told me he wasn't planning on getting a room at the Holiday Inn or stopping off for waffles at the IHOP later.

'Is there somewhere we can talk?'

His eyes were bloodshot, with fat sandbags beneath them. He suppressed a yawn.

'Let's get some coffee,' I said. 'Canteen's just down here.'

He took in the pristine cafeteria with its mounted cereal dispensers, snack baskets and soda machines.

'Beats the Yard.'

The FBI seal dominated the wall behind the gleaming chrome serving station, the American flag hung on a pole beneath it. And a big stars and stripes helium balloon bobbed over the muffin display.

On the wall outside was a series of FBI movie posters. *J. Edgar. In the Line of Duty. The FBI Story*, autographed in marker pen by Jimmy Stewart.

'Not easy to forget where you are, is it?' I said, handing him a flat white before leading the way to a window table overlooking the Bureau's landscaped gardens. Even at this time of year the grass was lush.

I sat down and took a sip of my espresso, extra shot.

I hadn't slept in my clothes like Barnwell but I needed a caffeine fix all the same.

'I'm sorry for the interruption back there.' He blew the steam off his coffee. 'I realise you weren't supposed to be coming home for another few months.'

Coming home? I raised an eyebrow. So, this wasn't just about getting my take on a difficult case.

'You're here to bring me back?'

He nodded.

'The thing is, this is something only you can help with.'

'I'm flattered, detective, but I'm not the only profiler on the Yard's books.'

'Right now, you may as well be.'

'I don't understand.'

His voice changed. His expression too. From the outdoor range came the distant sound of peppered gunfire.

'You've heard about the PRK?' he said. 'God, isn't that an awful nickname?'

He pronounced it 'gawd'. You don't get many posh types at the Yard but that's not what made my ears prick.

6

The Pink Rose Killer was big news, even on this side of the pond. So far, he'd claimed five victims over a four-week period. Each time he cut off a different part of his victim's face, leaving behind a single pink rose on the corpse.

And as yet the police had no leads apart from the Ripper-style messages he'd started sending to Duncan's best friend, Jack Wolfe over at the *Daily Telegraph*, after the most recent murder. Though why he was sending them to Wolfie was unclear.

I slurped the crema off my espresso while stifling a yawn. I'd been having trouble sleeping, my mind fizzing with the lectures I was giving and trying to fight off my black dog.

I had nothing on Barnwell, though. The guy looked like he was ready to fall into his coffin.

I'm familiar enough with what goes on at the Yard to know he'd have already clocked up a fortnight's worth of nineteen-hour days. And without an arrest, the pressure wouldn't be letting up any time soon.

'Couldn't we have talked on the phone?' I said. 'Saved you a trip? They do have video conferencing here, you know.'

Barnwell looked at his hands.

'A phone call isn't enough. We need you on this. Full-time. And given . . . developments, DCI Falcon wanted me to get you up to speed on the way back to London so you can hit the ground running.'

He was bouncing his knee up and down. His index finger danced on the table.

The killer was on a spree but these were still relatively early days.

So why recall me now? What wasn't I being told?

And what made him think I was the only one who could help?

CHAPTER 4

'What aren't you telling me, detective?'

Barnwell wet his lips, couldn't meet my eye.

'DCI Falcon's been getting phone calls. From Monster Mansion.'

My brows shot up.

HMP Wakefield is a Category A prison, the biggest high-security slammer in Western Europe. The nickname comes from the type of evil bastards that call it home. Ian Huntley, Harold Shipman and Michael Sams have all resided under its steel reinforced roof.

But which of the inmates dialled up the Detective Chief Inspector? And why?

Barnwell picked his nails.

'The caller was Dr Sange.'

A cold jet blasted down my spine. For a moment, both of us were still. The name, Vernon Sange, always has an effect. Even on me.

'Amazing to think they caught him because of you,' Barnwell said, breaking the silence, his eyes all big and round, glued to my face.

'Nearly ended up being for nothing, given everything that went missing before the trial. Without that anonymous tip, the bastard might still have got off.'

Barnwell nodded fast, like one of those bobbing-dog toys people stick on their rear parcel shelves.

'I managed to get a spot in the public gallery on the first day of the trial with some friends from the Yard. The way he convinced Judge Jewell to throw out that evidence. Wow. I mean, I know he's an Oxford don and everything, but he had no legal training. It was a bold move, representing himself, don't you think?'

'It had bugger all to do with boldness. Sange is a show-off. He wanted to be the star of the show. It's why he sacked his lawyers, he didn't want them hogging his spotlight.'

I shifted in my seat as I thought back to the way he'd winked and smiled at the jury during cross-examination. Sange is one of the coldest killers I've ever come across. Camouflaged in his university gown and surprisingly strong for his size, he lured his teenage prey with his charm and good looks before snaring them in a snake-like grip, his body wrapped round each victim, increasing the pressure as they struggled for breath, cutting off their circulation until their hearts gave out.

Yet there are still people out there who question his guilt. You hear them on breakfast TV sometimes. 'He just doesn't look the type to kill,' they say. 'He seems so nice, always smiling.' Rumour is, he's even got a cult following on the dark web.

Mind you, on the other side of the board you've got all the bloggers and Twitterati who attribute every unsolved murder to him. Three years after he was put away, and the Butcher of Balliol hashtag is still trending. Either way, there isn't a person in the country who doesn't have an opinion about him.

'So, what does he want with the DCI?' I said to Barnwell now.

'He's about to be extradited to the States. Florida. He's facing the needle.'

'I heard that. But why? I realise he's a US citizen, though shouldn't extradition cancel out the death penalty?'

'Funnily enough, there's a group of politicians who've raised a number of questions in the House on that exact point. Apparently, Dr Sange was honing his skills at Stanford before he came to the UK, so normal rules don't apply. But ironically it's the murder in Florida that they're pinning on him for extradition for the death penalty.'

'The system playing the man who played the system.'

There was something artistic about it.

I couldn't help smiling.

Barnwell didn't smile back. For the second time, he couldn't meet my eye.

I cocked my head. Waited.

'Thing is, the whole extradition business is a bit of a ticking clock for us.'

The flesh tightened on my frame as he lined up the shot.

'Dr Sange claims to know the identity of the Pink Rose Killer. And from what he's told us, we're ready to believe him. But there's a catch . . .'

CHAPTER 5

'What's the catch?' I said.

Barnwell hesitated, looked at his hands.

'He'll only talk to you.'

The demand wasn't as strange as it might have sounded. I'd almost been waiting for Vernon Sange to make a move.

I was the one who'd pulled off his mask, developing the profile that led to his capture after a year-long Scotland Yard investigation into a succession of killings came up empty. I'd been analysing offenders for years with the special forces, but this was the case that got me noticed.

Including by Sange.

After his trial he sent me a letter, the notepaper thin and prison-nondescript, unlike the embossed Balliol College stationery he'd have been used to.

The message itself was only one line long, written in Latin, the letters perfectly formed, almost unnaturally regular. An artist and a logician; highly organised, meticulous and intense. A man who left nothing to chance.

Alea iacta est.

It was a quote from Caesar, according to Google. *The die is cast.*

Typical, I'd thought at the time. Making sure I don't forget him. Peacocking just like he did in front of the journalists every day in court.

I'd scrunched it up and chucked it in with the kitchen waste, where it had gradually been buried by coffee grounds and the orange rind Duncan would peel away from the fruit in one long unbroken coil.

Shortly after my husband was killed, I received something else from the Butcher. An anthology of Latin poetry.

The card had simply been signed, *A concerned friend.* But the writing was the same as on the first note.

I was brought up to treat books with respect, but this one ended up in the same place as the letter.

Now, listening to Barnwell talk, I couldn't help wondering if they were both part of a bigger picture. There was nothing spontaneous about Vernon Sange, as his kills showed. I imagine if you played chess with him, his whole game would be in 3D. Just like the way he reeled in his victims.

He'd claimed to know the identity of the Pink Rose Killer and obviously said enough for Falcon to take him seriously, despite the terrible history between them. But that didn't mean he wasn't bluffing.

I'd watched the interview tapes back when he was arrested, analysed his facial expressions and body language. Consequences don't mean the same thing to him as they do to other people.

When faced with the prospect of life imprisonment, Sange's pulse rate didn't change, his ocular muscles didn't flicker. Months later, when he was led out of court to start his sentence, the only expression on his face was disdain.

'What makes you think this isn't just a bid for attention?' I said to Barnwell. 'Or an attempt to delay his extradition? The stakes couldn't be higher.'

Sange might not respond to punishment, but he did love himself. No way would he willingly offer himself up to Death Row.

Barnwell twisted his cup on its saucer. His nails were clean and buffed. His skin had a soft pink look.

'There was some debate internally. I mean, given the timing and everything . . . It took the DCI a while to buy it.'

No surprise there.

The stress of the Butcher's case cost him, besides what happened with Janie. A peptic ulcer, his wife very nearly leaving him, and a panic attack so severe he was rushed to hospital with suspected coronary failure.

DCI Falcon would be the last person to give Vernon Sange the benefit of the doubt. Nor would he want anything to do with him. He may have got his scars five years ago but, like his daughter's, they were still raised and raw. It wouldn't take much to make them bleed.

I watched Barnwell closely.

'What does he say now?'

'He thinks Dr Sange may not know as much as he's letting on. But he knows something.'

'What makes him think that?'

'He has information about the crime scenes we haven't released to the media.'

I raised an eyebrow.

'Go on.'

I clasped my hands together. My thumb rubbed against my knuckles. Under the table, my toes jittered. Even when I sleep my body doesn't quit moving.

Barnwell took a breath.

'The killer puts a pink rose on his victims' corpses. But that's not all he does. He leaves another item by each of the bodies.

13

Always something different. So far we haven't been able to find a link between them.'

'What sort of items?'

He rattled off a list, ticking each item off on his fingers.

'Wine-soaked bread. A charcoal drawing of a wolf. A little plastic horse, the sort you get in a kid's farmyard set. Charred sticks. And in the most recent murder, goat meat.'

'Goat meat? Bit bizarre. There can't be many places in London selling that.'

'More than you'd think, actually.'

I sucked the edge of my thumb. The items had to mean something, but what?

'There's more,' said Barnwell. 'Dr Sange predicted the date of the last murder. And he got it right. It wasn't a guess. He knew.'

CHAPTER 6

I ran a fingertip round the rim of my cup, nuking it out.

'Sange must be communicating with the Pink Rose Killer,' I said. 'There's no other way he'd know so much.'

'We thought that too. I went up to Wakefield myself to question the guards. I examined the visitor logs and his mail too. It's monitored, obviously, and the prison keeps records of who he's writing to and who's writing to him. But it wasn't an easy task. Dr Sange gets hundreds of letters every month and there's nothing even vaguely referring to the murders in any of his correspondence.'

'Still popular as ever then.'

Each day of his trial, women had queued to get a place in the public gallery, plenty camping overnight outside the Old Bailey to try and secure a spot. Scuffles broke out on a regular basis.

'You should see his fan mail,' Barnwell said. 'There's one woman who's written to him forty-eight times. A twenty-six-year-old virgin from Wyoming, apparently. Says she wants to marry him.'

I rolled my eyes.

'She signs off "Always yours", and tells him she's sad because she never got the chance to make love to him.'

'A killer with groupies. How original.'

He looked surprised.

'It has a name. Hybristophilia. Or Bonnie and Clyde Syndrome. A condition where people get turned on by evil bastards. It's actually more common than you'd think.'

'Really?'

'Aye. Richard Ramirez received thousands of letters from female fans. He even got married to one of them. Jeffrey Dahmer was sent money totting up to over $12,000 from his admirers. And Peter Sutcliffe, the Yorkshire Ripper, still gets swamped with cards and snaps of women showing too much skin. Lingerie too.'

Barnwell shuddered. He had dandelion-clock hair. It moved when his head did. You could picture it blowing off on a windy day.

'Doesn't make sense. I mean, I know everyone thinks he's so good-looking, but still.'

I shrugged.

There's nowt so strange as folk, Duncan would have said, his voice momentarily clear in my head as if he'd really spoken. He's always there, easily summoned. Though since arriving in Quantico, the memories have been calling to me more than usual.

I swallowed hard, pushed them down.

'I'd like to go through the letters myself,' I said. 'Compare them to a profile. It wouldn't be the first time a serial killer's admirer has tried to get her crush's attention by deadly means.'

Barnwell's eyes stretched wide. They were big and cornflower blue, gave his face a baby look.

'Really?'

'You've heard of Veronica Compton?'

'Who?'

What were they teaching them at Hendon? The police training college. Made me feel my age. Thirty-four and I've already lived a lifetime.

'She was part of Ken Bianchi's fan club. The Hillside Strangler. He got her to kill for him using his MO to make it look like the

16

authorities had got the wrong man. The girl bungled it, though. Ended up in Washington Correctional Center.'

'Shit!'

I smiled.

'My point is, we should dive deeper into the mailbag.'

Barnwell nodded but I could see his mind was moving elsewhere.

'What is it, detective?'

'Dr Sange has given us the next murder date. March 17th.'

It was my turn to swear. The 17th of March was just three days away.

We needed to get back to London on the double.

Because the Butcher may be playing a game, but the next move was mine.

CHAPTER 7

The Artist leans over the bath, pouring in a capful of Radox Muscle Soak and stirring the water until the bubbles fluff and multiply.

Herb-scented steam wafts off the water's surface. It settles on the window, clouding up the glass, obscuring the tiny carving on the inside of the frame made many years ago.

The thin-as-a-pin lines, once arterial red, are now a rusty brown. The colour, so well camouflaged against the wood, renders the drawing practically invisible. A secret talisman. A protection against evil spirits. An offering of love. 'Odi et amo. Sed sine te non potero vivere.' I love you and I hate you. But I can't live without you.

The Artist kisses the amulet, an always-worn locket containing the picture of a god, then hurries down to the kitchen to fetch Mother for her ablutions, pausing only to unwrap the new bunch of flowers purchased earlier from the stall by the station. In the background, the 'Nessun Dorma' aria reaches its crescendo on the record player as the ice-hearted princess succumbs to Prince Calaf.

'Why are you smirking like that?' Mother says, eyes narrowed. 'It's creepy.'

Then a beat later, 'What have you done?'

CHAPTER 8

Dulles International Airport

The departure gate at Dulles International was teeming with men in navy blazers and tasselled slip-ons. Out of the picture window, a 747 began its taxi to the runway, while inside the tannoy system pinged constantly.

I let out a sigh. Being in Quantico had catapulted Duncan's loss to the front of my mind, as I'd known it would. My black dog is nothing if not predictable. But despite that, I'd got a kick out of being there.

The Academy gave birth to behavioural science. No one values profiling like the FBI. All too often at Scotland Yard, I have to justify what I do to the senior investigation officers I'm teamed up with. At Quantico, no one questions the merits.

Next to me, Barnwell was leaving a voicemail for his mother. I couldn't help earwigging.

'Hope your flat's warm enough, Mama,' he said. 'Make sure the thermostat's turned up.'

Solicitous, I thought. Caring. He couldn't be much younger than I am. Twenty-seven tops, possibly not that long out of college. But given what he was saying, his mother was clearly elderly. Likely living alone. A widow, like me. Leans on him.

And with that thought, another followed fast. Jack.

The time difference between Virginia and London, combined with the long days spent in the lecture theatre and long nights putting in face-time at the Boardroom bar, meant I hadn't spoken to Wolfie more than a handful of times since I'd been away. And I'd missed him.

Before I'd left for the States, things had changed between us. We still got on as well as we ever had. Being with him, I don't have to think about what to say or what he might think of me. It's easy, like slipping into a hot bath after a long day out in the cold. But ever since he wound up in hospital after that car incident engineered by the same mamzer bastards who'd killed Duncan for getting too close to the 'Sunlight' conspiracy, there's been something else too. A possibility of more; unacknowledged but definitely there.

I glanced at my watch. 21.50. London was five hours ahead. But knowing him, there was a chance he'd still be awake.

There was a click as the lines connected.

You've reached Jack Wolfe. Sorry I can't take your call. You know what to do.

It was a long shot, but disappointment filled my belly all the same.

I didn't leave a message.

'I'll call you when we've landed.' Barnwell glanced at me. His message could have been a podcast, it was so long. 'Take care of yourself, Mama. Love you.'

Feels the need to look after her, I thought. They're obviously close then. An only child, probably.

I'm an only child too, though no one could accuse me and my mother, Emmeline, of being close.

'You were a surprise,' she used to say when I was a kid. I may have been in pigtails, but I knew enough to know unplanned meant unwanted.

We are now inviting those passengers seated in rows 1 to 30 to come forward.

'Ready?' Barnwell said, putting his phone away, his apple cheeks Braeburn-red.

'Aye.'

I took a last look over my left shoulder.

One of Duncan's silly superstitions. He used to say it meant you'd come back.

CHAPTER 9

Scotland Yard, London

It may have been the middle of March, but it was snowing when we arrived at the Yard, the flakes whirling round so thickly we had to strain to make out what was in front of our noses. Catching the red-eye then coming straight here didn't do much to help. Neither one of us could see straight.

Course, if we'd been on FBI business we might have been able to wangle a private jet, or at the very least go club. But this was the UK. Barnwell and I flew coach.

He took me through the files on board, laying them out on the tray tables, the shadow of his pen moving across the pages as he talked. We kept our voices down, our heads bent over the reports. The last thing this case needed was the other passengers listening in. In an ideal world, I'd have been briefed in private, but every minute we were stuck in the cabin was another minute closer to the next victim being killed. We didn't have the luxury of waiting for an office with a door.

The first body was discovered in Hampstead, north London, in the woods at West Heath. The sort of neighbourhood where people were more used to seeing Hermès than homelessness.

'Any staging?' I asked.

Barnwell nodded.

He dug the photos out and handed them to me. 'The body was in a kneeling position in the centre of a rough circle drawn in the ground with a foreign object, a stick according to Forensics, judging by the width and shape of the line. Plenty of those around. CSI also found a number of long hairs with the follicles still attached around the perimeter.'

'The victim's?'

'No. Tests suggest they belonged to an older woman. In her early seventies. No match on the system, though.'

'So, unless we're looking at a geriatric killer, he brought them with him.'

'Why would he do that?'

I shrugged.

'All I know is if he did, it's an important part of the signature.'

'The things a perpetrator does that are extraneous to the commission of the crime?'

I smiled. Someone had done their homework.

'This is the initial wound and also the one that killed her,' said Barnwell, indicating a throat laceration. 'He severed the carotid straightaway. Blood spatter patterns suggest he tilted the head downwards.'

So someone who knew what he was doing, who'd cut flesh before. Practised, probably. First time, there are always hesitation marks, regardless of an offender's lust for blood.

I pictured the offender leaning over his kneeling victim, slicing his blade through her jugular. This was a slaughter. But that's not all the photo showed.

I held it a little way from my face. My long-sightedness comes from my mother. It's one of the few things we have in common.

'You say the perp only needed one cut to kill her, but there are multiple stab wounds here.'

Barnwell nodded.

'They were administered after her throat was cut.'

'So, the kill itself is clean and controlled but then our guy loses it. Gets in a frenzy. High on the blood.'

He looked at me.

'What's that tell us?'

'That, like all serial killers, this perp craves power and order. Though in his case, what he craves most is command over himself and the impulses that rule him. He's trying to be someone he's not but he can only act the part for so long until his true self comes out.'

Barnwell ski-jumped his lip, looked impressed.

'Anything else?'

'There are definite sacrificial elements here. Victim kneeling. Ritual-type killing. Body placed in a circle. I wonder whether the items left by the body tie in with that. The goat meat and so on.'

'Maybe.'

'What about other markers? Any satanic symbols nearby?'

'No. But all the vics were found in similar positions and killed in the same way. The others weren't murdered in the woods, though. They were discovered on the steps of different Catholic churches around London.'

That much I already knew. The US papers were carrying the story on its front pages, same as in the UK.

'The girls were abducted from the West End?'

'Yuh.'

It sounded like 'yah'. I could have been talking to Prince Charles. Though he was missing the sure-of-himself posture that usually comes with an officer-class accent.

'The perp has a connection with both areas,' I said. 'But given where he dumps the bodies, Hampstead is likely to be the place he knows best, especially given the distance from the abduction sites.

It's either near where he lives now or where he spent his childhood. Either way, that's his comfort zone. His anchor point.'

I opened the autopsy file. The victims looked young. Children almost. I've spent my adult life hunting killers. But the sadness of murder, the lives ended before they've had the chance to blossom, the people left behind, gets me every time.

Means you care, Duncan used to say.

Not sure that's always such a good thing, I'd tell him. Caring blurs your vision, gets in the way of the job. It's why surgeons don't operate on family. And operatives with children don't get to bust paedophile rings.

These days I wonder if I got it wrong, though. Caring makes you human. It's the one thing that differentiates us from the monsters we hunt.

'No defence wounds,' I said now, examining the photos. 'No scratches on the hands or broken nails. So, no struggle. And no ligature marks round the wrists either. Means he lures them with a ruse, then drugs them.'

Barnwell nodded.

'There were traces of diazepam in their systems.'

'This is an organised killer, despite his issues with impulse control. He comes to his kills prepared. Forward planning suggests experience. High IQ too.'

Barnwell smiled in a shy sort of way.

'Profiling's amazing. The way you can deduce so much about an offender from what they do.'

'What plus why equals who.'

My mate Ressler again, the man who coined the term 'serial killer'.

Barnwell nodded, smiled again.

Good to know I've got an ally, I thought. Even if he does look like he's just out of short trousers.

By the time we walked past the iconic revolving sign in the courtyard of Scotland Yard and through the sliding glass doors, I had a pretty good handle on the case. Though I still couldn't work out where Vernon Sange fitted into it all.

How did he know so much about the Pink Rose Killer if he wasn't in contact with him?

'Ziba!' said DCI Falcon, coming into the reception area to meet us. 'I'm so sorry to drag you back like this.'

'Happy to help, sir.'

He clasped my hand in both of his. His skin was warm, thawed mine out.

'You look well,' I said.

There was more colour in his face since I'd last seen him and the swelling round his finger joints had gone down, the signet ring he always wore no longer cutting into his flesh.

'Marie's had me on some Mayo Clinic diet off the internet. Lots of green vegetables, herb tea and salmon. Supposed to be good for the gout. But I don't half miss my coffee.'

'I'm sure.'

Nothing would persuade me to give up lifer juice. Or red wine.

We walked over to the lifts, Barnwell insisting on hefting my suitcase. It might have been a suck-up move but the quiet way he did it showed it wasn't about impressing the boss. That impressed me.

Falcon hit the call button.

'So, Vernon Sange . . .'

We locked eyeballs. The blood left Falcon's face. Not surprising, given what the Butcher nearly took from him.

'I realise he seems to have intel, but I can't help wondering if this business with the Pink Rose Killer is just another ploy for attention. We both know how much he loves the show.'

Falcon nodded.

'I'll never forget him in court, pressing the CSI witness to give up every gory detail of the disposal site just so he could relive it. Sick fuck.' I raised an eyebrow. Falcon doesn't often drop the F-bomb. 'How in hell's name can all those people think the bastard's innocent? Did you read about that idiot student of his? Called Sange the nicest man he'd ever known. "A lovely guy", he said.' He shook his head. 'Pete's sake!'

'He didn't fool everyone.'

I thought of Jack, calling Sange out for what he was right from the start: 'A malignant narcissist with more than one screw loose.'

He got that one right, and it was a line that stuck.

The lift doors hissed open and Falcon stood back to let me go first.

'Christ knows, no one hates Sange more than me,' he said as they snapped shut. 'And I'd like nothing more than to write this off as one of his games. But unfortunately there's only one way to do that.'

'By going up to Wakefield prison,' I said, finishing the thought for him.

CHAPTER 10

Falcon led the way into the MIR, the major incident room; a hive-busy open-plan space papered with maps and crime scene photos the same way an undertaker's is decked out with images of headstones and urns.

Suck it up, MacKenzie, I thought, throwing off the memory. Duncan's ghost is always strongest here at the Yard. It's where we first met and fell in love. And where I came to rebuild my life after he was killed.

I looked around, counted eighteen detectives, nearly all white males; on the phone, tapping their keyboards, scurrying between desks with stacks of paper and cans of Coke.

I was taking it all in, when—

Jesus fuck, not him!

'Nigel,' said Falcon, waving over a skinny-wristed man with bone-white skin, whose face contorted the second he spotted me.

The feeling was mutual.

DI Nigel Fingerling and I worked together hunting the London Lacerator. And we didn't get on one bit.

'MacKenzie,' he said, his voice both patronising and cold at the same time.

I matched his warmth.

'Hello, Nigel.'

'The old team together again,' said Falcon with a big smile, a hand on each of our shoulders.

Politic as ever, I thought. There's no way he could have missed the mutual antipathy between me and DI Donkey Dick.

'I thought I'd sit in on the briefing this morning,' Falcon said. 'Mac, do you think you're in a position to give a preliminary profile? I realise it'd only be top line at this stage, but a steer from you would be helpful, don't you agree, Nigel?'

'Of course,' he said, dead behind the eyes.

Hocus-pocus, he'd called profiling when we'd first met. 'Nothing more than a fancy word for conjecture'. Never mind that it led to the arrest of a serial killer who'd eluded capture for the past twenty-five years. And solved a major cold case to boot.

Falcon called for attention and we all trooped into the briefing room next door, arranging ourselves in a horseshoe around the DCI and Nigel Fingerling, who perched himself on the edge of a desk at the front, his legs crossed over like a hooker at a bar.

He adjusted his tie, which as usual was knotted too tight, and introduced me to the team, his voice every bit as annoying as I'd remembered it.

'For those of you who don't know her, this is Ziba MacKenzie, a freelance offender profiler and serial killer expert.'

It cost him to say the 'expert' bit and if Falcon hadn't been there, my guess was he wouldn't have bothered. But clearly the DCI thought he hadn't gone far enough.

'Mac here has helped solve some of our toughest cases,' he said, butting in, to Fingerling's obvious annoyance. 'And she's the best profiler on our books.'

He gave a quick smile in my direction.

'She's also the person Vernon Sange has asked to speak to,' said Fingerling, glowering at me as if I'd somehow engineered the request.

There was a frisson in the air at the mention of Sange's name. A number of eyes darted to Falcon's face. The kinder detectives on the team had the decency to look at their hands.

'Ziba's going to give us an initial overview of the perp, but before I hand over, I'd like to run through the latest round-ups,' said Fingerling, either oblivious or indifferent to the effect Sange's name had had on his team.

'I want us to look more closely at Marc Gethen, the man who found the first vic up on West Heath in Hampstead. I don't buy his story. Nobody goes hiking in the woods wearing designer jeans and suede loafers. And he was as jumpy as an illegal at passport control when we interviewed him. Alibi checks out for the time of the murder but it came from his missus, so . . .'

There were a few nods round the room. Couple of smirks too. The Metropolitan Police aren't exactly known for their political correctness. Or original metaphors.

'And Officer Dale's coming in later this morning. He called me earlier, said he'd remembered something. I suggested he talk to you, MacKenzie.'

'Dale?'

Fingerling threw Barnwell a look.

'I thought you'd brought her up to speed.'

'Gosh, sorry. I was sure I'd . . .'

'Oh golly gosh,' said Fingerling, mimicking his posh accent. Dickwad.

There were a few snickers. Poor Barnwell went red.

There's only one way to deal with bullies.

'Why don't you fill me in, unless you'd rather spend a bit longer bigging yourself up by picking on someone who can't answer back.'

The DCI cleared his throat. Fingerling killed me with his eyes. Falcon answered for him.

'After the first murder, the offender sent a letter bragging about what he'd done to a West End beat cop, same area the victim was abducted from. We've managed to keep it out of the press and there's been nothing since.'

'Hang on, a beat cop? Surely one of you two makes more sense if he wants to gloat.'

I rubbed the edge of my thumb against my knuckles, thinking.

'There has to be history between them. We should look into the copper's background, check his arrest record.'

Unless . . .

'How can we be sure the letter's really from the killer? Maybe it's from someone else with a gripe against this Dale guy, trying to freak him out.'

'It's definitely from the PRK,' said Fingerling.

'How do you know?'

'Because he didn't just send a note. He also sent a chunk of the victim's liver.'

CHAPTER 11

Mailing a body part makes a hell of a statement. But why had the PRK gone to such lengths to send a low-level cop running to the bathroom?

There had to be some beef between them. Either in their shared past or relating to this particular string of murders. Though, how did the liver fit in?

The PRK was all about symbols, that much was clear from the bizarre items he left at each crime scene. Figuring out what they meant would be the first step towards catching him.

As anyone who's passed through Quantico will tell you, a killer's signature is as unique as a fingerprint. Serial murderers are defined by their rituals and this one was more ritualistic than most, despite him going postal on the bodies after he'd sliced their throats.

The kneeling position of the victim, the circle, the loose hairs. Paradoxically, though, like the post-mortem stab wounds, the emphasis on ceremony suggested that rather than being in control, this perpetrator was wild and violent, desperately trying to manage his explosive impulses in the same way a person with OCD will use repetitive behaviour to try to bring order to chaos.

But what else did the Pink Rose Killer's actions tell us? What patterns had Vernon Sange spotted that I'd missed? What clue was he capitalising on that could finally move us up the ladder?

'Over to you, MacKenzie,' said Fingerling. 'Let's have the profile.'

He spat the word out like it was mouldy fruit.

I walked to the front of the room.

'The mutilation is a critical part of this offender's signature. I'm not sure why he's cutting out their livers, but I have a theory about the facial parts.

'As we know, serial killers always experience a trauma prior to their first attack – a pre-kill stressor. The PRK will be no different. However, as well as undergoing a life-changing event, the butchering and symbolic elements of the crimes suggest he's also suffering from some sort of psychosis.

'Put those factors together, and it's possible he's trying to recreate the face of a woman he lost by harvesting parts from other women who resemble her. Alternatively, he could be looking to obliterate her, feature by feature.'

A detective with tired eyes raised his hand.

'Who do you think that woman is?'

'A lover or a wife who's left him. Or possibly someone he could never have. A person he admired from afar, perhaps stalked. Someone who rejected him. If the goal is to destroy, we could be talking about the true target of his rage.

'If he's building a face, that could indicate a finite number of kills, that he'll stop once he's assembled all the parts he needs. Though by then his addiction to the hunt could just as easily take over.

'His victims are all homeless women in their late teens, high-risk targets – in other words, easy prey. That suggests opportunism and low confidence, which further implies a relatively young perpetrator, likely someone in his early twenties.'

'Not a teen?' asked the sole female detective. Her voice was overly deep, she was wearing a man's style pinstripe suit. A chameleon in a roomful of penises.

'The distance between the abduction and disposal sites suggests he has access to a vehicle. While the first symptoms of psychosis typically emerge between the ages of eighteen and twenty-four, the onset is often slightly earlier among men. The level of fantasy on display here suggests a condition that's been developing for some time, all of which put our perp in his early twenties.'

'Didn't I tell you this lady was good?' said Falcon, grinning at me.

Fingerling's nose twitched like he'd caught a bad smell.

'He's out of control emotionally,' I carried on, 'which he compensates for with an excess of planning and organisation. These aren't crimes of passion. Rather they require planning and a studied attention to detail carried out by a man with absolutely no empathy.

'Harvesting body parts is a gruesome business. Yet even during the first attack, we know the offender wasn't freaked out by the act, given there was no vomit found at the scene.'

Even the British serial killer John Martin Scripps, who likened cutting up people to butchering pigs, was affected enough by his initial murder to puke while sawing his victim's arms off.

'So, we're dealing with a person so pitiless he won't second-guess what he's doing for even a moment. The initial abduction tells us some more things about him.

'He lures the girls with a trick, possibly the offer of food or drink given he drugs them with diazepam. So, he's not some dribbling hygiene-phobe who can't string a sentence together. However, the victimology and post-mortem blitz attack suggests he's afflicted with a physical condition that makes him uncomfortable around people.

'But he's not physically disabled. The forensics reports suggest he carries the girls from his vehicle to the kill site. In the case of the first victim, that meant a trek through the woods.

'It shows we're not looking for a man in a wheelchair or someone with a limp. Rather this guy is strong and physically fit. And not disfigured, otherwise he'd be remembered by witnesses and less easily able to persuade his victims to leave with him. Sad fact is, we tend not to trust people with ugly mugs.'

Fingerling sneered.

'A physical condition that makes him uncomfortable around people but he's not disabled or disfigured. What does that leave?'

'The Trailside Killer had a speech impediment. It could be we're looking at something similar here.'

'A speech impediment?' His eyes cruised the room for laughs. 'You can see the lisp patterns in the wounds, can you? Or perhaps there were stutter marks at the crime scene?'

Twat.

'The clue's in his victim preference. The easy prey, women on the bottom rung of society's ladder. Non-threatening targets. There's something about him he's ashamed of. Likely he was teased at school because of it – or by the woman who rejected him. Yet it wouldn't make him stick out in a crowd. And ironically it might make him appear less threatening to his victims.'

I caught Barnwell's eye. He was nodding vigorously, his face all lit up. He wasn't just being polite when he said he found profiling fascinating.

'The time of the murders suggests the perp lives by himself. Otherwise his frequent absences would be noticed. Don't underestimate him. Everything about his work points to a highly intelligent killer inhabiting a complex fantasy. He'll follow the case closely in the media and inject himself into the investigation where possible.'

'Like supposedly finding the body?' said a wiry DC with an impossibly small head.

'Aye, that would fit.'

Fingerling jerked his head up.

'Another thing pointing to Marc Gethen,' he said, as if he'd been the one to come up with the idea. He turned to an immaculately turned-out detective near the front. 'Joe, I want you to delve deeper into Gethen's religious background. Was he brought up as a Catholic? Go to Catholic school? Sing in a choir? And while you're at it, check out historic complaints about priests dating back over the last twenty years.'

'Why do you want to do that?' I said.

Fingerling's request had sweet FA to do with what I'd been talking about.

He raised his eyes to the ceiling.

'Because, unless you're coming to it, you've missed a glaring detail out of this profile of yours.'

'What's that?'

'Our perp has a gripe against the Catholic Church.'

The papers had mooted this point, picking up on a recent press conference. But I didn't agree.

'There were no satanic symbols at the crime scenes. Or references to Christianity.'

'No references to Christianity? Four of the five victims were found outside churches.'

I shook my head.

'This is a killer who deals in signs and symbols. He's incredibly cryptic. If this were about Catholicism, he wouldn't be so transparent about it.'

'Maybe you're just ignoring the obvious.'

And maybe you're just a giant shit-stick.

'Let's move on to what we can agree over,' I said, my words more diplomatic than my thoughts. 'The perp isn't a sadist, despite the gruesome nature of the crimes. There's no sign of torture, so he doesn't get off on inflicting pain. Rather the ritual elements show the attacks are based on a fantasy he may well have been harbouring since youth.

'Nearly all serial killers had troubled childhoods that upset their love maps, the blueprint for future relationships we develop as kids. Given the level of fantasy, you can be sure that's the case here too.

'And given the mutilation elements, chances are, growing up he killed and tortured animals. Look for reports of dogs and cats going missing in the Hampstead area over the last ten years and cross-reference those with truancy and social service call-outs.

'The first three kill sites are centred around Hampstead, which suggests it's an area the offender knows well. He may have spent his childhood there. It has unhappy memories for him.

'In his mind, he's righting a wrong, working his way up till he's ready to attack the true target of his rage. The person he blames for his sorry existence. And the fact he hasn't been arrested yet will be fuelling him, making him believe he's invincible.'

Vernon Sange thought he was invincible too. The day he started his sentence, he sent me another letter:

Audentis fortuna iuvat. Fortune favours the brave.

It's not over, Ziba.

Little did I know then, he was right.

CHAPTER 12

'Pop into my office a moment, would you, Mac?' said Falcon as everyone got up to leave at the end of the session.

His jowls wobbled, the buttons strained across his stomach. His wife might have him on rabbit food but he still looked like a bulldog in a suit.

He opened the door for me then shut it behind us with a soft click.

'No one on the team knows the way Vernon Sange operates as well as we do. He's made it clear that he's got information on the PRK and that he'll only speak to you. But that doesn't mean you have to talk to him if you don't want to. I won't sacrifice you to this man, Ziba.'

His eyes didn't leave my face, his voice cracked.

I touched his arm.

'I know what's involved, sir. And what I'm doing. It was different with Janie, you must see that.'

'She was younger, yes. And so vulnerable, poor love. But don't underestimate him. People are playthings for this monster. He lives off their pain. More so if he's caused it, you know that.'

'I do.'

Falcon's face tightened like it was being sucked from the inside.

'Bet you don't know this, though. While he was at Oxford, he volunteered for a suicide hotline.' He covered his eyes. 'Christ, can you imagine that? What he must have said to those people?'

I didn't have to think too hard. My eyes flitted to the framed photo on Falcon's desk. A family shot, a summer day. Only his daughter, Janie, was wearing long sleeves. Cut deep enough and the scars never fade.

Back when we were hunting Sange, DCI Falcon wasn't as camera-shy as he is now. His face was all over the news, a freshly promoted Detective Chief Inspector making his name on a big serial killer case. Sange took umbrage. He wasn't yet on our radar, but even so he didn't want to share the spotlight with anyone.

Later analysis of the Butcher's hard drive shows he went online, befriended Falcon's anorexic daughter. Groomed her the way all these shitheads groom kids, by making her think he was the only one who understood her, that he was the only one she could trust. Only this reptile wasn't trying to get in her pants. He was trying to get in her head.

It's all there in the binary code, how he nursed her feelings of low self-worth. How he told her there was a way out, that she didn't have to suffer. And how to slice her skin deep enough to sever the radial artery.

She blacked out on the bathroom floor. If her mother hadn't needed to get in there to do her make-up, she may have gone into hypovolaemic shock. Instead she's spent her life since in therapy.

Vernon Sange hadn't done what he had out of necessity. He did it because he enjoyed it.

Falcon looked hard at me now.

'I have to ask you. Are you absolutely sure you want to go down this road?'

'Want has nothing to do with it, sir. If the Butcher does know something about the offender, I need to find out what it is.'

'I don't like this, Ziba.' There was a pause while he studied my face. I looked back at him hard. He sighed. 'You've made your mind up, haven't you?'

'Yep.'

He teased his top lip through his bottom teeth.

'All right, then. Just be careful. And for Christ's sake, never forget for a moment what he is.'

He squeezed my shoulder, caring and avuncular. I looked up at him, my throat momentarily constricting as a faint cinnamon smell reached my nostrils.

I've been without Duncan for two years and without my father for ten times as long. Yet still they come to me in a stranger's expression or the trace of a scent caught on the air.

'I'll be on my guard,' I said. 'I know his game. I can play it too.'

'I'm sure you can.' Falcon smiled, relaxed a bit. 'Okay then, find out what he knows. And what he only wants us to think he knows.'

'Copy that,' I said, my tone jauntier than I felt.

Vernon Sange's mind is more twisted than the Minotaur's labyrinth – one of the stories in a leather-bound collection of Greek myths found in his rooms at Balliol after his arrest, annotated, like everything he reads.

I've made my living analysing people. For him it's just a hobby. But like everything else he does, he's brilliant at it. And as we'd seen from the business with Falcon's daughter, he uses his skill to snare his subjects.

The Butcher might be willing to share information about our perp. But it would come at a price.

He may be facing down the needle but experience told me the deal he was after would have nothing to do with delaying his travel arrangements.

He'd want something much more personal.

To destroy me. Payback for me destroying him.

40

CHAPTER 13

The child is sitting up in bed, rocking back and forth, pulling the stuffing out of a charity-shop Care Bear, screaming itself hoarse. Salty rivers of snot and tears run into its mouth. Its face is blotchy and ketchup-red.

From the other side of the wall comes a rhythmic creaking — eek-eek — like something out of a Halloween movie. A man, grunting. Mother praying. 'Oh God. Oh God . . .'

The child screams more urgently, pounds the walls with desperate little fists.

The bedroom door is locked from the other side, a big barrel bolt is drawn across. The windows are locked too. And barred. The child is in a prison; no way out.

The man's grunts knit closer together. The child's screams become lung-bursting loud. Its eyes are filmy with tears and impotence.

The grunts stop, replaced by shouting, the front door slamming and then the heavy fall of approaching footsteps. The bolt slides back.

Mother is in the doorway now, hair wild, purple lipstick smudged like a bruise, a wet red mark on her neck.

There's a ladder running down her stockings, the thin black rungs standing out against her paper-white skin.

'You evil little bastard!' she says, flying at the child, hand raised. Payback.

CHAPTER 14

Falcon and I walked back into the major incident room together. The board was close to the door, covered with photos of the PRK's five victims.

Five slit throats. Five mutilated faces. Five wet wounds beneath the ribs. And on the chest of each corpse, a single pink rose, the tips of its petals tinged with blood as though dipped in paint.

Normally we'd have 'before' shots to go alongside the 'afters', but these girls hadn't had anyone to capture their last days on camera. Likely their families didn't even know they were dead. Possibly some of their relatives hadn't seen them for years; others might not know they'd existed at all.

Vernon Sange was dangerous. But if speaking to him would bring us closer to catching the shit-bird responsible for these crimes, then that's what I was going to do. Screw the risk.

'I'll drive up to Wakefield after I've read over the letters the perp's been sending Jack Wolfe. And a quick shower,' I added with an embarrassed smile.

He lowered his eyes for a second, his hatred of Sange clouding his features. It'd be pushing it to say Falcon's like a father to me, but we are close. It cost him to send me to the Butcher's table.

'I wouldn't waste your time on his mail,' he said. 'The team's already been through it.'

'Another pair of eyes won't hurt,' I replied, diplomatic for a second time that day. Must be a bug I'd picked up on the plane.

'And while I'm in Wakefield, it'd be a good idea for you to hold another press conference. Manage the media. Send a message to the offender.'

Normally that'd be my job. I've never been much of a team player. Delegating doesn't come easily. I'm a woman, but that didn't stop me mansplaining.

'Share the profile,' I said. 'Turn the public into our eyes and ears. Someone may recognise who we're talking about and have noticed a change in their behaviour.

'And whatever happens, make sure you keep Sange's name out of things. He loves the limelight. But he's not the only one. The Pink Rose Killer has written to a journalist and a policeman. You can be sure he craves attention too. And he won't react well at having to share it.'

Once Falcon and I had wound things up and he'd asked me for the umpteenth time if I was sure about visiting Sange, I was shown to my desk and the office manager went off to retrieve the letters for me. Perhaps it was the prospect of going over them that made Jack butt into my head again. Or maybe it was just being back in London, working a case he was so closely connected with.

Either way, I was thinking about him more than I should.

Put up or shut up, my oppos would have said. Fair enough. Though what the hell should I say to him?

I'd need a bottle of wine to get the words out. Maybe two. Over dinner tomorrow then.

I reached for my phone and opened my contacts list. WOLFIE. The only name in my favourites folder.

I was just about to press it when the office manager came over.

'Should keep you busy,' she said, dumping a folder on my desk.

She was right. Speaking to Jack would have to wait.

CHAPTER 15

Suns will set and suns will rise again.

    O D!

    She was so young and pure, just perfect for my purposes; going to the slaughter like a good little lamb. But now she is throat-slit and dead and all used up and I am lying awake thinking about where to shop next.

    But O D, how silly of me. The details are what're important . . . how her blood geysered out of her throat. How her lips twitched after I made the cut, like she was trying to blow me a kiss. And maybe she was. Ha ha!

    Call me up folks. 4.1 10-5.16-7.11 16 20 21

I read the first letter from the Pink Rose Killer to Wolfie, sent just after the last murder. There was a definite whiff of Jack the Ripper in the lines. The same bragging tone and mocking elements as in the Dear Boss letter. Though, unlike the Ripper, there were no spelling mistakes or grammatical errors. In fact, this letter was almost poetic, written by someone who clearly loved language.

University educated, then. An English Lit grad, maybe. Psychopath definitely; a person devoid of empathy, with a massive superiority complex, despite his lack of confidence socially. And living in a fucked-up fantasy world.

Animal killer, I scribbled on my yellow legal pad. *Fire-starter.*

Two out of the three predictors of violent tendencies from the Macdonald triad. Possibly a bed-wetter too, or late to toilet train. The third variable.

I read the letter again.

O D, I thought. What's that all about? Oh dear? Oh damn?

Is he trying to avoid swearing? If so, that might imply a strict religious upbringing. Could there be a link to the Church after all? No, that still didn't chime.

I chewed my thumbnail.

And what about the numbers? What do they mean?

I checked the other letters. There was another string in the second letter but not the third. Why?

I gnawed my lip, drummed my fingers on the edge of the desk.

They weren't phone numbers. They were the wrong length and pattern for that. What about dates? But then how did 16, 20 and 21 fit? Coordinates? I opened up a map on my laptop. No, that didn't scan either. And anyway, like I'd told Fingerling, the PRK was all about signs and symbols. Phone numbers and dates wouldn't be cryptic enough for him.

But a code . . .

The London Lacerator had used a code too. But his had been a cinch to crack. A basic substitution cipher.

I spent an age experimenting with different coding principles now but I still had nada to show for it at the end. Unlike the Lacerator, nothing was straightforward about the PRK's cipher. It wasn't an ASCII code, a column key, a grid transposition or even a wig wag cipher. So, what was he using? And why was he using it?

His letters were full of bluster. He was writing to the press and police. Setting us a challenge, trying to demonstrate he was cleverer than us, would fit with that.

'Nigel, do you have a minute?'

'What's up?'

I showed him the letters.

'I think our perp may be using a cipher. If we fail to crack it, we show we're stupider than him. If we do, we get some new piece of information, a reward.'

He ran his tongue over his teeth. The action made his lips bulge. It wasn't attractive.

'Sounds like you'd better find out what he's trying to say.'

Easier said than done.

I checked my watch; I needed to make tracks soon. The journey up to Wakefield prison would take over three hours. And I still had to go back home to Little Venice and get my Porsche out of the garage. No way was I driving hundreds of miles in a smelly pool car. Or spending any longer than I had to in last night's clothes.

The way things were going, I'd be lucky to make it there and back before midnight. Cracking the code would have to wait.

I read through the next letter, sent to Jack the morning after the most recent kill.

> Dear Sir,
> You didn't put my last note on your front page. That upset me.
>
> If you do not print this on the front page of tomorrow's edition, you will leave me no choice. I will cruise the city, killing and killing until I have lined up a dozen bodies at your door. I hate to be ignored . . . Do not be foolish again.
>
> To prove I am the person the gentlemen of the press are rather banally calling the Pink Rose Killer, I am enclosing a little token. Do you like it?
>
> O D, I must tell you how well my work is going and how much I am enjoying it. That first cut, the

46

release that follows! The smell, the colour, the heat
of the blood.

>*Yet, still it is not enough for mad, mad me . . .*
>*Call me up folks. 1.15 23 24-2.2 3 9*

Plenty of serial killers write to the media. It's a way of getting attention and wielding the power they crave by shocking and terrifying the public. Some have even sent proof they're the real deal, like the Pink Rose Killer had done in his letters to Jack. A smear of blood on each page.

But why is he writing to Wolfie? I thought. True, he's the *Telegraph*'s crime reporter but like that beat cop, Jack's not especially high up in the paper. Surely the editor would make more sense.

Unless the lack of seniority is the key here. Certainly, it's a common link, along with the posting of body stuffs.

There had to be more to it than that, though. Something that had drawn the offender to both Jack and PC Dale. But what?

I read through the last letter, which Jack had received two days before Barnwell pitched up at Quantico. Unlike the others, it was only three lines long, unsigned and missing a number string.

>*Excellent work, that last job. My next night approaches, o sun cut short the light that's left to linger.*
>>*I'm getting better all the time.*
>>*How kind to write and tell you all about it.*

There was something different about this one, not just length and absence of numbers. My phone rang just as I was reading it for the fifth time, trying to nail down a thought that wouldn't hold still.

'Ms MacKenzie? You have a visitor in reception.'

Officer Dale. The PRK's other pen pal.

CHAPTER 16

I ordered up tea and chocolate chip cookies, then led Officer Dale into one of the 'soft' interview rooms we use to talk to witnesses. He was in civvies; signed off work as a result of the stress caused by the PRK's letter, and in and out of meetings with the Force shrink.

'I can't sleep. I can't eat,' he said, his voice so flat it was practically monotone. 'Every time I close my eyes I see that slimy sliver. Why would anyone do that? Why would he send it to me?'

He hung his anorak carefully over the back of his chair then sat down, running his hands over his wispy hair. It had been dusted with snow when he arrived. Now it was beaded with moisture. An earring of water dripped on to his shirt collar. His nostrils were pink.

'Everyone wants to talk to me about this. They don't understand I'm living a nightmare.'

He hung his head, picked at his nails.

'Everyone?'

Shit, were the journos starting to sniff around?

'You guys. The investigation team. I mean, I realise I'm significant, a part of all this. It's just it's really hard for me, you know?'

He put his head in his hands. His shoulders shook.

Outside, the snow was still falling hard. Can't wait to drive up the motorway in this, I thought, my mind more focused on the interview I was about to have than the one I was in.

Dale sniffed loudly. He was obviously having a hard time of it. Understandably so.

I needed to dial things back, get the guy to relax.

'Felip,' I said. He looked up, wiping his nose on the cuff of his shirt. 'I've not come across that spelling before.'

'I changed it. A friend said it'd make me sound more interesting.'

His shoulders dropped, he took a breath, moistened his lips.

'DI Fingerling said you'd flown all the way back from the States to help with all this. You're a profiler, right?' I nodded. 'What do you make of him?'

For half a second, I thought he was talking about Fingerling rather than the perp. Either way, I didn't give him an answer. Dale may be a cop, but I've been round the block enough times to know not to share details of the investigation with someone outside the team.

'I'm trying to understand why the Pink Rose Killer is writing to you, Felip. You're not on the investigation team. You weren't the responding officer. And the first victim wasn't found anywhere near your beat. Which means he must feel there's some sort of connection between the two of you on a personal level. Understanding what that is could bring us closer to catching him.'

Dale glanced down at his hands. His nails were bitten to the quick.

'Is there anyone from your past who you've had trouble with? A kid growing up? A love rival? Someone you arrested?'

He shook his head.

'No one I can think of.'

'There's got to be something that connects you to the killer. He's writing to you for a reason.'

'That's why I called. I think I've come up with something. Kind of a psychological link, it's your speciality, right?'

'Go on,' I said, just as the refreshments were brought in.

'I kind of forgot about it, it wasn't a big deal. But I saw her picture in the paper the other day and it triggered a memory. I'd not been letting myself read the news for a while or watch it on TV. I didn't want any more reminders, you know? This was on a stand outside the Tube station, though. I couldn't miss it . . . Sorry, I'm blathering. Point is, I broke up a row at the soup kitchen a month or so ago. Between the first victim and some guy who works there. She was upset, claimed he was sleazing on her. She was really creeped out.'

I leaned forward.

'Did you get a name?'

'It was one of the volunteers. Ian Heppe. I gave him a warning – told him his behaviour wasn't on and that he was upsetting the young lady. He seemed genuinely sorry so I didn't write it up.'

He squeezed his eyes shut, put his hands on either side of his head.

'Now I keep thinking, what if I were the last person she talked to? If I'd acted differently, she might still be alive.'

How many times have I thought the same thing? What wouldn't I give to have kept Duncan off the streets that night?

As I listened to the policeman talk, my thoughts coalesced.

What if the connection wasn't between him and the perp? What if it was between him and the victim? And what if the offender worked at the soup kitchen? That would explain the success of his ruse. His targets knew him.

If I was right, then sending the liver was about sending a message:

Officer Dale may have saved the first girl from being assaulted. But he couldn't stop her from being killed.

50

CHAPTER 17

The girl is huddled in a sleeping bag, puffa jacket and three sweaters from the clothes bank, but the cold slices through her all the same. It burns her hands, her toes are numb.

'Snow's on the way,' she heard one of the others say while she was queuing for soup earlier. 'Just our bleeding luck.'

Hard to imagine the temperature could plunge lower than this, it's already well below freezing. She imagines her fingers turning to ice and snapping off. This little piggy went to market, this little piggy stayed at home . . .

There are a few drops left in the can. She tips it till it's vertical, leans her head all the way back. Her mouth is dry. The lager leaves a dirty taste.

Her sleeping bag is dirty too, it stinks of onions. Stale sweat and city grime. She burrows deeper down all the same, till the lip is over her head and she looks like a big green caterpillar. The Hungry Caterpillar. Her nana used to read that one to her, long time ago now.

Sixteen years old and it's come to this. She'd sell her soul for a hot bath and a soft bed, she really would. But then again, a soft bed was why she'd had to run away in the first place.

Evil prick, she thinks, lying on her side, her chilled hands glued in prayer position between her clenched thighs, the warmest part of her turned-to-ice body. Shithead. How could her mother have believed him over her? Doubted her own flesh and blood?

The streets may be bad, but at least she's away from all that. And if the bitch wanted to side with him over her, then she could go screw herself.

Time passes. She hears the sound of footsteps approaching. Thwack. Thump. Only one pair of feet. It's the middle of the night. The streets emptied out hours ago. The bars shut and locked.

So, who is this?

More footsteps, they slow then stop. The girl's heartbeat quickens, her senses heighten. Whoever's here is right by her now.

There's a rustle of fabric as the person squats down beside her. Then a weight on her back, a hand.

The girl's heart is a demolition hammer loud in her ears. She scrabbles in her jacket pocket for the flick knife.

'Fancy a hot drink? I've got coffee over there if you want some.'

The girl pokes her head out of the bag, pulse slowing as she sees who it is.

She smiles, lets go of the blade. A hot drink is exactly what she wants.

She slithers out of her sleeping bag and they walk off together. Already she feels warmer inside. See, not everyone's bad.

She doesn't think to bring the knife.

CHAPTER 18

I stood at my desk, the photos from each crime scene spread out in a long line across it. Five victims reduced to carcasses, their graves marked only by a pink rose and a random object.

The objects couldn't be random. The attention to detail and consistent signature across all the murders showed they had to mean something. But what?

'Having fun, MacKenzie?' said Fingerling, in the whiny nasal voice that probably got the shit kicked out of him at school.

I raked my hands through my hair. I didn't think much of the guy but a second pair of eyes never hurts.

'The murders are part of a sacrifice. But if not to the Devil, then who?'

He shrugged, shoulders high to his ears.

'Not my field. When I think of sacrifices, all I picture are temples and priests in togas.'

'Togas, of course!' I slammed my fist into my palm, face lit up.

'Ever think maybe you should cut down on the caffeine?'

'Never. Excuse me, I need to make a call.'

Talking things through with Fingerling is one thing, talking them through with my lovely mother is a whole other bundle of fun. But when it comes to Ancient History, there's no one in my contacts folder who understands it better. The woman practically lives in her office deep in the basement of the British Museum.

I steeled myself and hit her up.

'Yes?'

No way she didn't know who it was, my name would have come up on her screen. An old Motorola flip phone because she doesn't 'trust' technology.

'Emmeline, it's Ziba.'

'Yes, dear?'

We hadn't spoken for months.

'I'm working on a serial murder case. Wondered if you could help me with something.'

'Really?'

She sounded confused. Fair enough, this would be like her asking me for my take on an archaeological haul.

I explained.

'There's a sacrificial element to the crimes. I'm wondering if there might be a Roman connection,' I said, spurred on by Fingerling's toga comment.

'Really?' she said again, though this time she sounded interested. We were in her wheelhouse now.

'This is confidential, but the perpetrator leaves things by the bodies. Different items each time.'

I reeled off the list.

'Bread soaked in wine. A drawing of a wolf. A toy horse. Some charred sticks. And a lump of goat meat. Does that mean anything to you?'

'Well, grain sacrifices were fairly common during the Roman period. Blood sacrifices too. The bread and meat could fit with that. Is your killer attacking men or women?'

'Women.'

'So perhaps offerings to a goddess.'

'Huh?'

'Don't say, huh, dear. It makes you sound common.' I dug my nails into my palm; there's a reason we don't speak much. 'In the Ancient World, male animals were offered to male gods and female ones to goddesses. And although it was rare, humans were sacrificed pre-Caesar.'

Interesting.

'What about the non-food items? Is there a link you can think of between them and sacrifices?'

'Yes, of course,' she said, as if I were being completely obtuse. 'But the link's not just to sacrifices.'

CHAPTER 19

'Fingerling, listen to this!'

I'd barged straight into his office, hot off the phone from my mother. He looked up, didn't seem too happy about the interruption.

'The perp isn't just sacrificing his victims, he's killing them on Roman feast days. The items left on the bodies tie directly in with them.'

Fingerling held up a hand.

'Slow down and take it back one, MacKenzie.'

I read out the notes I'd made while talking to Emmeline.

'The first murder was on 13th February. That was the beginning of the Roman festival of *Parentalia*, a nine-day holiday to honour dead ancestors and exorcise evil spirits. Offerings included wine-soaked bread, the item found by the first vic.

'The second one took place on February 15th. *Lupercalia*. Another festival about exorcism but also fertility, of which wolves were a symbol. It ties in with the Romulus and Remus story about the founders of Rome being suckled by a she-wolf.'

'Lovely.'

'Right! But it also connects with what was found at the kill site.'

'The drawing of a wolf?'

'Exactly. Next murder date was February 27th, *Equirria*, a horse-racing festival to honour Mars. We found a plastic horse by the victim. Then, March 1st, New Year's Day in the Roman world. The CSIs found charred sticks at the scene. Want to guess how the toga wearers used to mark this particular holiday?'

'Lighting bonfires?'

'Close enough. By renewing the sacred fire of Rome.'

'Shit.'

'And 7th March was a festival for a god called Vediovis. She-goats were common offerings.'

'The meat?'

'Exactly. That's not all. Did you know that, during supplications, older women called *matronae* would sweep the ground with their hair? It might be a stretch, but it could tie in with the hairs found at the first crime scene. Barnwell said they belonged to a woman in her seventies.'

The corners of Fingerling's mouth turned down; it gave him a codfish look. He nodded, impressed.

'How did you come up with all this so fast?'

'I asked an expert.'

As I said the words, my breath stuck in my lungs.

'What's wrong, MacKenzie?'

'The murder dates. My mother isn't the only expert on the Ancient World. Vernon Sange is one too. What if he made the same connection she did? That'd explain how he could predict when the PRK was going to strike again, same way we now can.'

'You mean—?'

'What if the Butcher doesn't know the killer's identity at all? What if he just wants us to think he does?'

Fingerling tapped the end of his pen against his mouth. When he spoke, his voice was so quiet I had to ask him to repeat himself.

'Maybe it was a good guess. But what if it wasn't? You really want to take that chance?'

I did not.

CHAPTER 20

M1 Motorway

The snow was coming down thick as feathers. Even with my wipers and heating up all the way, I was struggling to keep the windscreen clear. And the salt spray from the road wasn't doing much to help. But after weeks driving round Quantico in a rental, it felt good to be back with my baby – despite where I was headed.

> *This is the coldest March for nine years with heavy snow forecast for much of the country and temperatures set to plummet to as low as minus 17 degrees Celsius in parts of Scotland.*

> *Aid groups are providing hot food and blankets for the homeless and businesses are advising workers to stay at home, with authorities warning of dangerous conditions on the roads.*

I switched the radio off; it sounded too much like DCI Falcon.

'Maybe you should delay until the weather improves,' he'd said hopefully when I'd stuck my head round his door to tell him I was off.

I don't usually have much contact with him on cases but this one was different. The difference was Sange.

'The PRK's not going to delay,' I said. 'And if he is going to strike again in two days, we can't afford to cool our heels till the sun comes out.'

He pinched the loose skin on his neck, a sign of rapid weight loss.

'The roads'll be treacherous.' He glanced at the photo of Janie on his desk, thinking of the last game the Butcher played. 'At least wait till the snow stops.'

A difficult journey was the least of my concerns.

'I'll be fine. And anyway, my Porsche could do with a run. Sitting idle in these temperatures isn't good for her.'

The car's the closest thing I have to a kid. A 1988 911 Turbo. Always 'her', never 'it'.

I glanced at the clock on my dashboard now. Two hours and I'd only just passed Northampton. I wasn't even halfway yet. Damn it, I should be out in front of the media, drawing the killer out. Not stuck out here in the boonies.

I called the prison to give a revised ETA then rang Jack again; we'd been playing phone tag ever since I'd landed. Not that I was going to lay it on the line right now. The plan was to ask him over for supper tomorrow night. Crack open a bottle. Cook for once. Steak, maybe. The only thing I can make aside from eggs.

Duncan was always the chef in our house. I'd perch on the kitchen stool with my wine glass while he tossed chopped shallots and garlic into the pan. They'd sizzle and spit as they hit the butter, smelled amazing. Even better once he'd added the chicken and sherry.

Since he died, I've been living largely off toast and take-outs. Trying to cook reminds me too much of him and I never could be bothered washing up for one.

59

Jack picked up on the second ring.

'Hey, Mac! Can't believe it's you, not just a recording. How are you, how was the flight?'

'All good. Wasn't expecting to come back to snow, though.'

'Tell me about it. Can't see me taking GIRY up any time soon.'

He was talking about the little plane he has a share in, refers to it by its call sign as if it's the name of his kid. I make fun of him but I'm as bad about my wheels.

'Your message said you're working on the PRK case. I had a feeling you'd get recalled.'

Bet you can't guess why . . .

'Want to get together tonight? Swap war stories? You must be tired. I could pick something up on the way over, save you schlepping to the shops.'

I don't like keeping things from Wolfie. But spilling my soup cooler about Vernon Sange wouldn't just be unethical. It'd also put him in an unfair position.

Asking him not to write about something that big would be like standing me in front of a suicide bomber and asking me not to take him out.

So, rather than telling him I was on my way up to Wakefield, I invited him for supper the following night instead.

'I'm beat,' I said. 'All I want to do is have a hot bath and fall into bed.'

It wasn't a lie. It was what I wanted to do.

Instead, I'd be spending the evening with a serial killer.

CHAPTER 21

The child is playing chess with Penelope. Penelope never argues or makes a fuss when the child suggests a new game. She's always so sweet and agreeable, always does what she's told.

She wears the same thing every time she comes over: black patent shoes, knee-high socks and a blue pinafore dress with a white apron over the top. Underneath is a crinoline that makes her skirt stick out like an umbrella. Her blonde hair is loose in a headband.

Really the child should have named her Alice since that's where she came from, the Alice in Wonderland book at the library. But Penelope is a much more interesting name, the wife of Odysseus, another favourite story. And that's the best thing about having an imaginary friend, the child gets to choose her name — and everything else about her too.

'You sound like a halfwit talking to yourself in that stupid baby voice,' Mother says, plonking down in front of the TV with a glass of Tanqueray. 'No wonder the kids at school think you're such a freak.'

The child looks up, eyes brimming, but says nothing. Mother flicks to another channel. Indifferent.

CHAPTER 22

Her Majesty's Prison Service, HMP Wakefield

'I realise it goes against protocol, but I need to take my iPhone into the interview room,' I said to the governor after a clammy handshake.

I glanced at the loudly ticking clock on the wall of his office. It was late, a combination of heavy traffic, bad weather and the over-cologned man who'd waylaid me in the prison parking lot asking for directions.

The governor leaned back in his chair behind a desk so wide it grazed the walls, and looked me over with bulging goldfish eyes.

'A mobile phone? You do realise we're a Category A prison. We can't take the chance of contraband getting into the wrong hands. I'd like to help, but I really can't make an exception here. It's procedure.'

'I understand the rules. But I thought DCI Falcon had explained why we'd be grateful if you'd make an exception.'

His gaze rested on my breasts. I folded my arms, imagined finger-scissoring his eyes.

'We're in the middle of a murder investigation, five women have already lost their lives and Vernon Sange claims to know the identity of the person responsible. Time is of the essence. If he reveals something, I have to let my team know right away. And by the same token, if they find out anything new that might be pertinent to the interview, I need to know while I can still use it.'

The governor flushed. With his fishy eyes, it made him look like a big pink salmon. This wasn't a man who enjoyed being taken to task by a woman.

He rubbed his lips together. They made a wet sound.

'Very well, dear.'

He smiled, oblivious to my internal growl.

'You're quite convincing, Miss MacKenzie. Or are you one of those girls that goes by Ms?'

I haven't been a girl for fifteen years.

'Actually, it's Mrs,' I said.

And don't call me dear.

CHAPTER 23

Goldfish Eyes made a short phone call and a few minutes later a grey-faced guard with Brillo Pad hair and a perspiration problem appeared at the door.

'Could you take Mrs MacKenzie to the fifth-floor legal visit room? She has an appointment with Vernon Sange.'

'So, you're meeting the Butcher, eh?' the guard said as we walked along the corridor through a series of iron gates to the meeting point. 'He's not human, that one.' He shook his head. 'Want to hear a story?'

'Sure.'

'He managed to catch himself a sparrow, made a pet of it. Tied string round its leg. Fed it scraps. Bread. Bits of cereal. Catullus, he called him.

'I'd hear him talking to it in his cell after lights out. He'd sing to it too.

'Course, he wasn't allowed to keep the bird. I told him he had to give it up. He didn't want to, though. Tried to sweet-talk me round. In the end I said if he didn't let it go, he'd get put on report and lose all his books.

'Well, I thought that got through to him. He slipped down off his bunk and untied the creature. Next thing, there's a muffled cracking sound. He'd squeezed the bird to death.

'"What did you do that for?" I said. I couldn't take my eyes off the poor little thing. A second earlier it had been chirruping.

'"It's your fault, James," he said, in this deadly calm voice. "You made me do it. The poor critter would be alive if it weren't for you."'

His story had all the rhythm of one that's been told many times.

'Want to hear another thing?' the guard said as we went through yet another metal gate. Outsiders must be a novelty in a place like this. Women too, what with 740 male lifers on the roll.

'We introduced a new scheme recently. Idea was to try and decrease inmates' aggression by painting the walls of their cells in soft pastel colours. Mainly pale blue. You'll see it in all the cells. But in Vernon Sange's room the walls are grey up to head height.'

'Why's that?'

'Said he didn't like blue. So, he peeled off the paint and ate it.'

I stopped pacing the interview room now and listened. There were steps echoing along the corridor. Two pairs of feet stomping. Guards in black combat boots. And alongside them, the clip-clip of thin-soled shoes.

The Butcher of Balliol was on his way in.

CHAPTER 24

Vernon Sange walked into the interview room flanked by two guards, but somehow managing to look as if he were the one escorting them.

The last time I'd seen him was just before his verdict came through. He'd been wearing a three-piece suit and an over-large bow tie, showboating to the media up in the gallery, telling them he was looking forward to getting back to Balliol College in time for Formal Hall.

A part of me was expecting the same pantomime today. Instead, he seemed relaxed. His hair was tousled, his face unshaven. Horribly, he looked just my type.

'Ziba, so glad you could come.'

His voice was full of Californian sunshine, his smile warm and easy. I'd been there when they excavated his disposal site, but a part of me couldn't help feeling seduced all the same. On the surface he seemed so *normal*. And yet I knew what those hands had done . . .

'We've got fifteen minutes,' I said. 'Then they'll take you back to your cell. Uncuff him,' I told the guards. 'I'll buzz when we're done.'

Sange brushed past me as he took a seat at the table. He gave off a scent of pine and leather. It felt wrong in here, out of place.

He caught me looking at him, tilted his head and smiled.

'Aren't you going to sit down, Ziba?'

From the floor below came the sound of inmates shouting and metal doors being slammed shut. In the distance, a siren screamed.

Sange leaned back in his chair, his ankle resting across his knee, a sheen of light from the caged bulb overhead reflecting off his glossy hair.

Whenever I'd seen him before, on the interview tapes, during the trial, he'd been buzzing with energy. Everything about him had been expansive, his hand gestures, the way he moved. In here, though, he seemed calm and relaxed. The pageantry had gone. But what had wrought the change? Being in prison, or being in this room with me?

'Tell me what you know about the Pink Rose Killer,' I said, straight to it, no games.

We both knew why I was here. The clock wasn't just ticking for us, it was also ticking for the perp's next victim.

CHAPTER 25

'You've done a pretty good job convincing my DCI you know who the Pink Rose Killer is,' I said, mirroring his body language.

I didn't want to come across as desperate. The second I became a supplicant, I'd be in his power.

'What do you make of that moniker?' he said. 'Bit banal, don't you think? Typical tabloid hyperbole. A mere whiff of the salacious turns those little headline writers into spittle-flecked hysterics.'

His lips tightened, the muscles round his eyes twitched. Was he thinking of his own moniker, the Butcher of Balliol? Another example of 'tabloid hyperbole'. Inaccurate too, suggesting nothing of the stealthy way he'd closed in on his prey, constricted them in his coils.

It must piss him off, I thought. A man so in love with control not being able to control the story told about him.

But it wasn't just Sange's non-verbals that got my attention. The language he used made me sit up too.

'Banal' was the same word the PRK wrote in his letter to Jack. Is that why Sange chose it? And had he deliberately mentioned reporters too? A way of referring to Wolfie, the first person to call him out for what he was, his description so dramatic it captured public imagination and stuck?

He must have known I'd pick up on both those factors. He was playing me, then. Showing he understood the perp better than me, letting me know he had it in for Jack.

Or had he just slipped up?

No. Vernon Sange doesn't waste words, everything he says has a purpose. I'd seen that during the cross-examinations at his trial as he eviscerated witness after witness, leaving them whimpering and confused on the stand. As they spluttered and hesitated, he'd make faces at the jury, shrugging and rolling his eyes. More than one smiled back at him.

'How is the Detective Chief Inspector?' he said now. 'His daughter must have given him a nasty fright.'

I looked at him. His expression was neutral, his voice level. There was nothing in either to suggest cruelty or excitement. And yet wasn't he claiming credit for what Janie had done? Wasn't he goading me?

The thinking part of me wanted to smack him in the face. The animal part was suckered in.

I'd come here expecting Hannibal Lecter, a man who ticked all the boxes on the Psychopathy Checklist. Instead, I was sitting across from a man in the street. An office crush. The guy next door. A friend, fiancé, husband, lover.

Unlike most psychopaths, he didn't talk in a monotone or brag about himself. He didn't um and ah more than anyone else or speak predominantly in the past tense. He wasn't preoccupied with basic needs or focused on cause and effect.

I tried to picture how his face would have looked as he squeezed the life out of his victims. But all I could see was the man in front of me: handsome and charming.

I batted away his question about Janie, worked to keep my tone reserved.

'DCI Falcon's well. His daughter too.'

'Pleased to hear it,' he said, with another of his buttered-on smiles.

Again, his voice and body language didn't change. But he didn't blink once and his eyes didn't leave my face.

I had the unpleasant feeling I'd said exactly what he wanted to hear. By toughing it out, had I revealed the fear I'd tried to keep hidden? Had he set a trap? Had I fallen in?

Flustered, I stood up. I didn't come here to be played, especially not with a killer lining up his next target. I tried a different move. Offence.

'You don't know anything about the PRK. This is just sport for you, isn't it?'

I moved to the buzzer.

I felt Sange's gaze on my back. He waited for the last moment.

'The next girl will lose her lips. Blonde this time. A goddess for the goddess.'

Eerily reminiscent of what my mother had said. Before I could question what I was doing, I'd sat back down.

CHAPTER 26

'We already know the offender's either constructing or deconstructing a face. It's basic reasoning. I'm disappointed, Sange. I must say, I'd hoped for something a little more impressive from you.'

I was trying to provoke him, make him show off what he knew. The thing all psychopaths have in common is the belief they're special. Challenge that illusion and they lash out.

Only Sange didn't react. No shadow of anger passed across his face, no ocular twitch. Instead, he looked at me with his unblinking eyes and smiled the way a friend might.

'You're right, it is obvious. Though I haven't seen the papers make the connection.'

Another swipe at Jack? Or was he implying he and I were a cut above? A way of flattering me, putting us in the same boat?

'What no one seems to know about what he's doing is *why.*'

Sange shrugged, smiled with his eyes.

'We can't all be satisfied with what we have.'

A chill ran through me. Was he right? Were the murders about the offender recreating himself rather than someone he'd lost? Was the PRK making a mask?

And was this just another deduction, like the date of his next kill? Or a detail born out of first-hand knowledge?

Sange leaned back in his chair, angled his head.

'Tell me, what do you make of Scotland Yard's take on your perpetrator? That he's got it in for the Church?'

It's a bucket of rat shit.

'It's a logical extrapolation based on the facts.'

He raised an eyebrow, smirked as though we were sharing a joke.

'It's trite, is what it is. A real C student came up with that theory.'

I hid a smile, threw down a glove.

'How would you describe him, then? Go on. Anything. How he dresses. His childhood.'

A darkness passed across the Butcher's face, fleeting but enough to momentarily change the set of his features.

Vernon Sange has always claimed to have had an idyllic boyhood, shaking off questions about the mother who continues to sell her story to the highest bidder and the father who abandoned him as a baby.

He told *GQ* magazine he spent his summers swimming in streams and building forts with the neighbourhood kids. That he excelled at sport and as a child prodigy who graduated summa cum laude from Harvard aged fifteen, school was a breeze.

'Didn't your peers resent you?' the interviewer asked. 'Were you bullied?'

'They loved me,' he said. 'I was a hero for those kids.'

Not my experience of childhood. Where I came from, brainboxes were tortured – lunch money stolen, wedgies in the corridors, bog-washes – or else they were side-lined. Certainly, no one put them on a pedestal. Hard to believe things were much different in Southern California.

The cloud over Sange's eyes did nothing to counter that. It made me think. When it comes to serial murder, a miserable childhood is usually what sets the dominoes falling. But what was the Butcher's backstory? What explained his violent tendencies? Or did he just like to kill?

'I'll tell you something about your perpetrator without even seeing the files,' he said, leaning back in his chair, legs elongated in front of him. 'The person you're looking for used to have an imaginary friend. A pretty little girl with blonde hair and blue eyes. No one else came to play in that house, it was always cold in there from fall right through to spring. The mother was too cheap to pay for heating, every night the child went to bed shivering.'

A shiver ran through me too. He could have projected his own childhood on to the offender's background or profiled him, same way I do, to come up with the imaginary friend idea. And there was some rationality behind it. If the offender was building a face, it wasn't unreasonable to suggest he'd had a rich fantasy life as a child focusing on the idea of creating a perfect person.

But the bit about the cold house had no link to the crime or signature. In showing off, Sange had gone too far and let something slip. It meant one thing. He knew the killer.

Though where did he know him from?

Before his incarceration, Sange had danced in a large number of circles. As well as his involvement at Oxford, he was also a patron of the London Symphony Orchestra, on the board of trustees at The Wallace Collection and a Fellow at Eton College. Likely he knew hundreds of people, any number of whom might fit the profile.

But with just two days to go till the next PRK murder, going through his address book wasn't an option.

I glanced at him. He looked back at me, tilted his eyebrows and gave a boyish smile. His irises twinkled, soft dimples formed in his cheeks.

Despite everything Falcon had warned me about and what I knew he'd done, I felt my guard slipping. The man was a snake. And yet I couldn't help falling for his charm.

I watched his mouth move. His top lip was a perfect Cupid's bow.

'You're an attractive woman, Ziba.'

My face burned.

He was still talking as I scrambled for a comeback.

'Your clavicles are quite pronounced. Have you lost weight? It'd be understandable under the circumstances. Eating alone is such a bore, isn't it? A woman like you should have someone to dine with. Don't feel bad, Ziba. It's perfectly natural you should be seeking out a new companion.'

It was an ambush. He'd slid up silently behind me and ensnared me, drawing up my guilt, toying with it. And now he was squeezing hard, the pressure increasing bit by bit.

But there's no way he could have known about my supper plans with Wolfie, so how did he get it so right?

I'd been seduced before, now I was angry.

'I didn't come here to discuss my private life,' I said, my voice firm and unequivocal. 'Give me a name or I'm going.'

Sange smirked, nodding gently as if confirming something to himself.

'Jack Wolfe, I believe. I do hope he feels the same way. Then again, the pleasure's so often in the waiting.'

For a moment I was too winded to speak. He couldn't have known how I felt about Jack, not till I walked in here. It was my fault. I'd given myself away somehow, hypnotised by his snake dance, not realising with each answer and outburst I was allowing him to wrap his coils tighter around me.

And I still hadn't got what I'd come for.

'I'm going to ask you one last time, Sange. Who is the PRK?'

'There's only one name that matters to your killer. Do you like classical literature, Ziba? *The Aeneid*, perhaps? Such tragedy must strike a chord. Or perhaps you prefer the Greek myths. They're not just children's stories.'

'Are you going to give me a name, or not?'

'Are you going to come back?'

No chance.

'Give me something.'

'I just have.' He smiled. 'This was lovely. We must do it again.'

Before I could respond, he'd jumped up and buzzed for the guards.

In control to the very end.

CHAPTER 27

The child is sitting at the top of the stairs, rocking, knees to chest. Breathing hard.

The Gorgon's going to get me, it thinks, rocking faster, trying not to cry. If only there was a way to keep her and Mother apart. To keep her away.

The child calls Mother's friend Medusa, because of her horrid hair; all dreadlocky and dyed green at the ends. A head of snakes, like Medusa from the fat book of Greek myths at school, one of the three Gorgon sisters with vipers for hair and the power to turn anyone who looked at them into stone.

She's in the kitchen now, turning Mother against the child. Both of them drinking gin; the ice tinkling in their glasses, their voices slurred at the edges, loud, rising up the stairs.

'The child's six, Lily. Bit old to still be in Pampers, surely? What does the teacher say?'

'That they all go potty in their own time. Still phones me to come in whenever the kid needs changing, though. It's ridiculous. I can't have any sort of life of my own going in and out of there every two minutes.'

'Ever thought maybe that's why the child won't use the toilet?'

'Hmm,' Mother says, 'I never thought about it that way. You're very insightful, Sally.'

The child listens to every word, hate forming like a stone in its chest.

CHAPTER 28

'Did you get what you came for?'

Governor Goldfish licked his lips, addressed my breasts, leaned in. Nothing about him made me want to answer that question honestly.

I took a step back, zipped up my jacket.

'It was very helpful. We appreciate you allowing me to come in.'

The 'we' was deliberate. I didn't want this guy thinking I owed him a damn thing.

He smiled, finally moved his eyes up to my face. Stepped closer.

'A pleasure. Look, it's late, you must be hungry. There's a steak-house not far from here. How about it? My treat.'

I answered quickly.

'That's very kind but I'd best be getting back to London, it's a long drive home.'

His eyes glinted.

'You can forget about sleeping in your own bed tonight, Ms MacKenzie.'

There are laws against that sort of talk, you fat little worm. And it's 'Mrs'.

I made for the door, resisted sending my knee to his groin on the way.

'It was good meeting you, Governor.'

'You haven't heard?'

I turned round.

'Heard what?'

'The Met Office has issued a red weather warning. Part of the motorway's been shut heading southbound. No one's sure when it's going to reopen. The roads are treacherous, too. Couple of nasty collisions already. They're threatening power cuts. Bloody snow.'

The words were very much out of sync with his pleased expression. His voice was silky, on his face the suggestion of a smile.

'So, what d'you say? Want to change your mind about dinner?'

I'd rather starve.

'It's very kind, but it sounds like I'd better get a hotel room sorted.'

He shrugged, lost interest.

'There's a Travelodge up the road. Some of the inmates' wives stay there on visit days. You wouldn't believe how far these women travel to see their ratbag husbands.'

I thanked him and reluctantly shook his proffered hand. It was moist and sticky, like he'd been licking it.

In the prison corridor, the lights flickered twice and went off.

I was stranded in Wakefield and now the power was out.

CHAPTER 29

Travelodge, Wakefield

The power was out at the Travelodge too. The corridors were in shadow, half-lit by the low beam emergency lights, and silent too; the outside world muffled by the snow.

I inserted my key card into the lock. Nothing. I slid it in and out, rattled the handle, pushed the door.

Broke dick piece of shit.

Finally, just as I was thinking I'd have to go down to reception and get a new one, the lock gave way.

Inside, I switched on my iPhone torch and shone it round the murky room. 'Box' would have been a better word for it. The place was tiny, not much bigger than a cell.

But that's not what was plaguing me. Ever since my interview with the Butcher, I'd only been able to think of one thing.

Vernon Sange knows I love Jack.

I destroyed Vernon Sange.

Vernon Sange wants to destroy me.

To destroy me, he has to destroy Jack.

Deductive reasoning, same as the Butcher's. Jack was in danger and I'd put him there. Again.

My mind snagged on the memory of him in that hospital bed, connected up to wires and tubes, his face graffitied with lacerations and bruises – because of me. I'd been working with Scotland Yard in its hunt for the Hillside Slasher, a serial killer targeting women who looked worryingly like me. At the same time, I'd been conducting an investigation of my own into my husband's murder. And I'd begun to attract some unwanted attention – though, as it turned out, I wasn't the only one being watched.

If I hadn't involved Jack in my quest to get to the bottom of Sunlight, the investigation that had got Duncan killed, he'd never have been hurt. And the purple scar just below his left eye would still be unblemished skin.

My phoned buzzed in my pocket. A text from Wolfie. Jeez, it was as if I'd summoned him with the power of negative thought.

Can't wait to see you tomorrow! Let me know what I can bring.

SMS 23.19

I started to type – Just yourself. Then stopped and hit delete. Might sound like a come-on, I thought. From now on, I had to pick my words as carefully as Sange.

On the drive up to the prison, I'd been focused on what to say to Jack when I should have been planning how to get the Butcher to give up his intel on the Pink Rose Killer. But having made the decision to tell Wolfie how I felt, I'd been able to concentrate on little else.

I felt his lips on mine, hot and rough. Felt his hands on my back, in my hair. The taste of him. The smell.

Except now it couldn't happen.

As a high-functioning psychopath, Vernon Sange would be keenly attuned to the human psyche, to non-verbals and the emotions they betray. A fact I knew but hadn't managed to shield myself from.

I'd been tough, asking basic questions, letting him talk. But in trying to come across as strong, I'd shown him where I was weak. When he hit a nerve, it made me easier to read. I'd been studying him so carefully, I forgot he'd be doing the exact same thing with me. As a result, I'd laid myself open.

When he pulled Jack's name out from between his teeth, I couldn't help thinking he was psychic. But of course, like all the best illusions, it was a cook-up of tricks and theatrics rather than real magic.

He'd have registered my micro expressions when he made that comment about journalists. He'd have known I knew he was referring to Wolfie, given their history. He'd have registered my reactions again when he said I should have someone to 'dine' with, testing me and then picking up on the flicker of shame and embarrassment that would have passed over my face.

Telling him in such a sharp tone that I hadn't come to discuss my personal life would have confirmed it. I was interested in someone new and I felt bad about it.

From there, the rest was easy.

My husband's been dead for over two years, no one would frown on me for dating again after so long. So why did I feel guilty? If not for moving on, then it had to be who I was moving on with. Duncan's best friend would fit that bill. And it would explain my physical response to his remark about journalists.

Sange is a logician, not a physic. But that doesn't mean he can't read minds.

Possibly he'd also seen the photo the papers printed after Duncan's funeral with that godawful caption, *Cop's Widow Grieves*.

Me shuffling out of the cemetery, a wide-eyed zombie with Jack's big arms supporting me. Another piece of evidence to corroborate the Butcher's theory.

I slumped down on the hard bed, thinking it through.

Jack Wolfe . . . I do hope he feels the same way. Then again, the pleasure's so often in the waiting.

It was a threat, but from where I stood now it was a promise too.

Jack was in danger. But only if he and I got together.

Which meant the one way to keep him safe was to keep us apart.

CHAPTER 30

I was jetlagged to the eyeballs and hadn't slept a wink on the plane, but I was too chewed up with guilt and fear to even think about going to bed. My flesh crawled with it. My stomach was bilious.

How could I have been so stupid? How could I have exposed myself like that? Sange had cut me down and I'd given him the bloody axe to do it.

He was an evil bastard. But I was a fool, allowing myself to be taken in by his charisma like the rest of his idiot fan club. And my stupidity had put Jack in danger.

I had no idea what Sange would do with his intel, but I knew he'd do something. No way he'd ignore his new-found power over me.

Normally when something's bothering me I'll jump straight on the phone to Wolfie. He'll stay on the line till he's talked sense into me. Or else he'll pitch up on my doorstep with a Chinese takeout and a bottle of Pinot Gris.

I'm perfectly capable of kicking troublemakers into touch. I enjoy doing it too. But all the same, it's good to know he's got my six.

He couldn't be there for me now, though. Whatever other mistakes I'd made with Sange earlier, I was clear on that. Jack and I couldn't be together. And I couldn't tell him what had gone on in that room.

Wolfie's a bit like me in some ways, he has a tendency to jump into things feet first. Taking that approach with the Butcher could be fatal. Literally.

Prisons are villages, minus the church spire and picket fences. Word gets round quickly. Everyone knows everyone else's business and who to ask for a favour.

Vernon Sange may be locked up in a maximum-security jail, but he'd know people on the outside. Given his infamy, most low-lifes would be only too pleased to have him in their debt. And if the rumours about him were true, they wouldn't be the only ones he could call on for a favour.

If only there was someone I could talk to, someone who'd listen while I got things off my chest, found some perspective.

Fingerling was out, for obvious reasons. Falcon too. I respected him too much to tell him about the giant clusterfuck I'd unleashed, didn't want to lose his good opinion.

My mind flashed on Barnwell at the airport leaving that message for his mother. Turning to my mother should have been the natural thing to do. But there's nothing's natural about Emmeline. Even as a child she insisted on me calling her by her first name.

'I'm a person in my own right,' she used to say. 'I refuse to be defined by biology.'

Some people shouldn't have children. My mother's one of them. She's never forgiven me for the mistake she made bringing me into the world. Not being allowed to call her 'Mummy' had nothing to do with preserving her identity and everything to do with generating distance.

My father was the opposite. He was always *Bâbâ*, 'Daddy' in Persian. I couldn't imagine ever calling him by his first name. Couldn't imagine what he'd have said if I had.

'You and Emmeline are so different,' I said to him once. 'How come you got married?'

'We weren't so different once. But life changes people, Zibakam. And when I changed, your mother changed too.'

'Iran?' I said. 'The revolution?'

He nodded, took a long drag on his cigarette, letting the smoke out slowly in rings around his face.

'The day my family was murdered, my heart shattered into a thousand pieces. *Ghalbam shekast*. A break like that can never be fixed. A person can never be the same again. Don't blame your mother for being the way she is, *azizam*. Her heart is broken too.'

Bullshit her heart's broken, I thought now. You have to have a heart for it to break.

And I have to get my hands on some wine.

No way would I get any rest tonight without a few glasses.

I pocketed my room key and headed downstairs to the bar, already tasting the Merlot on my tongue.

CHAPTER 31

'Large or small glass?' the barman said.

'A bottle. To go,' I said, glancing round the shadowy bar. Still no bloody power.

A man with his hood up and a nine months' pregnant stomach looked me over the way men do when they want you to notice them. He was sitting on a stool, kicking his Nikes against the side of the bar, supping a pint. Didn't seem like it was his first of the night. Or his last.

'Thanks.'

I took my bottle, and a packet of salt and vinegar ridge cuts, and walked off, studiously avoiding Beer Belly's eye. I felt them on me all the same, all the way to the door. His aftershave followed me out. Old Spice, sprayed on thick.

'Lifts aren't working, love. You'll have to take the stairs.'

The receptionist sounded bored, went back to playing on her phone.

I was one flight up when I heard it, the squeak of the stairwell door opening. I glanced behind me through the banisters. Beer Belly was coming up.

I took the next few steps two at a time, instinctively wanting to increase the distance between us, then slowed my pace as I approached the second floor. Behind me it was silent. He'd gone.

Out in the corridor, the dust got in my throat, tickled my nostrils. The residual heat was fading fast.

I shivered, wished I were home.

I was fumbling in my pocket for my key, shifting the wine bottle and crisps packet to my other hand, when I smelled it. A stagnant cloud of Old Spice and BO. Close. Though in the dark, I hadn't seen him coming. Or heard the soft tread of his trainers on the carpet.

'Well, hello there.'

Had he followed me?

I shoved the card into the lock. Nothing.

'You not talking to me, princess?'

I jiggled the key. The red light was resolute.

In my peripheral vision, I saw Old Spice in outline glance quickly to the left and right. There's only one reason a man does that when he's alone in a corridor with a female he doesn't know.

I spun round, though I was too late. He lunged forward, gripping me round the throat and slamming me against the door, his other hand raised to do damage.

But this time I was ready for him.

I dropped my purchases, grabbed his nuts and squeezed. Hard.

Aargh!

He tipped forward, his hands clutching his groin. But I wasn't done with him yet. Gripping him by the shoulders, I sideswiped at his ankles with my right leg and pushed him to the ground.

Oof.

'Ever asked yourself why women don't talk to turds like you?'

I stepped forward, stamped hard on his nose with my boot. There was a loud crack.

'And don't call me princess.'

It was only after I'd given a statement and the police had taken him away that it struck me. This wasn't the first time I'd smelled Old Spice today.

The guy who'd asked me directions out of the prison parking lot earlier had been wearing it too. I hadn't got a good look at my attacker prior to the assault, not least because I'd been avoiding eye contact.

But I had noticed one thing. He had a bushman beard, just like the man outside the slammer.

Was it a coincidence? Or could it have been a set-up?

And if so, did Vernon Sange have anything to do with it?

CHAPTER 32

It's late, only the sound of drunks stumbling home comes up from below. There's a bar down the street. Spice, it's called. Mother goes there at night dressed in high heels and the scooped vest top that makes her boobs look about twice the size they do in her daytime clothes.

She locks the child in its room before she leaves, deadbolts the front door.

'Stop your nonsense. You're safe as houses,' she said when the child kicked up a fuss.

Only houses don't feel that safe, not when the men come.

The child cried harder, didn't want to be left alone, begged to tag along.

'For fuck's sake! I'm entitled to have a life of my own, you know. If you hadn't driven your father away into the arms of that little tart with your constant bawling, I wouldn't have to leave you. Now go to sleep, goddammit.'

She's back now, with another man. But he's going. Ear to the door, the child listens.

'I like you, Lily. But . . . well . . . it's just your kid, you see?'

The child smiles, despite the hiding that's coming.

Another one bites the dust.

CHAPTER 33

I spent the night in a half-sleep and when I woke at dawn it was like I hadn't slept at all.

Was the attack outside my room yesterday really instigated by Vernon Sange or was I just spinning out? Was my imagination playing tricks, or were my instincts right?

The weak morning light filtered through the dark plum-coloured curtains, giving the room a bruised look.

Like my flipping ribs, I thought, lifting the blanket to take a look at the damage. It was less bad than I was expecting, a blueish-purple mark, faint and strawberry-sized.

I rolled over. The bed was small, the walls pressed in on either side.

In my head I heard Sange's taunts again. The inherent threat to Jack. But was I overreacting to that too? Was there really any reason to think Wolfie was actually in danger?

I pulled back the curtains, let the daylight in.

I needed to get back to London. We only had one more day till the PRK struck again. Lying on my back in a hotel room hundreds of miles away wasn't going to help me stop him.

I powered up my iPhone, switched off last night to preserve the battery. If the motorway had reopened, I could be on my way in ten minutes.

I was just opening Google to check for updates when an email alert popped up. My stomach tightened, a sudden pain pounded my skull.

I've infiltrated al-Qaeda cells and taken down drug lords without firing a shot. I can hit a target at 800 meters and incapacitate a guy twice my size with a double palm strike through the centre line. And I can outsmart most people by using their minds against them.

But Vernon Sange is different. He frightens me. A constrictor, calculating and cruel. A person I can't predict but who can predict me. A man who sits watching, waiting, sliding into position, killing slowly. A man with friends.

When he was first arrested, there were rumours he had people beholden to him in the upper echelons of government, perhaps even in Scotland Yard. The rumours were never proved, but they didn't go away. And it looked like he had minions in Monster Mansion too.

How else could he have sent the email, the one now in my inbox, after lockdown? My spine crawled as my thoughts lined up in front of me, a parade of badly dressed soldiers.

Is this how he's communicating with the PRK? Or has he just cracked the code? How the fuck had he managed to get hold of my email address? And if he can do this, what else can he do?

I clicked on the link, read the message.

> *Dear Ziba,*
> *It was good of you to pop in and see me this evening.*
> *I do admire you, most especially for your ability to*
> *start afresh. I imagine few people would be able to*
> *move on so quickly after a loss as sudden and tragic*
> *as yours.*

I wonder if your interest in Jack Wolfe stems from his connection to your late husband. Though of course that must be something of a drawback too.

Tell me, does the sting of betrayal add to the excitement? It certainly adds to it for me.

I'd like to see you again. Come tomorrow and I'll have something for you. In the meantime, perhaps you might enjoy this. It's an extract from The Aeneid, a work I've always considered to be the very pinnacle of Western artistic achievement:

'And more than anyone, the Phoenician queen,
Luckless, already given over to ruin,
Marvelled and could not have enough: she burned
With pleasure in the boy . . .
And she with all her eyes and heart embraced him,
Fondling him at times upon her breast,
Oblivious of how great a god sat there
To her undoing.'
Virgil has such a way with words, doesn't he?
Vernon Sange

The meaning was clear.

I was the queen burning with 'pleasure in the boy'. Sange was the god.

And his goal was my undoing.

CHAPTER 34

I sat up in bed, the walls closing in, trying to decide what to do about the email.

'Break your problems into manageable chunks,' my special forces instructor used to say. 'Beat them down one piece at a time till they're soft as pulp and you can flush them down the pan.'

There was a pan in the bathroom next door. But my problems couldn't be flushed away without clogging up the pipes.

Vernon Sange claimed to have something for me. Possibly it could help us catch the PRK before he struck again tomorrow. And given what he'd let slip during our meeting yesterday, there was a strong chance he knew the perpetrator.

But what would getting the intel cost me?

My brain doubled back to yesterday evening, to the windowless room and the single bulb in the ceiling, painting a sheen on the Butcher's hair.

I'd like to see you again . . .

I'd like nothing less. But not only could a second visit prevent another innocent victim from being killed, it could also save Wolfie. The message inherent in the email was simple: give me what I want, and I won't hurt Jack.

Trouble is, to remove the threat to him I had to increase the threat to myself.

I balled my fist and thumped the headboard in frustration. That'll be another bruise, I thought. And with that one came another.

Vernon Sange thinks Jack and I are already an item. If he stops believing that then he loses the hold he has over me.

Except bluffing wouldn't cut it. A man as emotionally perceptive as Sange would be able to see through a lie. To get him to buy that I wasn't with Jack, I had to make a relationship an impossibility. In other words, engineer a situation where I wouldn't have to lie and risk my body language giving me away.

And there was just one way to do that.

I stroked the edge of my phone with the side of my thumb, the same way Duncan used to stroke the base of my neck when he kissed me.

I shook the memory off, thinking what to say to Wolfie. It needed to be more than a fob-off. For this to work, I had to build a wall between us, one that couldn't be knocked down.

Face to face wouldn't work, nor would a phone call. Jack knows me too well. He'd see through the deceit. And hearing his voice, I wouldn't have it in me to say what I needed to.

So, an SMS then. The most impersonal form of contact.

I began to type, fingers shaking.

Do you mind if we rain-check this evening? Thing is I've met someone. I really like him. He wants to take me out tonight...

SMS 06.27

There had been something growing between Jack and me, something bright and golden and reaching towards the light. This would yank it up by the roots. He'd move on, meet someone else, maybe fall in love with them.

But I had to do this . . . Didn't I?

My finger hovered over the arrow icon. What if I was making a mistake, sabotaging a relationship that could be wonderful? What if—?

Tell it to the chaplain, MacKenzie.

I closed my eyes, took a breath and pressed send.

Moments later the phone started buzzing, his name lit up on the screen: WOLFIE.

I could still take it back. Put this right. Tell him everything.

Except I couldn't.

I held the phone against my chest, the vibrations pulsing through my skin. By the time it stopped my face was wet, my throat squeezed tight like I was being choked.

It was the best thing I could have done for him. But the worst thing I've ever done to myself.

Because saving Jack meant sacrificing myself.

CHAPTER 35

Her Majesty's Prison Service, HMP Wakefield

Stuck in Wakefield overnight. Motorway has reopened now.

Meeting the Butcher again then coming back to the Yard.

SMS 06.48

Nigel Fingerling

OK. Call me when you're done.

SMS 06.49

Getting into my Porsche was like slipping between the sheets with a glass of vintage wine, but as I approached the turnoff to the prison my baby's magic started to fade. I was meeting Vernon Sange; no amount of turbo-charged beauty could put a shine on that. Not just because there was a very real chance he wouldn't be taken in by the precautions I'd set up regarding Jack, but also because he was still our best hope of stopping the PRK before he struck again.

And if what he'd said was right, we had thirty-six hours before the next attack. No pressure then.

I'd have loved to believe that Sange was bluffing, making out he knew more than he really did. But inconvenient as the truth was, I could tell the Butcher was giving it to us straight. He knew the person we were hunting. Though that didn't mean he'd give me a name. Not unless I gave him what he wanted. A piece of me.

Thing is, who's to say he'd keep up his end of the deal? Vernon Sange is a serpent, this was a Faustian pact. And it's not as if I haven't been played by killers before. Ones behind bars.

There was Alvin Monsun, all pudgy and polite, with his gentle handshake, sitting where and when he was told. The guy claimed to have intel on a case I was working. Begged me to bring him the crime scene photos.

'There's something in them,' he said. 'I need to see.'

He wasn't lying. He did need to see them. But only so he could get his rocks off. Right there in front of me.

And what about Rupert de Lupa? I thought, pulling up to the roundabout. One of the first serial murderer interviews I conducted and the rat fuck tries to kill me.

De Lupa was a massive bloke. Over six foot five, must have weighed three hundred pounds. And highly intelligent behind those cold, dead eyes.

We'd been talking for hours, zeroing in on his depraved fantasies, when I felt the time had come to wind things up. I buzzed for the guard. But no one came. I buzzed again.

Most killers are highly aware of other people, their hobby depends on it. And despite my best attempt to appear calm, de Lupa sensed the apprehension behind my mask.

He smiled, slow and lazy.

'Must be changing shifts.' He got up, leaned his huge frame over the table, resting his bulk on hands the size and shape of baseball mitts. 'Could be ten, fifteen minutes before they come back.'

'Doesn't matter. I've got time on my parking.'

No way was I going to let him know I was rattled. But he knew anyway.

He smiled again, showed all his teeth.

'I could bite your head off. Leave it on the table for them. No one would hear. It's been a long time since I was alone with a female.'

He drew the word out. *Fee-male*.

The room was small. The door bolted from the outside. I've been trained by the SAS in close quarter battle, but even so, I didn't relish the thought of a fight with this guy. There was a foot and a half in height between us. Two hundred pounds in weight. And I didn't have a gun in my belt.

Way I saw it, reason was my best weapon. And an 'I'm not taking you seriously' attitude.

'Apart from the fact my hair could do with a wash, is biting my head off really worth the trouble it'd get you in? It's not like they wouldn't know who'd done it.'

He laughed loudly, right from the belly.

'I already lost my TV privileges. Not much else they can take away from me.'

'No, but they could put you in the hole.'

It wasn't a nothing punishment, inmates have been known to go mad in solitary. But de Lupa shook it off.

'It'd be worth a bit of alone time for the prestige I'd get for offing a pig.'

I was about to retort that I'm not police when a better idea presented itself. During the hostage training part of the SF pro-gramme, we were taught that getting an aggressor chatting is the best way to defuse a difficult situation and buy us time to plan an escape.

'You honestly think I'd come in here alone if I couldn't defend myself?' I said, acting all casual.

'Bullshit. They don't let weapons through here.'

I laughed.

'I don't need a weapon to take you, de Lupa.'

He laughed too. The tone changed.

'Martial arts, is it? You gonna whip me with your little black belt?'

'Well, I wasn't planning to beat you up with a little black dress.'

He sat down, leaned back in his chair. A leer on his great big face.

'I'd like to see you in a black dress,' he said.

'You like women's clothes, don't you? You used to keep items from your victims, right?'

And so I steered the conversation back to where I'd first broken it off. Until I heard the reassuring march of heavy black boots. This time when I buzzed, the door opened.

Right then I made the decision never to interview a serial killer or rapist alone again.

Until yesterday, when I had locked myself in a room with Vernon Sange.

And I was about to do the same thing again now.

CHAPTER 36

I was back in the same legal visit room as before, only it seemed smaller than the last time. There was a low buzzing sound coming from the overhead light as if it were about to die. And the ghost of the governor's cologne. He'd insisted on escorting me over himself.

'I heard your husband passed away,' he said, unlocking yet another steel gate.

He touched the small of my back. I considered putting my foot through his.

I closed my eyes now, took a breath, tried to ground myself.

I'm in a better position than before, I thought. I've already had a one-on-one with Sange. And I know what his game is, which tells me how to play mine.

My self-talk was just that, though. Talk.

The Crown Prosecution Service thought they had their case tied fast, used their top dogs to argue it out in court. Yet the way things played out at the Old Bailey, Sange very nearly slithered out of their ropes, until the anonymous tip came through.

I took another breath. Despite myself, the fear seeped in. It left a taste, hard and bitter in my mouth.

Are you sure you want to go down this road?

Falcon's words from yesterday.

'Want' has nothing to do with what I'm doing here, I told myself. I've got a job to do and I'll be damned if I'm going to let some pretty boy with an Oxford doctorate get the better of me.

I paced the room, buttoning down my approach. Profiling the Butcher the way I profile all my targets. Figuring out the best way to net him.

Serial killers are territorial, they don't like anyone else pissing on their doorstep. If I could make Sange believe we had another source of intel, he'd want to show his was better. And to do that, he'd have to reveal more about the perp.

My tongue was clacking on the roof of my mouth, keeping time with the fist now smacking against my thigh.

He won't give me a name though, I thought. Like I'd said to Fingerling, there'd be no fun for him in that. And once I got what I came for, he'd know I wouldn't come back.

Sange hadn't named his price, but he hadn't needed to. I could guess what he was after from his questions yesterday. He'd made it easy for me, deliberately so.

And he hadn't once mentioned privileges or delaying his extradition. The man is a sadist. He takes his nourishment from other people's pain and the power he's able to exert over them.

He likes to show off too, exerting control by demonstrating his intellectual superiority.

That's why he killed his pet bird in front of that guard. He wasn't being petulant. He was peacocking. And if I lined him up right, maybe I could get him to do the same thing for me.

A name was too much to hope for. But a riddle I could solve was a possibility. Question is, would I be able to crack it before the PRK went hunting again?

Thin-soled shoes, two pairs of boots. Getting louder.

I smoothed down my hair, sat down, hands steepled in front of me, ready. And then my phone buzzed.

Another SMS from Jack, on top of the three missed calls already logged.

Can you ring me?

His timing couldn't have been worse. Seeing his name up on the screen sent the blood straight to my face.

Just as Vernon Sange walked in.

CHAPTER 37

The tiniest of smiles danced at the corners of Sange's mouth. His eyes flicked from the phone in my hand to the heat flooding my face. His nostrils flared infinitesimally.

He knew.

'Hello, Ziba.'

His tone was as charming as before, but raspy too, like there was something caught in his epiglottis. Who else had he spoken to today? How many hours did he spend alone in his cell? How many hours did he have just to think?

The guards left the room. I set my phone to record, ready to put the script right.

'That was a text from my DI. Someone's come forward with information. We're following up a strong lead. Looks like an arrest is imminent. I doubt you and I will be seeing each other again. So, if there's anything you want to say, now's the time.'

The Butcher tilted his head, fixing me with a blue and blinkless stare.

'Did it hurt?'

His tone was full of false concern, his voice almost a whisper.

A fresh rush of blood surged to my face, my heart drummed hard in its cage.

How did he know?

All he'd had to go on was my reaction to Wolfie's SMS and our conversation yesterday. Yet somehow Sange must have worked out I'd broken things off with him and was beating myself up over it. Not only had I lied to Jack for nothing, he was still in harm's way.

I needed to un-fuck this fast.

'Sounds like you're making quite the tent blanket fantasising about Jack Wolfe and me. But that's all it is, Sange. A pathetic little fantasy. Jack's my friend. Nothing more. Never will be.'

I eyeballed the hell out of him. Let the bastard read me as much as he wanted. Everything I was saying was true. It *was* over between us.

Nothing about my non-verbals would suggest deceit. That was the whole point of the text to Wolfie claiming to be seeing someone new.

My shoulders dropped, my pulse slowed.

Thank crap I'd gone through with it. My experience yesterday showed Sange would see through a cheap bluff. The message I'd sent made it real.

It had been a tough call. I've had knife wounds that have caused less pain. But knocking Sange off the scent made it absolutely the right move.

When he spoke, his voice was soft, on his face the whisper of a smile.

'I was actually referring to the bruise on your ribs.'

Shit.

CHAPTER 38

Rookie idiot! I'd shot my mouth off and revealed everything I'd wanted to hide.

Sange had asked if it hurt and I'd responded with a diatribe about how Jack and I were just friends. *The lady doth protest too much, methinks.* A blind person could see that.

Though how had the Butcher known about the bruise on my ribs? I'd covered the marks left on my neck by last night's attack with a thick layer of foundation picked up from the pharmacy by the Travelodge. Though even if Sange had noticed the make-up and made a connection, it didn't explain his comment about my bruise, which was only faint and hidden under two layers of clothing.

Had I unconsciously touched my side? Winced? Or was I right, had he set up the attack?

I took a deep breath and forced myself to drop my shoulders.

Move it on, MacKenzie. You can still get what you came here for. You may have blasted yourself in the foot, but at least the strategy still stands up.

'You said you had something for me. What is it?'

Sange pushed the hair off his face, lolled in his chair like he had all the time in the world.

'Did you know, the ancient Romans enjoyed drinking blood almost as much as they enjoyed their wine?'

For fuck's sake.

'Where are you going with this, Sange?'

'After the games, vendors sold still-warm blood from fallen gladiators to the crowd. There was quite a demand for it. It was believed to contain a "life force", you see. They believed drinking it would make them stronger.'

'Lovely.'

'They weren't the only ones to appreciate the health benefits. Marsilio Ficino, an Italian Renaissance scholar, suggested the elderly suck blood "the way leeches do. An ounce or two from a vein on the left arm barely opened", so he said.'

'Are you trying to tell me the PRK is a vampire?'

That didn't scan. There weren't any bite marks or puncture wounds on any of the PRK's victims.

'Let your mind listen and absorb.' He smiled. 'Are you familiar with Pythagoras? He's well known for his mathematical theories, of course. But he was a philosopher too, founded the Pythagorean school that influenced Plato and Aristotle so heavily.'

It was quite an eloquent way of telling me to shut it. If the clock hadn't been ticking so loud in my head, I'd have fired back a retort. Instead I kept schtum and let him finish. If this was the intel that'd finally nail the killer . . .

'I had other ways of getting what I needed,' he said, as casually as he if were debating the benefits of Amazon Prime. 'But the principle remains the same. It's why I was only interested in the best specimens. I thought he understood that.' He smirked. 'I'm sure he does now, though.'

A jolt went through my body, so violent I could have been strapped to Old Sparky.

I thought he understood that. I'm sure he does now, though.

Was it a threat? Had the Butcher's people got to Jack while I'd been stranded up here? Is that what he was hinting at? Why Wolfie had been trying to reach me?

Or was this just another of Sange's games?

I'd come into the room determined to be in control this time. But once again he'd snatched the wheel right out of my hands.

CHAPTER 39

Sange angled his head, eyebrow cocked.

'I'm surprised you haven't asked me about him.'

So, he *had* been alluding to Jack! Sonofabitch, what had he done?

'If he's broken so much as a nail because of you, I'll make what's left of your life so miserable you'll be begging for the chair.'

The Butcher smiled through closed lips; the expression in his eyes was almost fond.

'I do enjoy talking to you, Ziba. You're quite a firecracker.'

'Well, I'm glad you've had fun, because we're done.'

He might know who the PRK was. And he might have intel that could help catch him. But I could see now that he never had any intention of sharing either. I'd wasted over twelve hours on his drivel. Twelve hours I could have used to unpick the killer's signature and figure out the true target of his rage.

My chair made a loud scraping noise as I pushed it back from the table. The sound echoed off the walls. My footsteps too.

Like last time, Sange didn't speak until my hand was on the buzzer.

'How about a trade?'

I turned round. One arm was slung casually over the back of his seat; he was leaning on his other elbow, his forefinger stroking the space between his lip and nose.

This was almost certainly another one of his games, but curiosity got the better of me. And fear for the next victim.

'What sort of trade?'

He smiled.

'You answer one of my questions and I'll answer one of yours. What do you say?'

I pursed my lips, rubbed the dip at the base of my neck.

'You'll give me something I can use?'

'Of course.'

'And you understand there'll be repercussions if you don't?'

'Absolutely.'

He didn't give a damn about consequences, I knew that. But then again, what did I have to lose? Likely it would prove to be a raid on an empty house, but there was a chance it could reveal a weapons cache.

'All right. What's your question, Sange?'

He slid forward in his chair, fixed me with his unblinking stare.

'There's nothing like the smell of a shot hitting its mark. The sharp, spicy scent of the gunpowder mixing with the rusted iron fragrance of hot, fresh blood. Gets in your throat, doesn't it?

'Tell me, Ziba, did you feel guilty when the bullet hit Duncan's head?'

CHAPTER 40

Did you feel guilty when the bullet hit Duncan's head?

With those words, the Butcher sent me right back to that moment on the pavement.

I tried to rein myself in by focusing on how he'd done it; analysing his words the way Duncan analysed the extracts of poetry he'd read aloud to me over wine on the sofa, in bed at night, side by side on our bench by the canal.

Sange's technique was brilliant; on the receiving end, I still had to admire it. Nothing evokes memory as well as smell. It's the strongest recall sense there is. Which is why when we're trying to dredge up the suppressed memories of a potential witness, we'll often ask them what a place smelt like. Or a person.

It's also why soldiers with PTSD will spiral faster when confronted with an odour they associate with a war zone than when they hear a car backfiring.

Sange had conjured Duncan's execution perfectly with well-chosen words, hurtling me back to the worst minutes of my life. The minutes my black dog feeds off and which were already ripe in my mind from my stay at Quantico.

Rationalising my emotions usually helps me manage them. But it wasn't working so well now. I was raw from my trip, sleep-deprived, stressed about Jack and the case.

On top of that, the black hound was already loose. And Sange had just waved a nice juicy bone under its nose.

But it wasn't just describing so perfectly the smell of Duncan's death that got to me.

The language was colourful, certainly. It sent me back, reminding me of the split-second change in air pressure as the bullet fired at my husband. The splat and crack as it connected with his epidermis and broke through the front of his skull.

It was his question that laid me bare, though. *Did you feel guilty when the bullet hit Duncan's head?*

No one's ever got to the heart of what I felt that night, what I still feel. Not even Jack, and he understands me better than anyone.

Yes, I felt shock and grief and despair. Disbelief too, for a while. But what I felt most was shame. Guilt.

I was still in the special forces back then, though on secondment to the Yard at the time. 7/7 changed the playing field for us. The monsters were on our own soil now. The battlefield was at home as well as abroad. I wasn't just being called in to advise on serial murder cases any more.

But swapping camos for civvies didn't change the job and it shouldn't have changed the way I react.

In the SF we're taught to pick up on the most insignificant details, wherever we are. Even now, I can go into a packed room for ten seconds, come out and tell you exactly how many people are in there. What they're each wearing. And which of them would be most vulnerable and most useful in a crisis situation.

I've been doing it so long now it's become an instinct, but the night of Duncan's death my training left me. When the bullet hit, I froze.

I caught the make and model of the shooter's van. But I didn't catch the plates. And it took me six whole seconds to call the emergency services. Six seconds probably didn't make much difference as to whether my husband lived or died. But they made a difference to me.

The way I saw it, I failed him. And yes, Sange, that makes me feel guilty as hell.

CHAPTER 41

I took a breath, grounded myself. I was here to get intel on the PRK, not fall on my sword. I'd answer Sange's question, but I wouldn't give him what he wanted – a piece of me.

'I was shocked when my husband was hit. Shocked and scared and horrified. But guilty? No. Of course not. It's not as if I pulled the trigger.'

The Butcher exhaled deeply, folded his arms.

'That was a lie, Ziba. Did you think I wouldn't notice?'

Yes. No.

'Give me what I want. I'll pay well for it.'

'A name?'

He smiled his boy-in-a-bar smile.

'If you'll give name to your feelings.'

'How do I know—?'

He held up a hand.

'Enough! I've offered to help. All you have to do is answer a simple question and you'll save the life of that little blonde girl. Unless you'd rather walk away now and await the inevitable. Because it is inevitable, Ziba. Your perpetrator has a strict timetable and I'm the only one who can help you delay it.'

For once he was transparent, his phrasing blatantly provocative. But that didn't mean he wasn't right.

The last thing I wanted to do was let the Butcher into my head; however, doing so might be our best chance of stopping the killer.

So, steeling myself, I met his eyes and began to speak. Though I didn't once refer to Duncan by name.

There was a limit to how much of myself I was willing to sacrifice to this man.

CHAPTER 42

Vernon Sange watched me as I talked, interjecting with questions, pushing me deeper and deeper down inside myself. His voice was soft and quiet like a therapist's, but there was no couch in here. His questions were designed to hurt, not help.

Constantly, he brought me back to the moment of impact, to the bullet crashing through Duncan's temporal lobe. His eyes on me the whole time.

'How did it smell when he died?' he asked, head rotating on his neck. 'Did it leave a nail polish tang in your throat? Did his eyes go filmy? Describe it for me, Ziba. Tell me about the yellowing of his skin, his last croak.'

A pulse danced at his temple. His pupils dilated. His eyes never moved from my face.

I knew what he was doing but it made no difference, I felt my feet slipping all the same. Inch by inch he drove me closer to the edge, until I stopped seeing him at all and only saw Duncan.

I saw his eyes, that mix of grey and green that always made me think of mountain lakes. His strong jaw – often clenched, always covered in stubble. His mouth, I'd kissed how many times? And which grinned so wide it lit up his whole face.

Then I saw him right there in front of me the way I'd seen him that first time at Scotland Yard, standing in the Round Table

Room addressing the team, his whole being exuding confidence and authority. Not dying out on the pavement. But alive, doing what he did best. Inspiring others. Inspiring me. Fearless.

Sange had tried to break me, but in conjuring Duncan, he made me stronger.

I squared up to the black dog, and to him.

'Your turn, Sange.'

There was the briefest flicker on his pallid features. For once, I'd surprised him.

'A name. Who is the Pink Rose Killer?'

He stroked his lips and smirked. It drew his brows together, made his eyes seem darker.

'Pygmalion,' he said.

'What kind of—?'

'Remember Pythagoras, Ziba. Listen and absorb.'

He gave a playful wink, moved smoothly behind the desk. And buzzed for the guards.

CHAPTER 43

'The principle idea behind the Doctrine of Opposites is that opposites fit together within the cosmos just as they do microscopically within an individual . . .'

The child is trying to explain Pythagoreanism to a teacher. She's pretending to listen but her eyes have glazed over. The other kids are giggling and whispering, deliberately loud, wanting the child to hear.

'Weirdo.'

'Freak.'

Someone throws a pencil sharpener from the back row. It hits the child's head.

The teacher wakes up, bites down a smile.

'Stop it,' she says. But there's no rebuke in it.

None of these morons understand me, the child thinks, belly sinking. What I'd like to do to them . . .

Flipping to the back of an exercise book, mind turning inwards, the child begins to sketch Mother as the Vitruvian Man; her naked body contained in both a square and a circle, every detail perfectly captured.

Below it, the child writes the words 'Cosmography of the microcosm'. Reference to another doctrine. Da Vinci's theory that the *workings of the body represent the workings of the universe. And of the soul.*

The words are also tattooed on the child's thigh, high up where no one can see. Carved deep with the sharp point of a compass.

A protective amulet, just like the holy tattoos of Ancient Egypt.

CHAPTER 44

I stormed out of the prison, fists clenched, jaw tight with rage.

I'd been played again, the second time in two days.

Sure, the name 'Pygmalion' would mean something. But it was hardly going to lead to an arrest before tomorrow.

I should have known the wank rag would screw me over.

Duncan once told me that riot police never put polish on their boots because if incendiary material is thrown at them it catches fire. In other words, they assess a situation for threats and take precautions before going in. But what precautions had I taken?

Cooling things with Jack? Hoping Sange wouldn't sense my true feelings? Putting on a brave face?

I was an embarrassment, a disgrace to my old unit. I hadn't just opened myself up and got screw all to show for it, I'd also run my mouth off and possibly put Wolfie in even more danger than he was in before.

I threw myself into the Porsche and slammed the door shut, cocooning myself in a nest of metal and tan leather, with the crazy feeling that Sange's snake eyes were still on me, gloating through the snow-crusted glass.

I'd allowed him to close in and trap me.

Though what choice did I have? I thought, turning up the de-mister to the max. This is all a hunt for him, and I'm the meat.

But he knows the killer's identity, it's obvious. I could hardly leave without trying to get it out of him.

I drove up the not very aptly named Love Lane, correcting the Porsche on the icy roads. Outside, the snow was slowly suffocating the landscape. Everything was bleached and bloodless. Driving forward felt like driving nowhere. I was caught in a cloud. And my side, only twinging before, was now throbbing hard.

I pulled over, unzipped my leather jacket and lifted the hem of my sweater. At the Travelodge, the bruise from last night had been faint and strawberry-sized. Now it was dark purple and big as a fist, as though Vernon Sange had landed a fresh punch.

Stupid, of course, but the idea stuck all the same.

I drove on, passing a large DIY store and a car dealership, the vehicles uniform white under their snow shrouds.

'Come on.'

Still no phone signal. It took until I reached the motorway for the bars to stay steady. Though by then the battery was on its last legs.

I called Fingerling.

'I'm just in with the DCI,' he said, picking up. 'Hang on a second, I'll put you on speaker.'

'Hello, Mac. I hear you've been stranded up there. Are you all right?'

Falcon's voice was warm, made me think of butter and hot toast. My stomach rumbled. Breakfast felt like a long time ago.

I kept the sit-rep brief, unsure how long the juice in my phone would last.

Much as I'd have liked to lean on him, he was anxious enough about what the Butcher might do without me revealing how I'd been played. And no way was I bringing up anything personal with DI Dipstick listening in.

'Sange didn't tell me much. He says the PRK will leave a picture of a circle with an arrow in it alongside the next body. He'll

120

cut off the next victim's lips. And she'll be blonde. *A goddess for the goddess*, he called her.'

'What's that supposed to mean?' said Fingerling. 'Another reference to religion? Fits the Catholic angle, of course.'

Jeez, not that God-bothering bullcrap again. There was almost no evidence to support an anti-Church motive, aside from where victims two through five had been found. Though I had a pretty good idea why he was clinging to the theory.

The London Lacerator case had an effect on us both. The perp should have been called Mr Skippy, he was so damn nutty. Or maybe St Skippy, given his delusions.

'That's not what's going on here,' I said.

'Why don't you want to believe this is about religion?'

'Because the moment I start wanting to believe anything, I may as well pack up my gear and go home.'

There was a pause.

'Goddess for the goddess?' Falcon said. 'Could it be we're looking for a woman?'

I shook my head, though there was no one around to see.

'There's no way the PRK's a female. We know from the forensics report that he carries his victims to the kill site. The upper body strength needed for that points to a male. Plus, Sange is a riddler. He wouldn't want to make things easy for us. You saw yourself in court, sir. He's a master of misdirection.'

And at getting people to do what he wants, I thought, my mind flashing on the email I'd received this morning. Another thing I couldn't mention to these guys without showing how badly I'd ballsed up.

'I need to get started on the team briefing,' said Fingerling, yawning. I wasn't the only one firing up the two-ended candle. 'Suppose it's too much to ask that you got a name out of your friend?'

I bit down on my irritation.

'He's no friend of mine. And he was never going to give us a real name.'

'Are you saying he gave you something?'

'He claims the PRK is called Pygmalion. It's got to be a reference to whatever fantasy the perp's inhabiting.

'But I've got absolutely no idea what it means.'

CHAPTER 45

Scotland Yard, London

Fingerling called just as I was turning on to Grosvenor Place. My battery was on its last 4%. He sounded harassed.

'Where are you?'

'Just a few minutes out.'

'I need you to go and re-interview Marc Gethen, the bloke who found the first victim. And the soup kitchen guy, Ian Heppe. I realise you've had a long journey but we're up against the clock.'

Roger that.

My phone pinged.

'Just sent you the address details. Barnwell will set up the meets. You might as well take him with you. You should have a copper present and it'll be a treat for him. Mr Jolly Hockey Sticks seems to have a bit of a crush on you.'

'Don't be ridiculous.'

'What's ridiculous? You're an attractive woman, MacKenzie. He lobbied me big time to let him be the one to bring you back from Quantico. Quite the little groupie you've got yourself there. He was a junior on the Sange investigation. You probably don't remember him, but he definitely remembers you.'

From him, the flattery was like swallowing a live eel. I could feel it squirming all the way down to my gut. But it wasn't just the backhanded compliment that made my insides writhe. His words were creepily similar to Sange's yesterday. And thinking of him immediately made me think of Jack.

Everything about the way I was ignoring Wolfie felt wrong, despite the reason I was doing it. If only I could tell him what was going on.

Embrace the suck, MacKenzie.

How many times did I have to tell myself that keeping a distance from him was the only way to keep him safe? Head vs Heart, toughest battle there is.

Back at the Yard, I charged my phone and read through Gethen's statement to the first responders before marching over to Barnwell's desk – shoulders back, head high. Superwoman pose. If you act strong, you feel strong.

'Ready to roll?' I said. 'I'll drive.'

My car. My space.

'I'm parked in the lot.'

He grabbed his coat and we headed to the lifts.

'You use a lot of Americanisms, but you don't have an accent. What's the story there?'

I shrugged.

'I worked a number of joint ops with the Green Berets, US Special Forces. Guess some of their lingo rubbed off.'

Duncan's Scottishisms rubbed off on me too. He's been gone for over two years, and I'm still saying 'aye'.

We walked out into the March ice-box. So much for global warming. This was global fucking freezing.

We got into the Porsche and buckled up, my back protesting from sitting so long.

'It's left-hand drive,' said Barnwell, as if I didn't know what side my steering wheel was on.

'She was made in Stuttgart,' I said.

I could have shown him the VIN plate but something told me he wouldn't get the buzz out of it I do.

I slipped her into first, let off the handbrake and pulled out. When we were clear of the other cars, I let her go, flicking her left and right to straighten her out as she fought for grip on the ice.

I glanced over at Barnwell. He was clutching the edge of the seat. He'd better not be leaving nail marks in the leather.

'Can you open up the file on Gethen?' I said, the quickest way to get him to take his paws off my girl. 'Talk me through the alibi, see if there's anything we missed.'

'Okay. Says in his statement, he and his wife were home watching TV the night of the murder. He gives the names of the programmes he says they watched. But he doesn't give any real detail about what happened in them beyond a basic summary he could have read online.'

'And the wife is sticking to the story. They have kids. Two under five and a teenage son.'

He looked at me, cocked his head. There was something puppyish about it.

'What's the relevance of the kids?'

'Could explain why Mrs G is going along with his story. Perhaps she doesn't fancy dragging the kids all the way to Belmarsh if Daddy-o gets banged up.'

Daddy-o? Just the sort of thing Duncan would have said. It was like he was speaking through me.

I tapped my thumb on the edge of the steering wheel, setting up the play.

'We'll show her the crime scene photos. Let her see what kind of monster we're looking for. She may be less keen to lie for her husband if she thinks there's a chance he could be behind the attacks.'

The main road was clear. I accelerated hard through the gears.

It had taken Marc Gethen over an hour to report the body after finding it. Possibly taking the time to get his story straight.

I planned for it to take half that time ripping it to shreds.

CHAPTER 46

We pulled up round the corner from West Heath outside a large detached house on Hermitage Lane. Black iron gates. Cream stone façade. Bay trees by the door cloaked in snow. The Gethen residence.

'We're minutes away from where the first vic was found,' said Barnwell in his boarding-school drawl.

I went to boarding school too but the manners never latched on the way my mother hoped they would. I was a misfit the moment I walked through those big wooden doors in my second-hand uniform.

Barnwell probably feels the same way about the Yard, I thought. Snobbery sucks even when it's in reverse, especially with dicks like Fingerling making fun of your accent every chance they get.

I rang the doorbell. Mrs Gethen answered, a woman who could have done with a few cheeseburgers; fully made-up and in head-to-toe designer labels, despite no one having been in or out of the house all day.

That's the thing about snow, people leave tracks.

'Going somewhere nice?' I asked after we'd been through the introductions.

'No.'

She looked confused.

So, she'd dressed for us. On guard, then. Realised what was at stake. Another one going for the superwoman pose.

That told me something else. She wasn't comfortable about our visit. Deceit creates discomfort. Profiler 101. But what was Mrs Gethen trying to hide?

The toilet flushed upstairs and a moment later Marc appeared on the landing, wiping his hands on the seat of his jeans and wearing mismatched socks. His muscles were big, his T-shirt tight. A man who worked out and wanted everyone to know it. The sort who wouldn't have much trouble carrying a woman into the woods.

'The police are here,' his wife said, in case he hadn't clocked me and Barnwell filling up his hallway. 'I've put the girls in front of CBeebies. Should keep them out of our hair.'

The words were friendly enough. But she didn't look at him as she spoke.

She turned to me, smiled tightly. On edge. Close up, she smelled of Dior. Pure Poison.

'The television's the best babysitter,' she said. 'It's the only thing that'll keep them quiet, even on a snow day.'

Gethen came down, shook our hands with a tight grip. A show of confidence, but his palms were sweaty.

'My son's still asleep. He's sixteen. I don't expect we'll hear anything out of him till this afternoon. Even then he keeps to himself. Teenagers, eh?'

He was rambling, another sign of nerves. But if all he'd done was find the body, what did he have to hide?

Mrs Gethen opened the door on to a cream-carpeted sitting room. Every cushion was up on its point, nothing out of place. Even the photo-house hardbacks were lined up perfectly on the coffee table.

Buttoned down and repressed, I thought. Everything's about appearances. Only one reason for a person to be like that. They don't want you scratching too deep beneath the surface.

'Would you like anything to drink?'

Barnwell and I both declined, the countdown clock loud in our heads. The sooner we got on with the interview, the sooner we'd be out of here.

Mrs Gethen crossed her legs and clasped her hands to her chest. Closed body language. Protecting herself. Tightly wound.

Marc Gethen sat next to her. His wife angled her body away from him. He touched her shoulder, she flinched. Happy couple.

On the wall above them was a well-stocked bookcase; novels arranged not alphabetically but by the colour of their spines. And on the third shelf down, in the centre of a row of yellow, was *Catullus, Carmina*. The poet apparently favoured by the PRK.

A shiver traced my neck.

'Who's the artist?' I said, trying to keep my tone light.

'I'm sorry?'

'The bookcase.' I gestured with my head. 'It's very colourful.'

Marc smiled.

'I was going for a Damien Hirst look.'

'Isn't he the guy who chopped up a cow and its calf, then pickled the parts?' said Barnwell, nose wrinkling.

'That's right. *Mother and Child Divided*. Brilliant title, isn't it?' He grinned. 'I went to see it twice at the Tate. There's a similar installation at this funky steak restaurant in Shoreditch. Just the one cow there, though.'

He sounded disappointed.

Listening to him, I couldn't help thinking they should revise the Hare Psychopathy Checklist to include the question: 'Do you like Damien Hirst?'

I squinted at the book titles as though noticing them for the first time.

'Catullus? It's not often you see him lined up next to Ben Elton and Nick Hornby. Did you study Classics, Marc?'

'No, that's my son's,' Gethen said. 'He's into all that stuff.'

His wife interrupted before I could probe further.

'Do you mind if we get started? There's a limit to how long the kids will stay quiet.'

Not what she'd said before. Was she really thinking about her children?

Or had I touched a nerve?

CHAPTER 47

Fingerling was right, there was something up with the Gethens. But to find out what, I needed to break Marc's alibi.

Back in the desert, we had our own ways of getting a subject to change his story. Here on Civvy Street the rules are a bit different. But that doesn't mean we can't still play dirty. At least, I can.

The police aren't allowed to introduce misinformation. But I'm not a cop. The rules that bind them don't apply to me.

Thanks to the plethora of crime dramas on TV, the public is well versed on the resources at the fuzz's disposal. But what most people don't realise is it usually takes a good ten days to run DNA. Most CCTV cameras have blind spots. And the images captured are often too low-res to be much use.

Those factors combine to create a perfect bluff. My people-reading skills do the rest.

If someone's giving an honest account of their whereabouts, they'll quickly become angry if you suggest they're lying. And they won't deviate from what they're saying. If they're giving it to you straight, the truth is all they've got.

From there, the strategy is pretty simple. I imply there's evidence they may not be aware of, tying them to the scene. Mobile phone signals bouncing off a cell tower is a favourite. Cameras are another fail-safe.

Or else I ask a series of detailed questions then pull the pin on the grenade. That was my plan here.

'I understand you were both at home on the night of the murder,' I said. 'You were watching *The Big Bang Theory*? Is that right?'

Marc nodded.

'Yes. Channel 4 was running them back to back.'

'And you started watching at . . .?'

'Nine. I turned in around eleven. Couldn't keep my eyes open. There's a lot going on at work. When you're the boss you don't get to switch off. Stuff on my mind, I guess.'

Too much detail. Waffling. Both signs of dishonesty. Nervousness too. The two often go together.

I flicked through the file on my lap. Made a big deal out of it.

'Hmm, that's interesting.' Marc and the missus finally exchanged glances. 'Says here, there was a change to the advertised schedule. Do you remember that?'

Gethen's eyelids fluttered but the rest of him was statue-still.

'Er, yes. Vaguely. Can't remember what it was, though.'

Bullshit.

'Do you remember, Mrs Gethen?'

She shook her head.

'Perhaps I dropped off. I seem to recall it had been a long day.'

'Let's talk about when you discovered the murder, Marc. You found the body in the woods at six in the morning. Do you usually go walking that early, in the dark?'

His foot started jiggling.

'Sometimes. I like to clear my head.'

His wife's lips tightened.

'You were hiking in BOSS jeans and suede loafers?'

He paused. Then smiled.

'Like I said, there was a lot going on at work. I knew I wouldn't have time to change before going into the office.'

It was a good angle but he looked too pleased with himself when he said it.

Next to him, his wife clasped her knees and shifted her weight about like she couldn't get comfortable.

She knew something. It was making her anxious. Perhaps some visual stimulus would help her open up.

'Do you mind if I show you the crime scene photos?' I said. 'I realise they may be distressing. But something in there might jog your memory.'

Marc sat up, leaned forward, his features brightening.

'Of course, anything I can do to help. I can't stop thinking about how I was the one who found the first body. The *Independent* said it might have been hours before she was discovered if I hadn't got to her when I did. The *Mirror* published a timeline the other day. Apparently, she'd been lying there dead since 1 a.m. Awful, isn't it?'

Reading all the papers. Following the case closely. Giving himself importance.

'I took the little ones round the neighbourhood on their scooters over the weekend, handing out leaflets. Trying to jog memories, as you put it.'

Another way of inserting himself into the investigation.

'You and your son didn't go with him?' Barnwell asked Mrs Gethen.

'Actually, he's Marc's son. First marriage.' She cleared her throat, massaged the dip at the base of her neck. 'And no, we didn't go. I was playing in a bridge tournament at the Acol Club all weekend. It was very full-on, quite exhausting. Nicolai was spending time with his mother. Put up a fuss about it, though. They don't get on too well, she's not the warmest person.' She covered a smile.

Some rivalry there, I thought. Had this Mrs Gethen displaced her predecessor?

'Nicolai was sorting his portfolio out.' Marc gave a proud dad grin. 'He's very talented. Wants to study Fine Art at Saint Martins.'

I took the photos out of the file and passed them over, watching their reactions closely as they looked at them. Marc's expression hardly changed, though he made a big deal of tutting over them. Then he handed them to his wife.

She seemed reluctant to look, but then something seemed to catch her eye in one of the broad shots.

Her mouth opened slightly; bright spots of colour appeared on each cheek. Her head jerked towards her husband then turned away just as quickly.

'What is it, Mrs Gethen?'

She fiddled with the chain of her necklace, moistened her lips. 'Nothing.'

Her voice was strangled.

'Are you sure?'

'Quite sure.'

Another lie. Just like the one about the television.

There had been no change to the schedule on the night of the first murder.

Whatever Mr and Mrs Gethen had been doing, it wasn't watching *The Big Bang Theory*.

CHAPTER 48

'Thank you for your time,' Barnwell said to the Gethens as we walked out into the white-tiled hall.

He'd hardly spoken during the interview but not because he had nothing to say.

Most detectives I've come across would have been too busy swinging their dicks around to let me take the lead. And plenty of them would have had a problem with me twisting the rules the way I had. But Barnwell hadn't just done what I'd asked, he'd also shown respect.

I'm not much good with people, but I do remember my friends. Maybe one day I could return the favour.

Marc opened the front door and pulled a face. In these sub-zero conditions, it could only mean one thing.

'You going out in this too?'

'Yeah, to visit my mother. She's in her eighties, lives by herself. Thought I'd take her some soup, check her heating's working.'

Another good son. Barnwell was nodding as if he were thinking of doing the same thing for his old lady. Christ knows what Emmeline would say if I pitched up on her doorstep with a thermos. Not 'thanks', that's for sure.

'I don't know why you want to drag out in this weather, Marc. It's not like she'll appreciate it.' Then in a quieter voice, as he put on his big Canada Goose jacket, 'She doesn't appreciate anything you do.'

The perp's mother will have subjected him to emotional abuse growing up.

It was a key part of the profile. Did Marc Gethen fit that aspect too?

'Got your gloves?' his wife asked him in a tight voice.

'Yup.'

He patted his pockets and smiled, though his skin flushed and his chin dipped, both signs of discomfort. But what was he uncomfortable about? Surely not losing his gloves.

'So, how do you think that went?' I said to Barnwell after we'd left.

I wanted to get his take. I didn't need his opinion, but I did want to know if my instincts about him were right.

'There's tension between Marc and his wife. But she was the one putting the barriers up. The way her body was turned away from him. The fact she didn't look his way. She's pissed off with him about something but they're putting on a united front.'

I was impressed.

'Spoken like a profiler.'

He blushed, took it as the compliment it was meant to be.

'You don't suppose she has something to do with this, rather than him?'

I shook my head slowly.

'She's clearly intelligent and organised. But nothing else about her fits the profile. And you saw how skinny she was. A woman like that couldn't have wheeled a grown person into the woods, let alone carry one.'

'What if they did it together? A partnership.'

I thought for a moment. It wasn't a stupid idea. Certainly, the victims would have been more susceptible to a woman offering help than a man. And there have been several successful husband and wife killing teams. But I wasn't convinced.

'In partnerships, you always have a dominant and a submissive. The submissive goes out of his or her way to please the alpha. But no one was trying to please anyone in there. Like you said, there was obvious tension between them. That comes from two people each refusing to back down. Both standing their ground.'

Barnwell ran his hands through his hair. Something else was bothering him.

'How come you didn't call him out on that business with the TV schedule? If we'd tripped him up on a provable lie, we could have broken his alibi.'

I smiled.

'We did break his alibi. He just doesn't know it. Which gives us the upper hand when we question him again.'

'So, you think he did it?'

I chewed my lip.

'Alibi aside, he found the body. He lives round the corner from the first discovery site and fits key elements of the profile. He's intelligent. He's injecting himself into the investigation. He's following the case closely in the media. And that bookshelf alone tells us he's highly organised, obsessive too. And imaginative, which often ties in with compulsive fantasies. He's also a braggart, same as the perp, judging by his letters.'

'But?'

I smiled. Barnwell was learning to read me.

'Not only did we profile the perp as being in his twenties and living alone, but Gethen's married. So, if he was responsible for the homicides, statistically we'd have seen signs of sadism in the attack. Rage directed towards women. While there are plenty of symbolic elements to the crimes, there's nothing sadistic in them.'

'If he's not the killer, what was he doing in the woods? And what are he and his wife hiding?'

'You're asking all the right questions, detective. We just need to find out the answers.'

CHAPTER 49

A rainy evening. A knock at the door.

'Sal, thank God you're here.'

Mother falls into the Gorgon's arms.

'I don't know what it means. I've got all these questions going round in my brain. I just need answers.'

'Shh, it's okay, hon. I've got you,' Medusa says, snake head crawling over Mother's pretty brown hair, turn-to-stone eyes searching for prey to petrify.

They go into the kitchen and the door clicks shut. The child creeps down the stairs, puts an ear to the wood.

'I've never seen anything like it,' Mother is saying. 'I know teenagers can be weird but—'

'This goes way beyond teenage weirdness, Lily. It's sick. Seriously messed up.'

There's a sobbing noise, the clink of ice cubes knocking together, a glass being put down.

'When I unwrapped those bandages . . . Jesus, it had a collar on, Sally. It was someone's pet.'

So, she's found it, the child thinks, throat tight. But that's all she's found from the sound of it. The other deities are safe. The decapitated pigeon's head stuck on to the cat's body, the glue turned pink along the ragged edges. The doll's head replaced with a squirrel's, its beady black eyes fixed wide. And the pièce de resistance: a rabbit's head on a pug's body, with little brown sparrow wings sewn on to the sides with neat white stiches.

All the critters snared with the child's stealth and skill and patience.

A gallery of sculpted saviours inspired by the gods of Ancient Egypt. A mark of the child's transformation from ordinary mortal to hallowed artist.

The beginning.

CHAPTER 50

Before going off to meet Ian 'Wandering Hands' Heppe at the soup kitchen, Barnwell and I took a detour to the first crime scene, just round the corner from the Gethens' place.

It's called a scene for a reason. When offenders strike, they paint a picture of themselves, a mindscape. Look at it the right way and you've got a telescope pointing straight into their psyche.

An attack in a public place suggests arrogance and impulsiveness. Overkill implies pent-up rage and oftentimes a personal connection to the victim. Evidence of a signature, the actions a perp takes that are not necessary to the commission of the crime, implies they're acting out a fantasy.

These criminals are the most dangerous types. They're the ones who'll kill again and again until they're caught. Because however many times they murder, the execution never matches up to what they imagined – or recreates that first high.

I'd analysed the crime scene photos and post-mortem reports. But there's nothing like visiting the kill zone for getting a feel for the person you're tracking.

Unfortunately, like everywhere else, this one was covered in a thick fleece of snow.

Walking up to the woods in two-and-a-half-inch heel boots along uneven icy pavements wasn't my idea of a fun time, but it did at least give us a feel for how close our suspect lived to the kill site.

The walk took us seven minutes, twenty-three seconds according to the timer on Barnwell's iPhone. In normal conditions, I estimated it at closer to four. Either way, it put Marc Gethen bang in the middle of the hunting ground, given the other victims' bodies had all been found within the same one-mile radius.

When killers strike for the first time, they usually murder inside their comfort zone, often within walking distance from where they live. Marc Gethen fitted a number of aspects of the profile; the first homicide had taken place minutes away from his crib and his alibi was sketchy.

As Barnwell said as we walked up to the woods, 'He looks good for this.'

But the nature of the attack didn't fit with what I'd seen of him. Would the crime scene fit any better?

We took a turn off the path that hugged the road and plunged into the heath; our trousers wet, the frigid air snapping at our fingers like sharp-toothed animals.

Two minutes in, we stopped. Remnants of the cordon marking off the radius were hanging loose off the trees like discarded skin. The circle the PRK had drawn round the victim was now engraved in the frozen ground.

'Close to the road, so he didn't have to carry her far,' I said, scanning the vicinity. 'Yet secluded enough to give him the privacy he needed to take his time with her. He either scoped it out in advance or he's familiar with the area.'

'Scoping it out's good for us,' said Barnwell. 'Someone may have noticed him.'

I wasn't so sure.

'This guy's highly organised. He chooses high-risk victims – vulnerable young women. And he operates under low-risk circumstances, drugging them and killing them in out-of-the-way places. He'll have taken precautions, planned the murders carefully, made sure he wasn't seen. It's not that hard to be invisible if you know how.'

Barnwell looked at me, tilted his head.

'I know you're ex-special forces. Was that Reconnaissance Regiment?'

I smiled. There were definitely the makings of a good profiler beneath all that dandelion hair.

I don't make friends easily, but I couldn't help warming to this guy. And given the position I was in with Sange and Jack, an ally was just what I needed.

'So, what do you think?' said Barnwell as we traipsed out of the woods. 'Does the scene fit with your read of Gethen?'

I thought back to the guy's mismatched socks, how he'd wiped his hands on the back of his jeans when he'd come out of the bathroom and how he'd left his alibi exposed. None of that tied in with a highly organised perp who took precautions and planned his kills carefully.

Which circled back to the first question: If he wasn't the offender, why had he lied about the night of the first murder?

CHAPTER 51

St John's Soup Kitchen, London

It was warm inside the soup kitchen. There was a strong smell of baked beans and jacket potatoes. And in the corner a bunch of people were singing 'Happy Birthday' to a large black woman in a beanie hat and duffle coat who had the self-conscious expression of a person trying, and failing, not to grin.

On the pinboard by the door there were posters about free CV-building and mentoring services. Below it was a leaflet saying: *Your small change can save lives*. Another advertised a clothes bank.

We hovered at the side, trying to spot Ian Heppe from the photo we'd found of him online. Interrogations are all very well, but I find the best way to learn about a person is often by watching them when they think they're unobserved. If nothing else, it gives a good base-line reading.

'There he is,' said Barnwell in a whisper, nodding at a hunched figure in tinted glasses wiping down tables, limping slightly.

Heppe was running a J-cloth round and round in ever-decreasing circles. He was moving slowing and meticulously, never once looking over at the people singing, his face blank and expressionless.

Not comfortable around people, I thought. Out of place in his own skin. Careful. Precise. Cautious.

We walked over.

'Hello, Ian.'

I touched him lightly on the shoulder. He jerked round, a mixture of defensiveness and revulsion on his face. Doesn't like physical contact, I thought. Suggests an underlying pathology, a sensory processing disorder maybe? Or perhaps a learned response based on a childhood trauma. That'd certainly tie in with the profile.

I took a half-step back, gave him space.

'We spoke on the phone. I'm Ziba MacKenzie. This is Detective Constable Barnwell from Scotland Yard. Can we talk?'

'Y-yes. We can s-sit over here.'

He pinked up as he spoke. His stutter was very pronounced. He didn't look at me once.

I eased him in; thanking him for his time, asking about his work at the soup kitchen.

The policeman's description of him sleazing on the first victim had prepared me for a man not particularly engaged in his work here, perhaps using it as a way of getting close to vulnerable women. But Ian Heppe was full of enthusiasm for the place.

'We f-feed over eighty people a d-day. Give them a p-place to get out the c-cold, to b-brush their teeth.'

'It's a wonderful thing you're doing. What made you volunteer?'

He answered without hesitation, though he still couldn't meet my eye.

'I've g-got a warm b-bed, h-heating, f-food. But these p-people have n-nothing.'

The guy sounded like a saint, but he'd also ticked off plenty of points on the profile. Was he the real deal? Or was this just a good cover story?

I asked him if he'd been following the news about the Pink Rose Killer, phrasing it more softly as homeless killings so as not to spook him.

He nodded, looked down at his bitten nails. But his face didn't twitch. Not a muscle moved to suggest the subject of the homicides excited him. And when I asked about the business with him and the first victim, he fessed up straight away. Though his answer troubled me.

'I thought she l-liked me,' he said. 'I was making a r-real effort.'

Was this someone who couldn't read people and situations? Asperger's would certainly fit with him not wanting to be touched, and the other non-verbals. It would also create a sensory overload, which could easily result in a desperate need for order and control.

But given his issues with physical contact, he was unlikely to have got touchy-feely with the first victim, as Fingerling had put it. More likely, him making a 'real effort' could mean he'd overcompensated in terms of trying to appear 'normal'. Staring intently at her in an attempt to override his difficulty with eye contact, for example, or holding a smile for too long. Such body language could easily have been construed as creepy by someone who didn't understand it.

Did he react badly to her rejection, given how hard he'd tried to get her to like him? Did it rekindle old insults and insecurities, tipping him over the edge? Did the hunted become the hunter?

I kept the conversation light, didn't challenge him. Right now, I wanted to get inside the guy's head. If I pushed him too hard, he'd clam up. I'd be lucky to get a handshake out of him by the time I was finished.

'You live with your mother?' I said. 'Is that right?'

The team had already got the basics down. By asking non-challenging questions I already knew the answers to, I'd be in a better position to spot lies later.

Heppe nodded, started nibbling his cuticles with his front teeth like he was picking meat off a chop bone. Forget non-challenging, asking about his mother clearly hit a nerve.

146

'You don't like living there?' I said in a gentle voice.

He shrugged, nibbled faster. That was a 'no' then.

'She's g-got MS. I'm all she has.'

'Your dad's not in the picture?'

I knew that answer too but not how he'd give it.

He shook his head; his eyes started roaming the room as if scanning for predators.

'I never knew him.'

Bam bam bam. We were hitting bullseyes with every shot.

'He left before you were born?'

'D-divorced my m-mum when I was a b-baby. M-moved in with someone else.'

He licked his lips, shook his head rapidly. Signs of shame and discomfort. Did he blame himself for his father's abandonment?

'It must have been hard on you and your mum being by yourselves.'

'I was the m-man of the house.'

The sort of thing his mother probably said to him. I'm not a parent, don't have a broody bone in my body, but even I know that's a lot to put on a kid. Even if it isn't meant seriously.

I watched Heppe. He was pulling at his sweater – picking at holes, twisting the material out of shape. From such a softly spoken man, there was something aggressive about the action.

It wasn't too hard to imagine him as a child treating his toys the same way.

CHAPTER 52

Wolfie

Do you have a minute? We should talk.

SMS 17.32

For a moment I just stared at the screen, the blood gushing in my ears.

Maybe I could call him? Find a way to salvage things . . .

Dammit, MacKenzie!

I hit delete.

'I said, what do you make of Heppe?'

Barnwell buckled up, looked at me, waiting for an answer.

It took me a moment to line up my thoughts; Jack was still filling up my head. What I'd done, should I have done it?

'He's the wrong age bracket and he doesn't live alone but there's plenty about him that does match up with the profile. And it's interesting his mother has multiple sclerosis.'

Barnwell looked confused.

'How so?'

I shifted the Porsche into third as we hit the main road.

'Do you know one of the most commonly prescribed drugs for MS?'

'Diazepam?'

'Aye. The same drug used to sedate each of the victims.'

He grinned.

'Brilliant!'

He was looking at me as though trying to work something out.

'What?'

'This is potentially a big breakthrough, and it's largely thanks to your profile, only . . .'

He paused, embarrassed.

'Only what, Barnwell?'

'I don't mean to be funny, but you don't seem that happy about it.'

The guy really did have the makings of a good analyst. And unlike me, he had a few people skills to boot.

'I've just got a lot on my mind, that's all.'

He nodded.

'The case is doing my head in too. Somehow, knowing when he's going to strike again makes it worse, not better.'

'It's not just the case . . .'

It slipped out before I could stop myself, though strangely I wasn't sorry. I've never been one to wear my heart on my vest, but I was longing to talk to someone about the whole Jack/Sange dilemma. I needed some perspective, an outsider's take. And with Wolfie not an option, I had no one else to turn to.

Barnwell seemed pretty intuitive. And Fingerling using him as target practice put us on the same side. Screw it, what did I have to lose?

'You know I met Vernon Sange yesterday—?'

'Ah, of course. No wonder you're feeling overwhelmed.'

It wasn't the word I'd use, but it was spot on.

'Thing is . . .'

I hesitated. Barnwell waited, didn't jump in with a follow-up question. It didn't just highlight his skills, it showed empathy too.

'He thinks I'm in love with a friend of mine. He's trying to use that against me.'

No need for names; opening up like this already put me in a foreign field.

'Are you? In love with him?'

I snapped my head round.

'You're missing the point.'

'You were there, not me. But I'd have thought your real feelings are exactly the point. If you're not in love with this person, Dr Sange has nothing over you.'

Unlike the rest of us, it was always 'Dr' Sange with Barnwell. Bit deferential for my liking. Then again, perhaps the formality was just a hangover from his days at Eton.

Aside from the over-respectful reference to the Butcher, Barnwell was sharp. I had to hand it to him. He'd joined the dots much faster than I had. And his response told me I'd done the right thing with Wolfie, however much I hated it.

'I sent him a text. Whatever was there is over.'

Barnwell nodded slowly, taking it all in.

'Sounds to me like there's not much else you can do.'

Exactly what was worrying me.

CHAPTER 53

Scotland Yard, London

Back at the Yard, I brought Fingerling up to speed on our conversations with Ian Heppe and the Gethens. He didn't like my take on Marc.

'So, you want me to disregard him because his socks were different colours? Not happening, MacKenzie. Especially given the business with his alibi.'

There was an angry red pimple on his neck, just where it met the top of his collar. He scratched at it, made it redder.

'I'm not saying we should rule him out. Just that he's obviously scattered-brained, unlike our perp.'

'Your eyes ever get sore gazing into that crystal ball of yours?'

My fist clenched, itching to be used.

'It's called behavioural science for a reason, Fingerling.'

He rolled his eyes widely then called everyone next door for the afternoon briefing.

'Right, boys . . . and, er, girls,' he added quickly. 'If Vernon Sange is right, we have less than a day till the next PRK murder. So, let's make the hours count.'

Falcon wasn't in the room this time, but there was a shift in tension all the same at the mention of the Butcher's name. I felt more than one pair of eyes on me.

After I'd answered everyone's questions, many about what Sange was like in person, the DI thankfully moved things along.

'There's a chance the Pink Rose Killer may have come across Officer Dale at a soup kitchen the first victim frequented, over at St John's Church. Which, I'd like to point out, is a Catholic joint. So, another thing to suggest our perp has it in for the papists.'

Jesus, did this guy never listen?

'Apparently, Dale broke up an altercation between her and one of the volunteers the day she died. Chap called Ian Heppe. Seems he was getting a bit touchy-feely over the bean stew. Might be he got pissed at being rejected and did her in later. Then thought he'd teach Dale a lesson for sticking his nose in by sending him a little liver package. The soup kitchen could also be where he met his next victims.'

Not exactly how I'd put it when I'd presented him with my theory . . .

'We're checking whether his mother is prescribed diazepam following a conversation MacKenzie and Barnwell had with him earlier. Meanwhile, Butler and Reese checked him out yesterday. Reese, why don't you take the floor and tell everyone what you found out?'

Reese stood up and flicked through his notebook. He was wearing a yellow tie with orange and brown spots on it. There was chocolate on his chin. It was as if he was trying to parody himself. All he needed was a smear of peanut butter to finish the look and he'd be a walking candy man. Detective Reese's Pieces.

'Heppe's given us alibis for the nights of the murders, which we're checking out. But there are lots of tallies with the profile. He studied Creative Writing and English Literature at Westminster.

He lives off Shoot-Up Hill in Kilburn, which isn't too far from Hampstead. He's unconfident. Never knew his dad. And he speaks with a stutter.'

Inside the room the energy changed, the air began to pulse.

This was a man who argued with the first victim the day she died. Had a connection to Officer Dale. And who fit the profile.

Was it possible he was also the perp?

CHAPTER 54

The magazine is spread open on the desk, the pages open to the Artist's letter and Medusa's reply. The snake-haired Gorgon is an agony aunt for a girls' magazine, doling out sex advice to promiscuous teens on a fortnightly basis.

> Don't let him pressure you into anything you're not ready for . . .

> Just because your friends are doing it, doesn't mean you have to . . .

> There's nothing wrong with being different. Be proud of who you are.

Duplicitous witch, making out she's so liberal and inclusive after all these years of poisoning Mother against her only child.

'There's something not right with that kid.'

'EQ's more important than IQ. All the academic success in the world means nothing if you can't relate to other people.'

'You need to take a harder line, Lily. Get some space.'

The Artist never expected the letter to be printed. But here it is, in black and white and high-sheen gloss:

My mother's best friend hates me and is trying to turn her against me. I wish she'd die and leave us both alone.

It's clear from her textbook cliché response that Medusa had no idea who the author was:

Are you sure that's what's going on? When we experience difficulties in life (falling out with friends/bad grades/not fitting in), it's easy to think everyone's out to get us. Try speaking to your mother and explaining how you're feeling.

I can tell you're suffering. You don't need to be.

I can tell you're suffering?! Fututus et mori in igni! *Pernicious wretch!*

The Artist obliterates the words with a scalpel, hard enough to leave scratches in the wooden desk. But still the anger hasn't abated, or the pain. Only one thing can make it go away.

Unbuttoning, the Artist scratches again. Deep enough to draw blood. And the bow of Mother's lips on virgin skin.

A new tattoo.

CHAPTER 55

Despite Reese's announcement about Ian Heppe, I was scowling by the time I got back to my desk after the briefing.

I'd popped down the road to Starbucks, aching for decent coffee and a brownie, only when I got there, I found my wallet wasn't in my bag.

I definitely had it on me this morning, though. I'd paid my room bill before going back to the prison and distinctly remembered putting it back afterwards.

So where was it now?

I'd have to cancel my credit cards and write off fifty pounds' worth of cash, but that's not what was really getting to me.

Early on in our relationship, Duncan sent me a bunch of sweet peas: pink, purple and white. The previous evening, I'd mentioned they were my father's favourite flowers.

I'd been talking about my childhood, how he and I used to read together in his study. Arabian Nights. The Greek myths. The Golestan. And how we'd pick the sweet peas that grew wild in our garden and put them in little jam jars around the house. I never saw them growing there after he died. I suspect my mother may have pulled them up.

I'd been a little maudlin, not my usual charming self. The Chianti we'd been drinking probably hadn't helped. Nor the fact it was *Bâbâ*'s birthday. Duncan sent the bouquet the next day. On the florist's card, he wrote the opening stanza of Byron's poem 'She Walks in Beauty'. That night he told me he loved me.

It was the first time he'd said it, and the first time I'd ever felt like saying it back to anyone. I kept the card in my wallet as a memento. Since the shooting, I must have looked at it a hundred times, a reminder my life hasn't been all bad.

And now it was gone.

The office manager came over lugging a large cardboard box, straining under the weight. I got up to help her.

'DI Fingerling said you wanted these. Letters to Vernon Sange from his admirers.'

She dumped the box on my desk, rubbed her lower back. Inside were stacks of fat folders. Ten in total.

We were less than twenty-four hours away from the PRK's next murder. The clue we needed to zero in on his identity could be in here. Only the mood I was in, I wanted to rip every letter into shreds.

Get on with it, MacKenzie. No one's going to put these on iTunes for you.

As I opened the first file, it briefly occurred to me that if Vernon Sange could arrange a hit on me from inside the slammer, he could also pull a puppet's strings, perhaps get him to commit a string of murders.

I kicked the idea into touch pretty quickly, though. Sange was brilliant, a genius even. Maybe he did have contacts in high places. But despite what people said about him, he was hardly Moriarty with an organisation of hundreds of agents on the outside. Arranging a one-off favour was completely different to masterminding a set of homicides and getting some sucker to carry them out.

Though that didn't mean someone wasn't telling him about them. And apart from the code, cryptic fan mail was the other most likely way.

The letters were ordered by date. Sorting them by sender would help me spot development of tone and subject. I was building up piles of varying heights, reminded of all the unopened post waiting for me at home, when Nigel Fingerling strutted over, bringing the cold air with him.

'What's wrong with these losers?' He picked up a letter, knocked over the closest pile. 'Don't they know what he's done?'

I made a point of straightening it up, glowered at him.

'Some will believe he's innocent. A victim of the system. Others will be impressed by his crimes.'

Fingerling pulled a face.

'Makes them as sick in the head as he is, don't you think?'

Maybe. But unless they also get turned on watching the life leave a person's eyes, they're not the same beast.

I kept the thought to myself, though. Debating the meaning of evil with Nigel bloody Fingerling wasn't at the top of my want-to-do list right now.

Instead, I answered as if I hadn't heard him.

'If the PRK's sending mail to the Butcher, he'll fit into the second group. And he'll write frequently. The letters will start off flattering, saying how much he admires him. He might send gifts. Money. Maybe even something he's made. The handicrafts will be a tribute. The money, a way of putting him in his debt.

'Gradually, the letters will become focused on how much the fan believes the two of them have in common. He'll play up an interest in Classics to persuade Sange he understands him better than anyone else does.'

I thought back to how Sange had represented himself in court – leaning across the defence table, intimidating witnesses, posturing for the jury.

Had the PRK been watching the show from the public gallery, along with Barnwell and his pals? Had he been hanging around Warwick Passage every day with all the protesters and journalists, waiting for the Butcher to be brought in and out of court? Or had he simply tuned in for daily updates on TV and Twitter, like the rest of the population?

'We can't be sure what lengths he went to,' I said to Fingerling. 'But we can be sure the offender followed the trial closely. And he'll use what he learned about Sange to enhance their connection. That won't be enough for him, though. He'll want to impress him too, show that no one understands him like he does.

'Which is when our perp's name will start to stand out.'

CHAPTER 56

There were hundreds of fan letters to read through from the last month alone. A woman from Texas told Sange to keep his head up, and that she was praying for his exoneration. One wittered on about his 'beautiful eyes'. And another, who simply signed off as Lottie, said, 'I'll never forget what you taught me. Or what I promised. *Si vis pacem, para bellum. Sed vis bellum, para pacem.*'

With the help of an online dictionary, I managed a rough translation:

If you want peace, prepare for war. But if you want war, prepare for peace.

It made no more sense in English than it had in Latin.

Hours in, I finally hit the jackpot. A series of letters, written on an almost weekly basis, and progressing in tone just as I'd predicted to DI Dipshit.

I took copies and highlighted the key extracts with a yellow STABILO BOSS pen:

> *They say eyes are the window to the soul. I can see you've suffered, just like me.*

I make necklaces with your picture in them. I wear them under my blouse so you're always close to my heart, a secret lover no one else can see. I'm going to make one specially for you, but I'll have to wear it first. That way it will have touched my skin so when you touch it, it will be like you're touching me too.

I know what it feels like to live with demons in your head and to have to hide your true self because you can't share what you're really thinking.

I understand you. You don't need wine and drugs to make me stay.

You mentioned Ovid during your trial. I knew then we were kindred spirts. I've always thought he was the greatest Latin poet. He wrote: 'Every lover wages a war.' And so must we, my darling.

Then the letters started to change. They became darker, more explicit. Clearly the Butcher's doing. He was grooming his pen pal to give him what he wanted, making his crack-ass monkey dance. Manipulating her just like he'd manipulated Falcon's daughter to try and take her own life.

I imagined him reading what she'd written, the tip of his tongue poking out of his film star mouth, his pupils dilating the more turned on he got.

You were so right! You understand me so well! The first time I cut, I cried out in pain. But by the third or fourth time all I felt was this delicious release.

The blood was dark and thick and beaded up on my skin.
I licked it and yes, it did taste sweet.

He was getting her to hurt herself, same as he'd done with Falcon's daughter. But as disturbing as that was, the next letter was worse.

Okay, so I've picked someone. She babysits for the family next door, nasty little brats. Always fighting and screaming. I have to turn my music up so I don't hear them. She's tall and blonde, with this fat little face and too much make-up.

The dad likes her, though. I see the way he looks at her. Like he wants to gobble her up. Last night he drove her home. It was 1.30 before he got back. Pig!

I scribbled a reminder to tell Fingerling we should comb through the HOLMES 2 database for cases involving actual bodily harm, or possibly even homicides, involving blonde babysitters. It was a long shot but any hits on the system could help us identify our subject.

The database was our best hope of doing that since there was no way of knowing from the letters whether the person who'd written them had actually taken things further. And although the prison had records of all the people Sange wrote to, not only were there thousands of names on the list going back three years to the beginning of his stretch but a surprising number of his correspondents either didn't sign off or used little nicknames.

The note about the babysitter was the last in the batch from this particular penfriend.

Post to violent offenders is always vetted before it's passed on. Whatever special favours Sange had managed to weasel out of the guards, they didn't extend to the mailroom. In all likelihood, the content of these letters became too inflammatory to give to him.

Shame they didn't hold the others back too, I thought. He'd have worded his notes carefully so they'd slip through, getting her to hurt herself on his say-so and then tell him all about it.

I couldn't help feeling a gush of shame. Hadn't he done much the same thing with me by getting me to dump Jack? Then a second later, what if he'd set the whole thing up?

I'd thought by sabotaging things with Jack I was beating Sange at his game. But what if I'd played right into his hands instead? What if I'd done exactly what he wanted me to?

Without thinking, I reached for my phone and hit my favourites list. Then stopped.

Maybe it was what Sange wanted, and crap knows defence isn't my favourite move. But right now, it was the best way of keeping Wolfie safe.

We were taught early on in the SF to box up our feelings and leave them in our lockers. Emotions have no place on the battlefield, we were told. They're a bag of rocks weighing you down, tripping you up.

It's possible I was right that Sange had manipulated me into breaking things off with Wolfie, though it was just as possible my heart was trying to rule my head, giving me an excuse to be with him. I'm not in the special forces any more, but I was definitely fighting a war. And to beat the Butcher, I needed to dump my sack of stones on the side of the road.

I put the phone away at the same time as Nigel Fingerling swanned over and perched himself on the edge of my desk, leg crossed over his knee, hand on his hip like he was posing for bloody *Vogue*.

'Anything?' he said.

There was something green between his teeth. His breath smelled of onions.

'There's one correspondent that stands out.' I showed him the highlighted section, hand over my nose. 'The letters are unsigned so we don't have a name. But the writer's obviously female, given the content. There's a link with the letters Jack Wolfe has received. And clear tonal progression.'

'You think it could be our perp?'

He sounded excited.

'We should keep an open mind. The soup kitchen guy is still a potential suspect. But it is possible, yes.'

'And if this is the perp, then Falcon was right. We could be looking for a woman.'

CHAPTER 57

The Artist lies in bed, eyes open, staring at the ceiling, thinking of him, reliving their last glorious conversation, word for delicious word.

'Evil is relative,' he said. They were discussing the idea that the only true evil is ignorance, the debate grasshoppering as it so often does with them.

'What's right or wrong is determined by society. There is no absolute. What one culture applauds, another lambasts. During the Spanish Inquisition, the Church believed it was doing God's work by eliminating heresy through torture. These days such practices would get you hauled off to The Hague.'

'So, you're saying, the concept of evil is generational, built on shifting sands. Doesn't that make it meaningless?'

'Yes, I suppose it does. You're quite brilliant, you know. I've never met anyone like you.'

A smile spreads into the Artist's heart. A soulmate at last, someone with the same passions, the same fantasies . . .

Their first encounter had been a chance meeting in the street, accidental and embarrassing. He'd been carrying a coffee. The Artist had tripped on a loose paving stone, stumbling into him and slopping hot liquid over both of them.

'Oh, my goodness! I'm sorry. I'm always so clumsy.'

He smiled beatifically, helped the Artist up.

'I find life is largely a matter of expectation.'

He was quoting the Artist's favourite Roman poet, Horace!

Stammering and blushing with nerves, the Artist offered to buy him a fresh coffee.

He smiled a second time.

'Only if you'll join me.'

CHAPTER 58

Nigel Fingerling smiled; it didn't reach his eyes.

'A woman, eh? So perhaps Sange wasn't messing with you when he called the perp a goddess. You like overcomplicating things, don't you, MacKenzie? Sometimes the obvious answer is the correct one, you know?'

You're right, Fingerling, some things are obvious, I thought. The fact you're a shiny-arsed fobbit for one.

But with Vernon Sange, nothing is as it seems.

When he invited his students to his rooms for his famous 'soirées', they thought they'd been chosen because they were special. Instead, he'd picked them because he wanted to add them to his collection of broken dolls.

So, when he called the PRK a goddess, I couldn't be sure whether he was being literal or metaphorical. Especially as he never once referred to the PRK as either 'him' or 'her'. Only ever 'your killer'.

'So, what's the connection between these fan letters and the ones to Jack Wolfe?' Fingerling said, glancing at his watch.

'They both quote Latin poets.'

That Lottie character had used Latin in her letter to Sange as well. But unlike the PRK and the other fan, hers wasn't a poetical reference. Rather it was a play on a quotation from an old Roman general, according to what I found on Wikipedia.

That suggested she was well-educated, likely a private school background with a degree in Classics or History. She was also self-assured and articulate, which implied she was attractive too. Good looks and confidence usually go together.

But the fan I was interested in wrote in tiny letters with a backwards slant; a shy, introverted type. By contrast, Lottie's letters were large and pointy, her words crammed tight together. A brazen woman, with a tendency to crowd others and with some serious underlying aggression. Possibly dangerous, but not our perp.

I pointed out the passage in the fan letter with the Ovid quote.

'Look here.' I showed Fingerling the first letter to Jack. '*Suns will set and suns will rise again.* It comes from a poem by Catullus. Which, incidentally, is the same name Vernon Sange gave his pet bird in lock-up, according to the guard I spoke to. It could be a coincidence . . .'

'I don't believe in coincidences.'

Me neither.

'Interestingly, the "suns will set" line comes from a love poem. Which fits with the tone of the fan letters. Catullus wrote it for his girlfriend, Lesbia.'

'Lesbian?' Fingerling laughed; it sounded like he was blowing his nose. 'Wasted his time on that one, I imagine.'

I rolled my eyes.

'Lesbia, not lesbian. It was a pseudonym. She was married.'

'Well, well. I wasn't aware you were such a Classics whizz. Quite a few strings you've got in that bow of yours, MacKenzie.'

The guy was chippier than a tube of Pringles. I was about to make a wisecrack back but swallowed the insult instead. Were his old demons rearing their heads? The gambling compulsion

I'd spotted during the Lacerator investigation. That'd explain the snarkiness, I thought. And the acne smattering his forehead.

During another recent investigation, the Hillside Slasher case, in which the victims had looked disturbingly similar to me, I'd read heart-breaking forum posts written by a woman struggling with alcoholism. It had given me a new insight into the sort of hell addicts go through. Fingerling and I would never be friends but that didn't mean I couldn't feel sorry for him.

I dropped my shoulders, softened my stance.

'My mother's the Classics expert, not me. I just google that shit. I found the other quote online too. The one from the last letter.' I passed it to him, showed him where to look.

o sun cut short the light that's left to linger.

'It's a variation on a line by Sextus Propertius. A poet writing during the reign of Augustus. He was friends with Virgil, they shared a patron.'

'Sextus. Lesbia. Right randy bunch, these Romans.'

They probably got more action than you. Jesus, I was trying, but he really was hard to like.

'Anything else to connect these fan letters with the PRK?'

His eyes skipped to his watch again. Tick tick.

'They both go into detail about what it feels like to cut flesh and the release they get from it, which suggests a history of destructive behaviour and feelings of low self-worth.'

I paused, thinking.

'I'm not convinced we're looking at the same author, though. Certainly, the tone of the letters is very different. But then again, you'd expect that given they're written for different audiences. Way I see it, there are enough similarities to warrant further investigation. But first, we need to find out who this fan is.'

'How do you suggest we do that? The nut-job doesn't sign off. And the postmark doesn't tie in with any of the addresses Sange is writing to,' said Fingerling, pursing his thin lips.

They were dry and flaky, like he'd taken a grater to them. A sign of stress possibly, or an effect of the weather. Either way, it wasn't pretty.

'We find her the same way we found Sange,' I said. 'Behavioural analysis.'

CHAPTER 59

Scotland Yard, London

'So, how long do you need to put together a profile of this fan girl?' Fingerling asked.

'I'm ready now.'

'Okay then, let's hear what's in that crystal ball of yours.'

Taking him out would be so satisfying.

He clapped his hands together, called for attention.

'Stop what you're doing, folks. MacKenzie's got something to share.'

There was a brief kerfuffle as everyone congregated round.

Barnwell stood to my right, all big-eyed. Next to him, a detective with hot-dog rolls on the back of his neck was chowing down on a Big Mac, a trickle of grease dripping down his chin.

On the opposite wall, the clock showed the time. 21.47. This time tomorrow . . .

'As you know, we're exploring the possibility that the PRK might be one of Vernon Sange's groupies, a fan who's been writing to him during his R & R in the slammer,' I said. 'That would explain how he seems to know so much about the perp.'

Eighteen faces watching me. Only my protégé looked interested. So far, I hadn't said anything they hadn't already heard.

'I've been going through the Butcher's mail and one correspondent stands out as a potential person of interest. Trouble is, there's no way of identifying her from the prison's records of Sange's correspondents.'

'Her? I thought you said yesterday that the perp was male,' said Hot-Dog Rolls, wiping his mouth with the back of his hand.

'He most likely is, but we should keep an open mind until we've ruled this woman out.'

'How're we going to do that if we don't know who she is?'

'We profile her.'

Barnwell was nodding happily.

'From what she's written, we can tell she's obsessed with Vernon Sange. And given the nature of her obsession, it's clear she's shy, likely lives alone and has never been in a long-term relationship. She also suffers from acute anxiety and low self-esteem. Hence her desire to please and her attraction to what she would see as a strong, charismatic figure.

'Given the level of her fixation on Sange, it's likely she's fixated on other men in the past. As a result, there may well have been a restraining order out against her or a criminal record for some sort of interpersonal violence. And she has a history of conduct disorder as a child. She's what we call an Intimacy Seeking Stalker.'

Fingerling made a snorting noise.

'In English?'

My trigger finger itched.

'As with killers, there's a classification system for stalkers. Intimacy Seeking Stalkers develop an infatuation and the imagined romance becomes the most important thing in their life. The woman we're looking for fits into this camp. And because of the work the FBI's done understanding these people, knowing her type tells us a lot about her.'

It occurred to me that I wouldn't have had to explain any of this if I'd been delivering the same talk at Quantico. I wouldn't have to answer to Nigel Fingerling either.

'The woman we're looking for suffers from acute paranoia, possibly linked to schizophrenia, and depression. She will have received medical help for one or both of these conditions but is no longer taking the drugs she was prescribed. And although she has a good level of education, she will either have a menial job or be unemployed. Her father abandoned her when she was young. Possibly he had an affair with a younger woman, which broke up his relationship with her mother,' I said, thinking of what she'd written about her neighbours' babysitter.

'Her letters are posted from St Albans but given there are no matches with the area in the prison records, it's unlikely she lives there.'

'So why mail them from there? Do you think she's trying to cover her tracks?' said Joe, the only one on the team with any sense of style.

'It's possible,' I answered. 'Or she could be trying to create a connection with Sange. St Albans is built on the site of Verulamium, one of the largest Roman cities in Britain. Certainly it would play to the Butcher's interest in the classical world. It's less of a draw for tourists than the temple and hot springs at Bath, but it's still a big deal for people who are into that sort of thing.'

My mother dragged me there one summer. There was a new archaeological find she wanted to examine, something to do with whatever thesis she was working on at the time. My father had recently died, there was no one for her to leave me with.

'The postmark would have been a stamp of pride,' I told the team. 'The woman would feel it was a way of making her stand out from Sange's other pen pals.'

'Do you think she could be the perp?' said another detective, looking up from his flip pad.

'The only way to know is by finding her.'

Easier said than done.

CHAPTER 60

Livy is shivering in her spot outside the Underground station, knees drawn tight to her chest, hands tucked into her armpits, dreaming of hot chips and bacon sandwiches.

'Spare some change,' she says, rattling her begging cup at yet another commuter hurrying past blindly. The 'Hungry and Homeless' sign is working wonders.

Still, not long to go now though, she thinks. The thought makes her smile.

So does the sight of *him* coming towards her. He's gorgeous. That hair, those broad shoulders.

Despite the sub-zero conditions, a shiver of heat ripples through her emaciated body.

'Hey there, Livy,' he says, the only one of these pricks who's ever bothered to ask her name.

She watches his lips move, gives him her best smile. She doesn't answer, though, doesn't want him to be put off by her voice. *Weirdo*, the kids at school called her. *Freak*.

He bends down, smiles as he gives her a coffee from Subway. And a chipotle chicken melt.

'Thought you might like something hot.'

His kindness gets her right in the feels.

She smiles at him again, warms her hands against the sides of the cup. God, that's good.

He adds a coin to her collection. Two pounds. If only everyone were this generous.

'Look after yourself, Livy,' he says, walking away.

She watches as he hovers at the flower stand near her pitch. She used to do that. Buy flowers. It gave her such pleasure, choosing them, arranging them in their vases into a paint box of colours.

'You've got flair,' her art teacher used to say. 'A real eye.'

Every Friday after school, she'd get a bunch for her mother. To celebrate the weekend, she said. Though looking back, time at home wasn't worth celebrating. And her mother never seemed exactly grateful.

Don't know why I bothered, she thinks now. Although she knows full well what she was trying to buy. Waste of money. Her flowers never won her mother's love.

She watches the handsome man as he makes his selection. Tries to push down the jealousy rising in her throat.

Who are those flowers for? she thinks. Who's the lucky lady?

CHAPTER 61

'Mother, I'm home!'

The Artist shuts the front door, clomps heavily up the stairs, smiling, bouquet held aloft. An offering.

'I bought you some flowers, thought they might cheer you up.'

Mother doesn't look away from the show she's watching. 'Why did you do that? Stinking things are everywhere.'

The Artist glances round the kitchen. There's a jug of hyacinths on the shelf, lily of the valley, narcissi and a big vase of pink roses. Their scents intermingle, competing for prominence. Heavy and cloying. Pondy. In their containers, their stalks peel and turn to slime.

'I was trying to do something nice,' the Artist says, voice a whisper.

'Would you zip it? You've got no consideration,' Mother says, pointing her remote control at the TV, turning up the volume till it blares. 'Can't you see I'm trying to watch this? You're disturbing me.'

CHAPTER 62

Outside the sky was black, the streetlamps reflecting off the windows, casting shadows. Save for the odd car or taxi moving up the Broadway, the roads were still, the office workers and sandwich vendors gone long ago; home for supper time, bed.

In here, though, we were all watching the clock for a different reason.

Fingerling was on the phone in his side office, visible through the glass walls; pacing up and down, gesticulating widely. Barnwell was on the phone too, writing as he spoke, checking his computer screen. I was at my desk, trying to figure out the PRK's code, while my mind stuck resolutely in that airtight interview room with Vernon Sange.

'Pygmalion,' he hissed inside my skull. 'Your killer's name is Pygmalion.'

But what did it mean? Was the Butcher toying with me? Or might this be the clue we needed to unlock the case? Or code?

I plugged my earbuds into my iPhone and played back the recordings of our conversations.

I'm surprised you haven't asked me about him.

Hang on a minute . . .

I hit pause, my stomach clenching like a fist.

Jack had been texting and calling all day. Each message he left said the same thing: 'We need to talk.' What if my initial instinct had been right? What if Sange was talking about Jack rather than the PRK?

I'd been so fixated on the lie I'd told Wolfie that I'd assumed he just wanted the lowdown on the hot date I'd invented. Assuming anything was another rookie mistake.

Only now did it dawn on me that his calls and texts may have had nothing to do with my fictional love life.

What if he was in trouble? What if I'd put him there? And what if I was too late to save him?

When Duncan was shot, my body froze, my training and my instincts blown to smithereens by the shooter's bullet.

I didn't know what had happened to Jack. But no way was I going to freeze twice.

CHAPTER 63

Damn it! Why wasn't Jack answering his phone? I tried again and again and each time it went straight to voicemail.

You've reached Jack Wolfe. Sorry I can't take your call. You know what to do.

Except I didn't. I was trapped in the incident room, about to go into another briefing, hours away from the next PRK attack.

I called Jack's office number. Maybe he was working late.

A perky voice answered. Some intern or work experience kid for whom long hours at the coal face were still a mark of pride. He'd learn.

'I'm trying to get hold of Jack Wolfe. Is he available?'

I tried to button down the worry bubbling inside me like a shaken-up soda can.

'I can take a message.'

'I need to speak to him directly. Is he in?'

'Er, no.'

My turn to pick up on tone and nuances.

'Has he been in today?'

'I haven't seen him. He's probably been out in the field following up that serial killer story.'

Not a story to me.

I scrambled, thinking who else might have a better idea of his whereabouts.

'His editor there?'

'She's gone home. I can take a message.'

At least I imagine that's what he said. I'd hung up before he'd got the last words out.

I gave Jack's house number a go, even though he never answers it. He's always forgetting to put the phone in its docking station so it's forever out of charge.

The line rang but he didn't pick up. No surprise there, but it did leave me out of options.

Unless . . .

I gave Max a bell, an old oppo who set up a personal security firm after quitting the special forces. Not exactly original, but definitely useful.

The last time I'd thought of calling him I was tracking the Hillside Slasher, all the while Duncan's killers were tracking me.

He picked up on the second ring.

'Hello, Mac. What's up?'

Short, sharp and to the point, one of the reasons I like him. Neither of us is big on chat.

'I'm worried about my friend, Jack Wolfe.'

'Him again? Likes trouble that one, doesn't he?'

Max has helped me out with Wolfie before. Kept him safe another time he had a murderer after him. That was my doing, same as this. The only real friend I have and I keep putting his neck on the block.

'I need eyes on him.'

'Address and licence plate?'

'He had to get a new car after what those guys did to him last time. But he kept the registration and he's still at the same

180

address. I need you to locate him for me, Max. Let me know he's okay.'

'Copy that. What's the sit-rep?'

He's been getting love letters from a serial killer. And thanks to me, the Butcher of Balliol has him in his sights too.

I gave him a top line then cut the call.

Outsourcing my problems was only a short-term solution.

CHAPTER 64

It's so cold. Livy's fingers have turned purple, the circulation's gone from her toes. They feel like they've been sliced off at the knuckles. An open wound.

Not for the first time, she wonders if she made a mistake running away. Was it an overreaction? Was her mother really *that* bad? Bad enough to give up a warm bed and hot food for?

In her mind, she drifts back in time. Her mother clipping her stockings to her suspender belt, dabbing the inside of her thighs with YSL, sliding on her leopard print vest top, as tight-fitting as a second skin.

'Can't you stay home tonight?' Livy asks. 'Just this once. Please. I get scared by myself.'

'I get scared by myself,' her mother says, mimicking, pushing her tongue over her bottom teeth, shaking her wrists. 'Jesus, can't you speak properly? Have you any idea how half-witted you sound?'

Livy rubs her arms, her legs, bites back tears. Yes, her mother *was* that bad. But there's another question still unresolved.

A year on the streets, a year away from her. And still Livy doesn't understand what she did to make her mother hate her so much.

She has a fantasy that one day her mother will come looking for her. She'll tell Livy she got it wrong. She doesn't hate her. She loves her and will she please come home so they can try and be a family again?

It's stupid, Livy knows that. A dumb dream. It'll never happen. But she can't help hoping all the same.

CHAPTER 65

I was finally leaving the Yard, still no closer to cracking the PRK's code or the meaning behind Sange's riddle, when I got Max's call. The news wasn't good.

'Where is he?'

No hello, how are you. Just straight to the questions that had been banging about inside my skull ever since I'd listened to the Butcher's voice playing through my earbuds: Where's Wolfie? Is he safe?

'That's the thing. I haven't been able to find him.'

The blood beat in my ears like a hundred insects up against a pane.

What had Sange done? What had I done?

'His car?'

'At an auto repair shop in Willesden.'

Had he been in an accident? Chased off the road? Sideswiped? A hit and run isn't difficult to set up, as last time had shown. Not everywhere's covered by CCTV.

'Any idea what's wrong with it?'

I kept my tone light, but Max is ex-SF, like me.

'You know better than to go jumping to conclusions. Maybe it's in for its annual service.'

Maybe. But unlikely, given what else I knew.

'Have you been to his digs?'

'Course.' He sounded offended. 'I used thermal binoculars and an under-door camera once I got into the building. The apartment was dead. And judging by the post on his doormat, he hasn't been home today.'

'So, where the fuck is he?'

'Hot date?'

Not funny.

'Want me to sit tight? In case he shows. Or someone else does.'

Max has been doing this job long enough to know the script. But I know it pretty well too, and it was time for me to play my part.

Thanks to me, Wolfie was in trouble. I'd been ignoring him all day. That stopped now.

'I'll take over from here.'

I'd made the mess. It was for me to clean it up.

CHAPTER 66

West Hampstead, London

I pulled up hard outside Jack's apartment block. The street was deserted, the parked cars on either side of it looking like hibernating animals under their blankets of snow.

I slipped running up the icy steps to the communal front door, knocking my ribs hard in my sore spot, though the adrenaline my body was secreting by the gallon kept me moving.

Max had had to blag his way in. That at least wasn't an issue for me. Jack and I aren't neighbours, but we do have each other's keys on our rings. He's also given a set to his folks. Needless to say, Emmeline doesn't have mine.

I turned it in the lock and a moment later I was in his lobby, the heating turned up too high.

I took the stairs two at a time.

'Jack!' I shouted, pounding on his front door, holding the bell down with my other hand. I'd give him a minute then let myself in. If he wasn't home, there might at least be a clue as to where he was.

I tried not to think of the alternative scenario. The one where he was bleeding out on the living-room carpet. Three missed calls from him up on my phone. Three 'call me' messages in my SMS log. All ignored.

'Jack! Open up!'

I stopped. My fist hovered in suspended animation over the door. I strained to listen. Were those footsteps?

'Jack?'

The door swung open, tipping me forwards into him, my forehead colliding with his bare chest.

He was standing there, wrapped in a towel from the waist down; hair wet from the shower, face livid.

'Did he hurt you? Where is he? I'll kill him!'

My mouth dropped open.

'How do you know about Sange?'

And then it clicked. He wasn't talking about the Butcher. He was talking about my imaginary date.

I burst out laughing, bent double. Hysterical. It was better than crying, I suppose.

I'd gone and bloody done it again, talked at cross purposes and given the game away, just like I'd done at the prison earlier. Only this time a part of me was pleased. I don't like keeping secrets from Wolfie. Maybe that's why I'd let it out of the bag. One-nil to my subconscious.

He put his hands on my shoulders, bent down, looked at me hard.

'Ziba? What's going on? And what's this about Vernon Sange?'

The laughter dried in my throat. It didn't seem so funny any more, not with his face so close.

I took a breath.

'You were right,' I said. 'We do need to talk.'

CHAPTER 67

'You're shaking,' Jack said, parking me on the sofa. 'Sit down. I'm just going to put a shirt on.'

Halfway to the door, he turned and smiled.

'You didn't half give me a fright hammering on the door like that. But it's good to see you, Mac.'

'You too,' I whispered, trying not to look at the ripples on his abs.

In the corner of the room, his pet tortoise, Shorty, clucked and chirped in his pen. I don't much get the appeal of a pet you can't cuddle, but Wolfie loves the wrinkled old thing. Calls himself 'Daddy' when he thinks no one's listening.

He came back a minute later wearing a pair of jeans and an untucked shirt, straight out of the laundry basket judging by the state of it. In his hand was a steaming cup of peppermint and lemon tea. He's king of the herbal blend, forever trying to convert me.

'Sorry about that. Here, get that down you.'

'Thanks.'

I took a sip. Spat it back. There must have been six teaspoons of sugar in there.

'So, what's going on?' He gave me the once over, took in the way I was dressed. 'I'm guessing you haven't been on a date.'

I lowered my eyes, blushed.

'Not exactly. This stays between us? I don't end up reading it on the front pages tomorrow?'

He gave me a look. That's two men I'd offended tonight, the only two people in the world I can count on for anything, him and Max.

'Vernon Sange claims to know who the Pink Rose Killer is. He told Falcon he'd only speak to me.'

'Was he bluffing?'

'No. He's got intel but also a price. He wanted to mess with my head. Ask me questions about Duncan.'

A crease appeared between Jack's eyebrows. His mouth tightened.

'You didn't let him?'

I grimaced.

'Ziba!'

'What choice did I have? Another girl's going to die if we don't catch him.'

Wolfie sighed.

'There's more.' This time I couldn't meet his eye. 'Sange thinks you and I are . . . close. I thought it'd put you at risk. That's why I said what I did earlier about having a date, meeting someone. I thought if I put up a bit of distance between us, he couldn't get to you.'

'So, you lied to me?'

He stood up, shaking his head. Whether he was more hurt or angry, I couldn't tell. I stood up too. Slopped my horrible tea.

'I thought it was for the best.'

'No. You thought you couldn't trust me.'

'That's not true, Jack.'

'Yes, it is. It's what you do. All that tough as nuts crap you spout, it's an excuse not to let anyone in. There's no shame in needing people, Mac . . . There's no shame in needing me.'

'For fuck's sake, Jack. Don't make this about you.'

'Isn't it, though? You were in trouble but instead of coming to me, you ran.'

'I'm here now, aren't I?'

'Why *are* you here, Mac? It's the middle of the night. I'm guessing you didn't swing by to borrow a bag of sugar.'

My voice was quiet when I answered, inaudible almost.

'I came here for you.'

His face softened; he took a step towards me.

'Ziba . . .'

'I was worried about you, Wolfie. All those missed calls. I thought something bad had happened. I thought Sange had got to you. And Max couldn't trace you.'

'Wait. You put Max on me again?'

His facial muscles clenched. He stepped back, folded his arms across his chest.

I suddenly had the feeling that rather than cleaning up my mess, I was tossing it all over the floor.

CHAPTER 68

Jack laughed. It sounded bitter.

'So instead of answering your phone, or God forbid calling me back, you put one of your army guys on my tail and pitch up on my doorstep at one o'clock in the morning looking like you've seen a ghost.'

'First, Max isn't army, he's ex-special forces. And second of all, I did try calling you back. But you didn't answer.'

'I've had my phone on all day. There were no calls from you.'

His tone was confused rather than challenging.

'Aye, well, I didn't get round to calling till this evening.'

Jack's expression cleared.

'That makes sense. I was at the theatre.'

'Must have been a long play.'

His cheeks reddened. He glanced away.

My stomach curled into a ball as I put it together.

Out till the wee hours. Phone off. A middle-of-the-night shower.

'Who is she?' I said, in a voice that wasn't my own.

If I'd been better prepared, I might have bantered it out – asked if she liked *Infinite Flight* as much as he does, or how this new bird matched up to GIRY, the little single-engine plane he keeps up at Elstree Aerodrome.

'Someone from work,' he said with a shrug. 'She had a spare ticket to *Chicago*. It's nothing serious.'

'Right,' I said, but I wasn't buying it. Jack hates musicals. The only reason he'd have gone is if he liked the girl.

I tried to sound nonchalant, to swallow down the bullet lodged in my throat.

'A date?'

'Yep.'

'Will there be another?'

'What is this, Mac? Twenty questions? Bit rich when you wouldn't tell me anything about your bloke.'

'Jesus, Jack. How many times do I have to tell you? There is no bloke.' Then, 'Is that what you were calling about before? All those texts and missed calls. You wanted the lowdown?'

I'd been right after all.

He yawned, rubbed his hands over his eyes.

'I wasn't after gossip. I was worried about you getting back into the cockpit after all this time.'

I raised an eyebrow.

'Cockpit? Bit of an unfortunate metaphor . . .'

We started laughing. It wasn't that funny but it did break the tension. Though it didn't change the fact that Jack had moved on; living it up with an all singing, all dancing Lois Lane while I cosied up with a psychopath.

It was only as I collapsed into the Porsche and started her up that it hit me. Jack had tried to reach me six times after hearing I was seeing someone new. And then later the same day, he'd gone on a date with some girl from the office whose name he hadn't once mentioned.

Was he really concerned about how I'd feel getting back into the 'cockpit'? Or was he jealous?

In which case, was his date more about me than the woman he'd been out with?

192

CHAPTER 69

Blomfield Villas, London

I glanced at the dash. Zero one forty hours. If the timings of the last murders were anything to go by, we were just hours away from the next Pink Rose killing.

Tempted as I was to go back up to Jack's flat, have it out with him and offload the burden of my feelings, this wasn't the time. I'd allowed my heart to mess with my head too much already today. It had put me on the back foot with Sange and made me take my eye off the target.

My focus had to be on the case now, one hundred per cent. I couldn't afford any more distractions or screw-ups. Jack and I would have to wait. And if I was right about his little date tonight being a meaningless distraction, then taking five wasn't going to hurt anyone.

I had to go carefully on the icy roads but at this hour there was no traffic and I was back at my place in a little over ten minutes.

As I climbed the stairs to my apartment, my feet heavy with exhaustion, Vernon Sange seemed to climb with me, whispering in my ear: *Pygmalion. Pygmalion.*

What the crap did it mean? I thought for the umpteenth time. What game is he playing?

I added the new post I'd picked up from downstairs to the pile on my hall table. Already it was more than two inches thick. Made me less rather than more inclined to go through it. So instead of opening envelopes, I showered and fell into bed, my suitcase from Quantico open in the corner of the room, still unpacked. Another thing that'd have to wait. As I closed my eyes, a nagging thought beat loud in my brain, pulling me back from the brink of sleep.

We'd been working flat out. But we were no closer to catching the killer than when I boarded the plane home two days ago.

CHAPTER 70

Despite the jet lag and the bombs I'd been dodging all day, I didn't sleep soundly. The nightmares that so often haunt me were back with a nasty twist.

I was in a cell, surrounded by every killer I've ever interviewed – mocking me, taking turns to lacerate my face, my thighs. And conducting the show, choreographing and coordinating each ghastly act of violence, was Vernon Sange, standing up on a chair, his arms moving in time to a music only he could hear.

The dream shifted. Duncan was in the room now, falling to the ground over and over again as Sange fired bullet after bullet, not at his head but at mine.

'I'll give you what you want,' I shouted. 'Just leave him alone.'

Sange smiled. The other killers stood back respectfully, let the snake move in.

He circled me, edging in closer and closer, his body coiling round mine, squeezing the breath out of me, the life.

He hissed in my ear.

'Your perpetrator is Pygmalion. Catch him, Ziba. Make your mummy and daddy proud.'

The killers laughed, mocking me again, waking me with their jeers. Except this time, the laugh was on them.

I jerked awake and sat up so sharply I banged my head on the shelf Duncan had nailed above the bed 'because you never have enough room for all your books'.

I rubbed the top of my skull, my heart a war drum in my chest, my skin slick with sweat.

Maybe Sange had given me something after all.

Make your mummy and daddy proud . . .

My father used to read to me every night, the two of us holed up in his study. I'd lie at his feet playing with the tassels on the big Persian rug, munching sugared almonds as I listened to his soft, deep voice.

'The Shirazi club of two', my mother used to call us. She didn't mean it kindly.

But we were a club.

'You're never alone if you have a good book,' *Bâbâ* used to say.

Then one evening—

'Let's read *Pygmalion*, my *fereshte*. I have a feeling you might like that one.'

CHAPTER 71

After my father died, my mother went round our apartment boxing up his things as if she couldn't get him out of the place fast enough.

I remember the sucking sound the tape made as she pulled it back off the roll. The snip-snip of her Lakeland kitchen scissors as she cut it, taping box after box shut. Boxes of books and artefacts from a life before her, from my father's past.

Enamelled nutcrackers. A menorah engraved with swirling patterns taken out of Iran before the revolution. A Persian ceramic dish painted with flowers from the early seventeenth century.

'Your father was a hoarder,' she said. 'And this place is too small for sentimentality.'

That night I snuck out of bed and unstuck her boxes, salvaging the items that reminded me most of him. A letter opener, which I now keep on my desk. The almond bowl he kept on his. A silver beaker that had belonged to his grandfather, with Hebrew writing engraved round the top. And my favourite books. Among them, Ovid's *Metamorphoses* and in it, the story of Pygmalion.

Although it's up on my shelves, I haven't opened it since my father died, haven't been able to. But Vernon Sange had given me a puzzle. This book might help me figure it out.

I climbed on a stool, standing on tiptoes, stretching my arm up till it hurt. Duncan must have moved it to the top shelf, no way I could have reached up there to do it.

I fumbled, fingers grasping for the book.

Damn it. I'll have to get the ladder.

Out in the desert, my height was often an advantage. Somehow most people don't expect a five-foot female to have a Glock down her shirt or to be able to flip them over her shoulder in three quick moves. But right now, I could have done with a few extra inches.

The ladder was dusted with paint chips. A reminder of an incident not long ago when an ingrate had left scratches on my ceiling, trying to spy on me with the sort of listening device I used myself back in the day. Though, unlike him, I never landed in the slammer for doing it.

I climbed up and this time easily reached the book, a leather-bound volume dusty enough to make me sneeze.

I sat on the ladder, lost for a moment in memories of my childhood; the sun not yet up, the birds' heads still tucked under their wings.

As I was flipping through the pages, a piece of powder-blue paper, tissue-thin with age, fell out and fluttered to the floor.

Curious, I climbed down and retrieved it. It was a letter, the ink faded but still readable. The handwriting was my mother's, though the content sounded so unlike her I could hardly believe it had come from her pen.

> *My love,*
> *It is cold and grey outside but in my heart all the world has turned to Spring.*
> *The most beautiful thing has happened. Something wondrous, magical.*

*There is life growing in me, Aria. A child too
small yet to see but with a beating heart tucked deep
in my womb.*

*Perhaps I should have waited to tell you in per-
son but I'm bursting with this delicious secret. If I
have to keep it to myself any longer I think I shall
explode.*

Hurry home. I long for you.
Emmeline

I read it twice, my head dizzy as if I were hanging upside down.

It was dated before my father's family was murdered in Iran
following the revolution, seven months before I was born. The child
she was talking about was me.

I put my hand to my mouth; for once, I couldn't move.

Had my mother wanted me after all? My whole life, I'd thought
her pregnancy was a mistake. An annoyance. A stumbling block in
the way of her academic career.

She never tucked me in at night or made me breakfast in the
morning. I learned to accept her indifference, built up walls, told
myself I didn't need her. But had I got it wrong? Was my father
right? Was her heart as broken as his?

After his family was killed, he hardly left his study. He took his
meals in there and slept on an old futon set against the wall. He
literally withdrew into a cave and although I was always welcome
in it, my mother was not.

'Would you mind shutting the door, Emmeline?' he'd say when
she knocked. 'You're letting a draught in.'

Duncan used to say you can't assess a situation without 'ade-
quate data points'. Up till now, a crucial piece of information had
been missing.

I knew my father changed after his family in Iran was killed. It made him close in on himself just like I had after Duncan died, and as a result the romance between my parents was snuffed out.

But the letter I'd found showed something else.

For so long I'd thought my mother didn't give a shit about me, but what if she was just closing herself off, the same way my father had? What if she was frightened to open herself up and risk being hurt again?

What if there was still hope for us?

CHAPTER 72

Scotland Yard, London

I marched into the incident room at zero eight hundred hours sharp the next morning. My favourite person was over by the incident board.

'Nigel, can I have a word?'

'If you make it quick. I want to get started on the briefing.'

'Roger.'

'You're not in the army any more, MacKenzie.'

'A cop who doesn't like the military. You're so original.'

If I'd smiled, it could have passed as banter.

'Your background isn't the issue.'

The muscle in his jaw ground up and down.

'Aye, perhaps you'd feel better if I didn't come with lady parts.'

'I'd settle for ladylike.'

I grinned despite myself.

'You'll get old waiting for that to happen.'

He smiled back, a temporary truce. In other circumstances, without the pressure of a case and a killer to catch, might we get on better? I remembered how worried he'd been when he thought the Lacerator had made me his next target, the relief in his voice when he realised I was safe.

He was a dick, but I'm not the easiest person either. Perhaps I should try to cut him more slack, I thought. Especially if he is struggling with his addiction.

'It's about the name Sange gave me yesterday, Pygmalion,' I said. 'Have you heard of it?'

'It's a film, isn't it? *My Fair Lady*. I saw it when I was a kid. Rex Harrison. And some fit bird. But what's it got to do with anything?'

'Absolutely nothing.'

'MacKenzie, I'm not in the mood.'

'I'm talking about the original story, not some Hollywood remake. It was written by Ovid, remember him?'

'The dead Roman that Sange's fan girl has been banging on about?'

'Aye, the dead Roman. He adapted the tale from Greek mythology.'

I paused, thinking of what Sange had said in our first meeting.

Do you like classical literature, Ziba? The Aeneid, perhaps? Such tragedy must strike a chord. Or perhaps you prefer the Greek myths. They're not just children's stories. It made sense now; he was trying to tell me something – albeit by making me work for it.

'The story's about a sculptor called Pygmalion, who carved a statue of a woman so beautiful he fell in love with it,' I said. 'He went to the temple to pray to Venus, the goddess of love, asking her to bring his creation to life. And she did. I think the perp might be doing the same thing.'

'I realise you like to think out of the box, MacKenzie. But are you sure your little tête-à-têtes with the Butcher haven't addled your brain?'

'My brain's working fine, Fingerling.'

'And yet you're trying to tell me the Pink Rose Killer is some fictional character from hundreds of years ago.'

'Just under two thousand years ago, actually. And no, that's not what I'm saying.'

He pushed up his shirt cuff, made a show of looking at his watch.

'So, what exactly is your point?'

'I was wrong. The PRK's not constructing a face or trying to recreate someone he's lost. Rather, he's creating something he's never had. The perfect woman.

'And he's sculpting her out of body parts.'

CHAPTER 73

'He's building a statue out of dead girls? How the hell did you get there from Pygmalion?'

'It fits perfectly with the signature. And his fixation with Latin poetry. The sacrificial elements too, as well as with what Sange said about the perp wanting a "goddess for the goddess".'

'You've really lost me now.'

'Think about it. He's creating a goddess, a perfect woman – as an offering to another goddess, Venus in the Pygmalion story. Depending on how deeply he's inhabiting his fantasy, he may believe he needs her help to make his statue come to life. That could explain the pink rose left on each corpse. It's an offering, all part of the ritual.

'The bad news for us is that he's not going to stop killing once he's got the next victim's lips. He's going to keep slaughtering girls until he's harvested everything he needs to construct a whole person. That's a hell of a lot of body parts. Which could mean hundreds of victims, unless we stop him.'

Fingerling sniffed hard, shook his head.

'You spin a good yarn, MacKenzie. But that's all this is. A story. The anti-Catholic angle's the route we're pursuing, as I said at the briefing the other day. And to be clear, I don't want you bringing up this Pygmalion nonsense with the team. The clock's ticking. I won't have you confusing things with fairy tales.'

I bristled. I was trying, but this guy pushed all my buttons without moving a finger.

'It isn't a story, Nigel, and you're looking at this back to front. It's not about hatred of the Church, it's about love.'

He laughed through his nose.

'Love tokens in the shape of dead girls? Nice. Remind me never to ask you on a date, MacKenzie.'

I managed not to make the obvious response.

'My point is, Christianity became the dominant religion in Rome during the reign of Constantine. And like the old Roman religion, Catholicism incorporates plenty of ritual. Don't you see, if the PRK's associating with Pygmalion, praying for his sculpture to become real is part of the fantasy. Hence the sacrificial elements we've already identified. In the absence of a temple, he's going to the next best thing. A church. We have to bring the team up to speed on this. It's critical.'

'Calm down. I've said "no" and that's it.'

Fingerling was a good foot taller than me, but I could still bring him to his knees. An outside leg trip and he'd be on the floor. Might not do much for my career, though.

'Listen—'

'No, MacKenzie, you listen. The offender has it in for the Church. It's why he's left the last four victims on church steps, mutilated and in a kneeling position. He's making a statement. Showing the dog-collar wearers what he thinks of them.

'The team will be continuing to investigate historic complaints about priests. They will also be delving into Marc Gethen's religious past and trying to ID Sange's fan. That will be their focus today.

'If you can't support them, you may as well go home and put your feet up. God knows you look like you could do with some sleep. Failing that, perhaps you could make yourself useful and crack this bloody code you keep banging on about.'

And with that he marched off in the direction of the briefing room, leaving me wishing I'd gone for the outside leg trip after all.

CHAPTER 74

The atmosphere in the briefing room had the heaviness of an approaching storm. No one looked like they'd slept more than a few hours, everyone was amped and antsy, wearing yesterday's clothes, slurping Red Bulls. Only Barnwell would have passed a parade inspection. His shirt was freshly ironed, his eyes were button bright.

I used to be that way, charged by the hunt. It's been a while since I felt that sort of adrenaline rush, though. Another thing Duncan's death changed.

'Turns out MacKenzie was right,' Fingerling was saying. 'Ian Heppe, aka Mr Soup Kitchen, does have access to diazepam. His mother is prescribed it to help with muscle spasms.'

Barnwell caught my eye, grinned.

'You can put your teeth away, Barney Boy,' snapped Fingerdick. 'The mother's given him an alibi for the first four murders. They live together. She says he was home the whole time. Not exactly ironclad but we're going over CCTV in the area to corroborate it.'

'So, it might be him,' said the woman detective with the man's voice.

'Possible, but unlikely. Seems the night of the fifth murder, Heppe had an accident and wound up in the Royal Free Hospital. He was home the next morning, though she was asleep when he came in. We're checking the hospital records and the security tapes. Of course, it could be our boy's got himself a nice little cover. We'll see.

'Meanwhile, I've arranged for uniforms to go round the homeless community, warning them not to accept food or drink from strangers, given our resident profiling expert here thinks that's how the PRK is drugging and luring his victims.'

I fired bullets at him with my eyes, tried to explain that no girl freezing her ass off on the streets was going to turn down a bite to eat or hot beverage in these arctic conditions. But he wouldn't listen to that any more than he would to binning the anti-Catholic theory.

Forget 'Follow the evidence'. He was going round and round in circles, getting nowhere. And while he was off chasing wild swans, our bird was flying free.

Back at my desk, I had another crack at the code, but whichever way I looked at it, I couldn't figure it out. With everything else going on, my brain was blunt.

I rapped my fingers on the edge of my desk, trying to think what else I could do to help identify the PRK while Fingerling went off in all the wrong directions.

My old SF instructor used to say, when you've got a puzzle to solve, start with the outside edges and work your way in. He liked his metaphors, that one. Liked cussing us out too.

I flipped through my notepad. Marc Gethen's name was on the first page with lots of circles round it and a fair few questions. That's where I'd start, by going back to West Heath where he'd found victim number one. It was still freezing outside, but the snow was finally beginning to melt. With less of it around, maybe I'd find some answers.

Barnwell looked up as I was pulling on my jacket.

'Off out?'

'Aye, road trip. Want to come?'

My preferred play is to go it alone, but the guy was sharp, I'd already seen that. A second viewpoint wouldn't hurt.

We were walking through the lobby when we bumped into a harried-looking Officer Dale, the policeman the perp had written to.

'You all right?'

The guy was trembling. His eyes were red, like he'd been crying.

When he spoke, his voice was even quieter than the last time. He seemed smaller somehow, too.

'I got another letter,' he whispered. 'From him.'

He took a plastic wallet out of the old leather satchel he wore across his chest and handed it to me. The note was only two lines long. It was boastful and, unlike the letters to Wolfie, unsigned. But the brown fleshy material enclosed in a sandwich bag inside the folder showed it was definitely from the same person.

Dale watched me as I read, his thumb rubbing obsessively at the knuckle of his left hand.

The police think they're so clever but they won't catch me, ha ha! And tonight I will slip through the net again to take my next piece.

'Do you really think he's going to get away with it again?' he said.

He looked like he hadn't slept properly for days, poor bugger. We had that much in common. Killers taking too much interest in us was another thing.

'You know we're doing everything we can to ensure this guy is caught.'

I spoke firmly and confidently, but I could see from his face that Dale wasn't any more convinced than I was.

CHAPTER 75

I unlocked the Porsche and slid in behind the leather steering wheel. Barnwell clunked his door shut and we were off.

The roads were more manageable today, the ice turned to slush. Already London had a dirty look. The snow, starting to brown, was patchy on the pavements, like discarded rubbish. In other places, big blocks of it stood unmelted and incongruous on the concrete.

It would make the crime scene easier to examine, though, and at this point, with the PRK preparing to strike again tonight, we needed every bit of luck we could get.

Fingerling was still hot for Marc Gethen, the guy who'd found the first victim. But I wasn't so sure about him. If Barnwell and I could rule him out, it would narrow down the suspect pool.

Having said that, you didn't need glasses to see the guy was sketchy. There was his dodgy alibi, for one thing, and all the boxes he ticked on the profile – not to mention what he was really doing in his fancy-dancy get-up on the Heath at zero dark thirty.

And what about the tension between him and his wife?

Whatever was going on between the two of them, the anger came from her. He'd done something to piss her off. Though not enough to stop her trying to dissuade him from visiting his dragon mother.

'I don't know why you want to drag out in this weather, Marc,' she'd said. 'It's not like she'll appreciate it. She doesn't appreciate anything you do.'

She cared about him, then.

Did that also mean she was covering for him? Or for someone *he* cared about?

My mind zeroed in on what she'd said in the interview about Marc's son. The kid from the first marriage who kept to himself, had a difficult relationship with his mother and wanted to study Fine Art at Saint Martins.

A loner, mummy issues, and an interest in Catullus, the PRK's favourite poet.

My scalp tingled. Could it be we'd been looking at the wrong Gethen?

I slipped the 911 into an empty spot on the edge of the woods and cut the engine.

The veil of snow had lifted. Hopefully the face that had been hidden beneath it would finally yield some answers.

CHAPTER 76

West Heath, London

As we picked our way through the undergrowth towards the discovery site, I tried to ignore the throbbing in my ribs. The bruise hadn't just darkened since my meeting with the Butcher, the pain had intensified too.

'I still think the perp's a male,' I said to Barnwell, using the sleeve of my jacket to push a thorny branch out of my face. 'But Sange's fan mail shows we could be looking at a woman.'

'Didn't you say a woman wouldn't have been able to carry the first victim through here?'

I untangled a burr from my hair, stopped and looked around, taking in the exposed roots and wet ground, going over the CSI report in my head. There had been no mud on the victim's shoes. So, she hadn't walked to her death.

'If the killer's a woman, she had to have had help.'

I thought about the Canadian serial killer duo Karla Homolka and Paul Bernardo, who lured, raped and killed their victims together, starting with Karla's younger sister.

Could it be that's what we were seeing here, despite what I'd thought before? A twisted exhibition of teamwork? Two people inhabiting the same fantasy?

I let out a breath I hadn't realised I was holding, sidestepped a discarded condom wrapper and tutted. There were Durex packets everywhere. According to Barnwell, the place was a known hook-up spot, mostly for the gay community. It had been a factor in the CSI search.

'Thing is,' I said, 'there's no way the fan mail girl would have acted with anyone. She's all about impressing the Butcher, not a separate alpha male. If she took on a partner, she'd have forfeited the admiration she craved from Sange.'

Barnwell moistened his lips. The frosty leaves crunched under his boots.

'And you said it couldn't be Marc Gethen's wife because of the tension between them, right?'

'Exactly. It rules out a dominant/submissive relationship. Unless . . .'

My flesh crept.

'Unless what?'

'What if *she's* the alpha and the tension between them was about maintaining a hold over him.'

Barnwell made a face, scratched at the back of his neck.

'I don't understand.'

'The way she wouldn't look at Marc during the interview and then how concerned she seemed later over that business with his mum. It's classic controlling behaviour. Giving and withdrawing affection to dominate another person. It's called trauma bonding. You throw out scraps of kindness to keep your prey on the line then pull away, leaving them hankering for more.'

Barnwell grinned; the tips of his ears glowed pink.

'You could be on to something. She was definitely more in control than him. Those clothes she was wearing, could be power-dressing. And remember how she took charge when we arrived?'

'Exactly. Plus, if they're in this together, it explains why they're both sticking to that leaky bucket alibi.'

Barnwell was nodding so fast it was like there were springs in his neck.

'You saw how she went red when she was looking at the crime scene photos? Her hand was trembling when she passed them back.'

'Maybe she spotted something she thought might incriminate them.'

'Holy moly, Ziba! You do realise we might have just cracked the case?'

I couldn't help smiling at his enthusiasm, though he didn't half make me feel my age. When had I last felt excited like that?

'We're not there yet, but we do need to re-examine those photos. Come on, let's hurry. I'll buy you a coffee back at the Yard.'

I was just bouncing a call from Jack, not wanting to talk with an audience, when I noticed it.

An abandoned glove that could both incriminate Marc Gethen and put him in the clear.

CHAPTER 77

Scotland Yard, London

Ha! I thought, checking through the CSI photos from the first crime scene and cross-referencing them with the list of 'foreign' items found in the vicinity. Ha, I knew I remembered seeing a glove in there!

I was just gaming it all out when my mobile rang. Jack again.

I knew him well enough to know why he was phoning without having to pick up. He's the only person in the world who calls me out on my shit and gets away with it. He's also got too much empathy for his own good. Always after having a go at me, he'll want to check I'm okay and that he hasn't upset me.

I hate people treating me like I'm made of glass. Enough of Duncan's old Yard mates do it, terrified they'll say the wrong thing and break the weeping widow.

My whole adult life, I've never cried in front of anyone and I don't need Wolfie or any other bugger passing me the Kleenex.

So instead of answering the call, I let it go through to voicemail and put my phone on silent. I wasn't ignoring him, not like yesterday, but I didn't have time to make nice right now. There was only a matter of hours left to catch the PRK before he struck again. And things weren't looking good.

As Barnwell and I had walked into the woods, I'd had a flash-bulb moment about the Gethens being behind the murders. Now I was back in the dark. I'd talk to Jack when the real perp was behind bars. Strung up by his toes, if I had my way.

I strummed my nails on the edge of my laptop, clucked my tongue on the roof of my mouth, tapped my foot against the base of my chair. The detective at the neighbouring desk glanced over crossly, not enjoying my body's percussion orchestra. We were all on edge, feeling the pressure.

I'd have to question Marc Gethen to confirm my new theory, but the more I thought about it, the more it made sense given what I'd spotted in the photos and on the list. Not to mention all those foil wrappers in the undergrowth.

Fingerling walked past, a muscle working in his jaw. A sign of teeth grinding, and stress. I wasn't the only one fixating on the PRK's timetable.

'I have an idea what Marc Gethen was doing on West Heath when he found the first vic,' I said, getting up and blocking his path.

'Having his way with her?'

'Half right. Only not with her.'

'You're talking in riddles again, MacKenzie.'

'Barnwell and I went back to the crime scene. The snow's melted, I wanted to see if there was anything I'd missed.'

'And was there?'

'Indirectly. There was a glove on the ground, kid's size, so nothing to do with our killer. But it got me thinking.'

He cricked his neck.

'Let's make this quick, shall we?'

'CSI found a man's leather glove in the outer perimeter. Beige. Distinctive pattern around the top. It was tested, obviously. Nothing to link it to the victim. Nearby, there was a necklace snagged on a

216

tree. Also found to be unrelated to the crime, but very distinctive. A real statement piece.'

'So?'

'So, you can see both items in one of the broad shots. I think the glove might belong to Marc Gethen, which is easy enough to check. And I think his wife noticed it when we showed her the crime scene photos. Combined with the necklace, I believe it confirmed her suspicion.'

'What suspicion?'

'That Gethen was having an affair.'

'Bit of a stretch, isn't it?'

'Not necessarily. We know the woods are a popular hook-up spot.'

'For the gay community.'

'No reason a straight person wouldn't want a bit of al fresco fun.'

He gave me a squinty-eye look. His idea of fun was probably the missionary position with his socks on. And a blow-up doll.

'It all fits,' I said, pushing away the grim mental image of Fingerling in flagrante. 'Why Gethen was dressed the way he was when he found the victim. Why he was out in the woods at oh silly hundred hours. Even why it took him so long to report the body. He had something to hide.'

I paused, putting myself in his skin.

'Given the proximity of the necklace to the discovery site, it's possible he wasn't the only one who stumbled across the body. What if his lover was with him – only, unlike him, she was freaked out by what she saw and ran off? What if he hasn't just been covering up the evidence of the affair? What if he's been covering for her too, keeping her name out of all this? It must have been quite a secret to carry around. The pressure could explain the strain between him and the wife. And now this.'

Fingerling ran a finger round the inside of his shirt collar.

'What makes you so sure his missus picked up on all this from this image?'

'The glove is only visible in one of the shots. The first few she looked at, her expression didn't change. And then suddenly she went bright red. When she handed the photos back to me, this one was on the top of the pile.'

I showed him the photo in question.

'There's the glove, it's in the foreground so easy to see. And the necklace too. It's very stand-out. The sort you'd notice someone wearing. It's possible Mrs G recognised it. Which would mean she knew the woman it belonged to.'

Fingerling stuck his tongue in his cheek, nodded slowly.

'If she already suspected Marc of having an affair, it'd explain her overreaction to the picture,' I said. 'The connection wouldn't be hard to make.'

It also explained why she made that snarky comment about his gloves when he was putting his coat on.

'She's his second wife. Perhaps she was Gethen's mistress during his first marriage. If so, she'd know he's got form. And there was already tension between them.'

Fingerling sucked air in through his teeth.

'What about the alibi? You've got to admit it's dodgy.'

'If I'm right about the affair, it's possible they weren't watching TV the night of the first murder. Maybe they were arguing about his infidelity but didn't want to admit that to us. Mrs Gethen is all about appearances,' I said, thinking back to the way she'd been dressed and the house that could have been lifted off the pages of *Ideal Home*. 'She wouldn't want us to think anything was awry in their marriage. To her mind, it would be a mark of shame. And Marc wouldn't have wanted us probing, asking questions about his extra-curricular activities. If his lover is also married, it'd put her in a bind.'

Fingerling perched on the edge of my desk, his ass on top of my papers.

'Lots of maybes in all this, MacKenzie. Got anything concrete to support it?'

'I told you before that Gethen's wife seemed pissed off with him. She loves him, though. That comment about how he shouldn't waste his time visiting his mother since she never appreciates him. It's why she's sticking around. She wants to make this work.'

If a guy cheated on me, I'd feed him his balls. But not everyone's made the way I am.

Fingerling pursed his lips.

'Doesn't mean Gethen didn't kill the girl. He could still have rowed with his missus, done the victim in, then supposedly found her after banging his bit on the side.'

'True. But this murder is part of a series. Up till now he hasn't been able to give us proper alibis for the nights of the other four crimes, claiming to either be asleep at home or out of town alone. But what if he was with his lover? What if that's why he wasn't forthcoming? He just needs to prove where he was during one of the murders to show he's clean. Even if he is doing the dirty.'

CHAPTER 78

Fingerling slid his skinny ass off my desk. My notes were creased. I tried not to think they'd be warm too.

'Any luck cracking that code?' he said.

I shook my head.

'Nope.'

'Well, keep at it, and it'd be helpful to get some more search parameters on the nutter writing to Sange. The boys have narrowed down the prison records pool, but it's still too big and nothing's flagging up on the system about attacks on babysitters either.'

'Copy.'

He gave me a look but kept his anti-military comments to himself this time.

'Did you hear, the perp's sent a second love letter to Officer Dale?' he said instead. 'Poor chap's in nervous decline. Or should I say, even more of a decline.'

'Aye, I saw him. Can't be much fun tipping a dead woman's liver out on to the kitchen table while you're chowing down on your Cheerios.'

'You certainly have a way of putting things, MacKenzie. Anyway, I'd better go brief the DCI. Let me know how you get on with the mad girl profile.'

I rolled my eyes. He had a way of putting things too. Trouble is, I wasn't sure how to go about the task he'd set me. I'd already presented a detailed portrait of Sange's fan to the team. Based on the scant information available, it was hard to see how much more detailed I could get.

I spent the next few hours going over the letters again. Data diving, we call it. And each time I came up empty.

James Fitzgerald, an FBI profiler straight out of training, employed linguistic analysis to examine the Unabomber's manifesto. His idea was to look at peculiarities of language to hone in on the killer.

Fitzgerald noticed the Unabomber referred to a well-known proverb, only he wrote it in an outdated way. Instead of saying 'You can't have your cake and eat it', he wrote 'You can't eat your cake and have it too'.

This unusual turn of phrase was one of the things that led to his identification and later capture. Another was his use of terminology reflective of an upbringing in Chicago.

It was a brilliant approach, but Fitzgerald had more than twelve hours and counting to get it right. And nothing stood out to me in the fan girl's letter to indicate a strong regional association.

Tick tock. Tick tock.

It was the afternoon now and still I had nothing new to share with the team.

By sixteen hundred hours I was ready to hang up my holster when an idea came to me. I'd like to take credit for it, but really it belongs to Fitzgerald.

He'd made the controversial call to publish the Unabomber's manifesto in the hope the way it was written would ring bells with a friend or family member. And it worked.

In profiling, there's no such thing as plagiarism. You steal with pride.

Time wasn't on our side. But there's no reason Fitzgerald's approach shouldn't work for us.

I just had to persuade Nigel Fingerling to let me try.

CHAPTER 79

We were all aware the next PRK attack was imminent, but we were still no closer to catching him. Though for what it's worth, I had been right about Marc Gethen. Not that I liked him any better after speaking to him.

This time, Barnwell and I had met up with him without his wife present.

'How long has the affair been going on?' I asked, straight off the bat.

A direct question usually gets a direct response, of the non-verbal variety anyway. Without the chance to prepare, a person's body language is unguarded and therefore easier to read.

Gethen went as red as his Hummels, his shoulders gravitated up to his ears. He was a cheater, and he'd just been caught out.

'Please don't tell my wife.'

'Why? She already knows, doesn't she?'

He chewed his lip.

'She suspects.'

'And she called you out on it the night before you found the body. You denied it, but she wasn't convinced.'

His voice raised a notch.

'You spoke to her already?'

'Not yet, and if you tell us what we need to know we may not have to.'

His shoulders sagged. I'd got him where I wanted. He started to sing.

Turned out, the night of the third attack he and his lover had snuck off for a night of passion at some seedy hotel in Paddington. As far as his wife knew, he was at a business conference in Reading. It meant an alibi, though. Barnwell scribbled down the details on his flip pad. Easy enough to follow up.

'Claudia's so uptight,' Gethen said, warming to his subject, relieved to shrug off the burden of deception. 'I like to mix it up a bit. Outdoors. Rough. Handcuffs. That sort of thing. She was always up for it when we first got together, but as soon as I put a ring on her finger it all changed. "The kids wear me out," she says. "I'm so tired." It's bullshit, though. She's just got boring. It's not my fault I've been forced to look around. I have needs. She should understand that.'

'She knows your girlfriend, doesn't she?' I said, thinking again that Mrs Gethen must have recognised the necklace to make the connection.

Marc grinned. His teeth were coffee-stained.

'They're in the same book club. Our kids carpool to school. Adds to the frisson, if I'm honest.'

The guy was a lowlife, but his story checked out. He was off the suspect list. And when we got back to the Yard, we found Ian Heppe was off it too.

What his mother had told us about him having an accident was true. Seemed he'd managed to slip down a pothole the night the fifth victim was killed and, suspecting a broken ankle, he'd called an ambulance, which had taken him to the Royal Free. His injury was actually just a sprain, but his long wait in A&E coincided with the band of time the medical examiner had estimated the victim died in.

We didn't have to take his or his mother's word for it. It was all there in the hospital records and on the security tapes. And with a fresh sprain, there's no way Ian Heppe could have carried anyone up a flight of church steps. He was in the clear too.

That left Sange's fan girl. Not that it did much to help us, given we still hadn't managed to get an identity on her. We were no closer to finding the perp than when Barnwell turned up at Quantico three days ago, despite me going all James Fitzgerald.

Fingerling had given the okay for me to brief the press office and put out her letters. By now he was desperate enough to try anything. Though, as he said, 'By the time they hit the stands tomorrow, it'll be too late for the poor cow the PRK's lining up for tonight.'

The evening titles all carried the story. It was on TV and radio too. But so far, the hotline had been quiet, save for the usual crackpots wanting their five minutes of fame.

I glanced up.

Nigel Fingerling had stopped by my desk on his way out of the MIR, a thick sheaf of papers under his arm, a pulse going full throttle in his temple.

'Have you spoken to your friend, Jack Wolfe?'

Was there news? Another letter to the *Telegraph*?

'Why, what's going on?'

'He thinks he's being followed. Some incident on the Tube earlier. And something dodgy this evening.'

Bile rose in my throat.

How come didn't he call me, I thought, before realising he had. Several times. Only I'd gone and bounced his calls again. Then set the phone to silent.

CHAPTER 80

I was out of my chair before Fingerling had finished speaking.

'We have to keep an open mind. Him being followed may be nothing, or it may be connected to the case,' he was saying. 'The PRK has been writing to Wolfe. Maybe he's decided it's time he got to know him better.'

Or maybe this has nothing to do with our perp. Maybe it's about Vernon Sange.

Had my worst fear come to life? Me and my big damn mouth.

'Where is he now?' I said, mind working through scenarios and options as I spoke.

'He's in one of the soft interview rooms. He was asking for you. Butler has just given him a pep talk.'

'What sort of pep talk?'

'Usual crime prevention guidance. You know the drill. Keep your phone handy. Ring 999 if you're worried about anything. Don't meet up with anyone you don't know.'

In other words, bland reassurances. And as a journo, the last bit of advice would be almost impossible to follow.

'I'm going down to speak to him. Text me if anything comes up.'

Fingerling nodded his okay, not that I was asking permission. 'He's in Room 5.'

Roger.

I took the stairs down two at a time. I was too wired to wait for the lifts. And mad at myself. All those times Jack's been there for me, I should have been there for him.

Anyone else and I would have knocked. But this was Wolfie. I barged right in.

He was sitting on the sofa, talking quietly into his phone.

He looked up, raised a finger. One second.

'Yeah, I'm fine. They've given me a talk. Taken a statement.'

A personal call, judging by the softness of his tone. His mother probably; she's a worrier, thinks she can sort the world out by feeding everyone lasagne and apple pie. My stomach rumbled. Lunch was a distant memory.

'I've gotta go, Char. Yeah, I'll keep you posted. Speak later.'

Not his mother then.

'Who's Char?' I said, though it didn't take a genius to guess the answer.

'The girl I'm seeing.'

Seeing? It suddenly sounded a whole lot more serious than it had last night.

'You like her, eh?'

I tried to sound nonchalant, though my tight jaw probably gave me away.

'Yeah, she's sweet. Clever too. Went to Oxford.'

'Really? Buddies with Sange, was she?'

I was being a bitch. Didn't care.

He gave me a 'what the hell' look. I shrugged it off, didn't much want to talk about 'Char'.

'So, what's this about you being followed?' I said, changing the subject.

'I did try to call.'

He sounded apologetic, like it was his fault I'd put my phone on silent.

The tension from last night had lifted as though it had never existed. Fear does that, it makes you focus on what's important.

'Start from the beginning. Fingerling didn't say much.'

I sat next to him, curling my feet under me, back against the arm of the sofa. Same way we've sat hundreds of times together, but never in a Scotland Yard interview room.

'It started on the Underground this morning. Char and I were coming back from a meeting when I got the sense we were being followed. She tried to convince me I was imagining it, but I knew I wasn't, though the train was packed so I couldn't identify anyone.

'Then, when I got back to the office, I found my wallet had disappeared. I'd used it to check through the barriers, so I definitely had it when I left the station. Someone must have picked my pocket between there and work.'

'And you think the person tailing you is responsible?'

He ran a hand over his eyes.

'I dunno. Maybe. It doesn't end there, though. I met Char for a bite to eat in Marylebone this evening. She'd been out of London chasing a story all day.'

Bloody 'Char' again. What kind of stupid name's that, anyway?

'Hang on, you lost your wallet. How were you going to pay for this dinner?'

'She offered to treat me, Sherlock.'

'Okay. Go on.'

'I walked down there, wanted to clear my head. I was still a bit shaken up from the Tube incident earlier. I was trying to persuade myself it was nothing, but I couldn't get rid of the idea someone had been shadowing me. I knew I was het up, probably overreacting, but you know what it's like, you can't always rationalise your feelings away.

'Between us, I'm not sorry to have the scoop but the PRK's letters are getting to me. I mean, why's the guy writing to me? It's not like I'm the only crime reporter in the UK. And there're plenty of other papers with bigger circulations.

'The fresh air helped, though, calmed me down. I started thinking I'd got the wrong end of the stick this morning, let my imagination run a bit wild, like Char said. Only . . .'

He paused, took a deep breath.

I didn't have Barnwell's patience.

'Only what?'

'Only when I got to the restaurant, my wallet was back in my pocket.'

CHAPTER 81

Far as I could see, there were only two ways Jack's wallet could have magically reappeared in his pocket. Either it had been there all along and the stress of the day and the PRK's letters messed with his head. Or whoever had taken it decided to put it back.

Though what were they hoping to achieve by doing that? To screw with him? Or send some sort of message? And how would they have done it without him noticing?

'The lab's shut now. But there're some Zephyr brushes upstairs. And BVDA Gellifters, in case the wallet's too porous for powder. Either way, we'll be able to see if there are any latent finger marks that don't match yours.'

He shook his head.

'They've already checked for foreign prints. There were a couple of partials. But not enough detail to get a hit.'

'So, it was definitely pinched then.'

'Yep. But nothing's missing, so I don't know what they were after.'

I gave him a look.

'Okay, what *he* was after. That what you're trying to say? You think it was the PRK, don't you?'

I was through lying to Jack.

'He's obviously taken an interest in you.'

I chewed my lip.

'But?'

'But, this could just as easily be the work of Vernon Sange.'

Jack rolled his eyes.

'Jeez, I thought I was the paranoid one. Sange is locked up, Mac. Maximum security, hundreds of miles away. Unless the guy can teleport, he's got a pretty good alibi.'

I thought of my would-be attacker from the other night.

'He doesn't need to teleport,' I said. 'He just needs to call in a favour.'

I tapped my lips with my index finger.

'Do you have your wallet on you now?'

He nodded, confused.

'Let me see it.'

He handed it over, a small brown leather square warm from nesting inside his pocket.

I took a pair of blue latex gloves out of the Ziploc sack I keep in my bag and slipped them on. One day they'll make a size small enough to fit me properly.

Jack grinned.

'This your way of robbing me without leaving any evidence?'

I pointed at the camera tucked in the corner of the ceiling.

'Don't think I'll get away with it, do you?'

I started emptying the wallet, item by item, on to the table in front of us. Credit cards. Starbucks loyalty card. RAC breakdown cover. Phone numbers and login details scribbled on Post-it notes, with names and times scrawled next to them in handwriting as messy as his hair.

Cash. A ten. Two twenties.

Jack was sitting very close, head bent, watching my hands work. I could hear him breathing, felt the heat coming off his skin.

My heart began to pick up speed, my stomach tightened.

Maybe I should I tell him? It sounded like he'd only just started seeing this girl, it couldn't be serious yet. But what should I say?

I focused hard on the wallet, slipped my fingers behind the credit card holder. I couldn't look at him. It was like jumping into water. You can't do it with your eyes open.

Now or never.

'Jack, listen. There's something—'

I stopped, my insides turning to liquid.

I angled round, the words I'd been about to speak evaporating in my mouth.

'Have you seen this in here before?'

I held out the white card I'd just found tucked away in the back of his wallet. It was my business card, my name and contact details printed on the front. And on the back, written in purple felt-tip pen, the letters perfectly formed and unnaturally regular, were four words:

The die is cast.

It answered all my questions. Jack's wallet had been stolen and then returned to send a message. That message was from Sange.

But it wasn't meant for Wolfie. It was meant for me.

CHAPTER 82

'Ziba? What's wrong?'

I thought about fobbing Jack off, rejected the idea just as fast. Apart from anything, the fact Vernon Sange had chosen to communicate his message to me through Wolfie meant we were in this together. He had a right to know the details – not that I knew them all.

'*The die is cast*. It's word for word what Sange wrote in the letter he sent me after the trial.'

'Shit. This *is* about him, then?'

'Looks like.'

'What does it mean?'

I sighed, pressed my lips together.

'I think it's his way of saying "Game on".' And depending on how long he'd had my card, it explained where he'd got my email address from. I paused. 'Jack, did I give this to you?'

'Why would you have done? It's not like I don't have your number.'

Just what I'd thought.

'So how did Sange get hold of it? I mean, I wasn't exactly touting for business up in Wakefield. And how did he get it out of there?'

For a moment we were silent, each lost in our own heads. Then—

'Hang on a minute,' Jack said. He rifled through the cards spread out on the table, checked his wallet. 'Shit. It's missing.'

'What is?'

'My driver's licence.'

We locked eyes, both thinking the same thing. Whoever took Jack's wallet now knew where he lived. Sange, the PRK or both.

'You know what this means, right? You're staying at mine tonight.'

'It's good of you, but—'

'It's an order, not an offer.'

He laughed.

'Well, when you put it like that.'

He glanced down, then back at me.

'Look, I'm sorry about yesterday, ripping you a new one like that. It was wrong.'

I felt myself flush.

'I'm sorry too. I shouldn't have lied to you. Or kept you in the dark.'

He smiled.

'Now we've got that out the way, how are things with you? Apart from work, I mean. I feel like we haven't talked properly for ages.'

We hadn't.

'There is something, actually.'

I told him about the letter I'd found inside my father's old book, the one my mother had written when she'd found out she was pregnant with me.

'I'm not saying she's not messed up,' I said. 'Or that she's ever going to change. But maybe her distance is a shield. A barrier to stop her getting hurt again.'

'Now who does that remind you of?'

'Sod off, Jack.'

'I'm being serious. Maybe you two aren't as different as you think.' He shifted position on the sofa, his thigh brushing momentarily against mine, making my stomach twist. 'So, are you going to talk to her about it?'

'Aye. When the case is over, though. There've been too many distractions as it is.'

He looked confused.

'What sort of distractions?'

Me and my mouth.

'Sange,' I said quickly. 'He's like a bloody earworm. I can't get him out of my head. And the case too, obviously. We're in countdown now. The killer could literally strike at any point tonight.'

My phone buzzed before Jack could ask how I knew so much about the bastard's timetable. An SMS from Fingerling. I read it and leapt to my feet, grinning.

Yes! My plan had worked. Against all the odds, someone had recognised Sange's fan from the letters we'd shared with the media. Her name was Rosie Linger.

Finally, we had an ident. But was she our perp? And if so, could we trace her before she attacked her next victim?

It was only as I was racing back up to the incident room that a second name lit up my brain. The girl Jack was seeing, 'Char'. A diminutive of Charlotte.

Just like Lottie, another member of Vernon Sange's fan club.

CHAPTER 83

I stopped dead in my tracks. Char. Lottie. Were they the same person or was I seeing smoke signals that didn't exist?

I'll never forget what you taught me. Or what I promised.

Si vis pacem, para bellum. Sed vis bellum, para pacem.

If you want peace, prepare for war. But if you want war, prepare for peace.

From the letter I'd read, I'd profiled Lottie as either a History or Classics grad and thinking back to what she'd written, she clearly knew Sange. It's also possible she'd been taught by him.

Jack had made no bones of the fact Char had been to Oxford. Had she met Sange there, been taught by him?

Maybe it was coincidence. But what if it wasn't? What would that mean for Wolfie?

I'll never forget what . . . I promised.

What had she promised? And what did it have to do with war?

I was both het up and exhausted, fully aware I wasn't at my sharpest. Even so, I couldn't shake the thought that Jack was dating one of Sange's groupies – and from the sounds of it, a highly intelligent one at that. Which also made her highly dangerous.

I ground the balls of my hands into my eyes. I needed to focus, to be rational.

What else did I know?

I replayed the conversation with Jack in my head, going over the facts.

He and Char had been on the Tube together. Jack had got the feeling they were being followed but she told him he was imagining things. When they got back to the office, his wallet was gone.

Then later, he met her for dinner, only to find his wallet back in his pocket.

My heart began to gallop, my chest tightened. It was her! She took his wallet!

It would have been a cinch. She was there with him when it went missing. And when it was found.

Walking to their office from the Tube, she could have easily slid a hand into his jacket and pinched it. Then, kissing him 'hello' at the restaurant later would have given her the perfect opportunity to slip it back.

And the card that had appeared in it afterwards tied her directly to Vernon Sange.

She had to be the woman writing to him, it was the only thing that made sense.

But what was I going to do about it?

And did she have any connection to the PRK?

CHAPTER 84

My initial instinct was to race back downstairs to Jack.

'Your girlfriend's a psycho,' I wanted to say. 'She's got a thing for the Butcher. And she's messing with your head.' Followed by, 'Ditch her. Be with me.'

But that follow-on thought was the very reason I couldn't tell him anything. How could I be sure I wasn't acting out of self-interest? And why would he believe me anyway?

I had a theory. It made sense. But I'd never met the girl or watched the incident with the wallet unfold.

On top of that, he'd rightly be quick to point out I had a lot on my plate. If he could persuade himself that he'd been imagining things when he thought he was being followed, he could just as easily persuade himself that I was imagining things too. Not least because he wouldn't *want* to think I was right.

With few exceptions, people see what they expect to see and believe what they want to believe. Most of us don't want to prove ourselves wrong. We want to prove ourselves right.

I could tell from his voice on the phone that he liked this 'Char' character. It would take more than a crazy hypothesis from me to change that. And given what I felt about him, did I have the right to try?

After all, she had (probably) taken and later returned his wallet. But the message Sange had written on the card showed I was his focus, not Jack.

If being romantically involved put him in danger, it wasn't by being involved with her. It was by being with me.

Much as I wanted to tell him everything and get his woman out of the picture, I had to button it.

It may even be a good approach, I thought, starting up the stairs. Vernon Sange has a pawn in play and I'm on to her. But he doesn't know that, which gives me the upper hand. And possibly the opportunity to feed back misinformation.

Plus, if Jack's all loved up with Char-de-da, that gives credence to my line that there's nothing going on between us.

Yes, I thought, coming out of the stairwell. I might not like the idea of Jack cosying up with one of Sange's minions. But perversely, doing so might be the best way for him to stay safe.

CHAPTER 85

I walked back into the incident room, mind back where it was supposed to be – on catching our killer.

'There you are, MacKenzie.'

For once, Fingerling looked happy to see me. He was actually smiling. First time for everything.

'So, we've got an ident on the fan . . .'

'We do indeed. I have to admit, I was doubtful your little stunt would work but—'

'Hardly a stunt, Nigel. It's what led to the capture of one of America's most wanted killers.'

'I wasn't looking for a history lesson. If you'd let me finish, I was going to say you did a good job.'

It occurred to me that if I'd leapt to the wrong conclusion just now, I could just as easily have leapt to the wrong one about Jack's woman too. I was all over the place, jumpy as a bouncing bomb.

I mumbled an apology then asked how things had played out.

'A number of news channels ran the story. The BBC put out a tweet. We got a call to the hotline while you were downstairs with your boyfriend.'

I snarled but let it go. Fingerling didn't want a history lesson and I didn't want to rehash old arguments.

So instead of saying it was a pity his mother hadn't faked a headache the night he was conceived, I asked instead –

'Who called it in?'

'Some girl Linger works with. They're both hairdressers. Doesn't think too highly of her. "Right whiny cow" were the exact words she used.'

'What makes you so sure she's not just ratting out someone she has it in for?'

'First off, a lot of what she said fitted that profile of yours. Linger moans all the time but apparently she's shy as shit. It was a problem with the clients, the caller said. Seems you ladies like to chat when you're having your hair done.'

I don't. Then again, I've never been much of a lady.

'She suffers from what the caller described as "social anxiety".' He made air quotes like it was a made-up thing. 'She takes pills for it. Has an eating disorder too, the caller reckons. Which fits with the whole low self-esteem business you talked about.'

I nodded. Eating disorders and lack of confidence do tend to go hand in hand.

'What else?'

'She lives on her own, and she's obsessive when it comes to men. Apparently, she screwed some bloke she met in a bar. Just a one-night stand but she went all Glenn Close on him afterwards; hounding him with phone calls, showing up on his doorstep in the middle of the night, throwing eggs at his windows when he didn't respond the way she wanted. The caller said things got so out of hand the guy had to take out a restraining order.'

All right in line with the profile so far.

'Does the restraining order check out?'

He grinned so wide I could see his fillings.

'Yes, it does. That's not all, though. It never made it through official channels, which is why there's nothing on the system, but it seems Linger caused quite a scene in front of a load of onlookers not so long ago. Word is she was screaming and shouting obscenities at this poor seventeen-year-old kid and shoving her. Want to guess who she was?'

'Babysitter for Linger's neighbours' kids?'

'Exactamundo!'

It was a direct link to the fan letter:

Okay, so I've picked someone. She babysits for the family next door, nasty little brats they are.

'Sounds like a match. Anything else to connect her and the Butcher?'

Fingerling's eyes got even wider. A yes, then.

'Rosie Linger makes jewellery. Lockets with funny symbols on the front. She showed our caller one once. Inside was a picture of—'

'Vernon Sange?'

Fingerling nodded, licked his lips like they were covered in cream.

'I've dispatched a uniformed response team to her address. It won't be long till we've got this bat-shit bitch in cuffs. Just a shame we've got cameras in our interview rooms, if you know what I mean.'

It's not just serial killers who have violent fantasies.

CHAPTER 86

'We can't go in guns blazing,' I said to Fingerling. 'If we want a confession out of Rosie Linger, we'll need to take it slow, empathise with her, draw her out.'

From what her colleague had said, the woman was unstable. She'd require careful handling, whatever the DI might secretly like to do to her.

But Fingerling was only half listening, carrying on as if the threat to the homeless community had already been neutralised. The way I saw it, though, we weren't at the party popper stage yet.

'How's a girl with an eating disorder going to be able to carry the first vic deep into the woods?' I said.

'Barnwell, show her what you found in the DVLA records.'

Driver and Vehicle Licensing Agency.

I hovered over his shoulder as he opened up a photo of Linger on his laptop. Rather than being the skinny anorexic I'd envisaged, possibly because the term 'eating disorder' made me automatically think of Falcon's daughter, Rosie's problems were on the other end of the spectrum. She was enormous, around five foot six and easily 250 pounds.

Meanwhile, our first victim was malnourished and petite. It wouldn't have been so difficult for a woman of Linger's size to heft her to the kill site.

My misgivings began to dissipate. The anticipation inside the MIR was palpable. You couldn't be in that room without getting infected.

In many ways, this had been a perfectly handled case – profiling and police work coming together to nail a perp. And despite our fears to the contrary, if we were right about Rosie, we'd close in on her before she had the chance to attack her next victim.

Sange could say all he wanted about the die being cast, but if this panned out, I wouldn't need him any more. And once we'd wrapped up everything here, I could sort things out with Jack too – if only I could find the right words.

Vernon Sange would turn out to have been a blip, nothing more.

Fingerling's phone rang. The unit must have arrived at Linger's house. The bird was about to be bagged and stuffed in the pot!

I wasn't the only one watching the DI as he answered. The room went silent, everyone holding their breath, listening.

'DI Fingerling speaking. Right. Okay then. Force an entry.'

He hung up, waited; only the thumb rubbing against his knobbly wrist betrayed his tension.

The phone rang again. He picked up before it had got through the first ring.

'I see.' His shoulders slumped. 'Search the premises . . . Shit.'

He looked round the room. When he spoke, his voice hardly carried.

'The house is empty. Rosie Linger appears to have left in a hurry. And her phone's off. She could be anywhere right now.'

We'd celebrated too soon.

The bird hadn't been bagged. It had flown.

CHAPTER 87

Livy is curled into a foetal ball, stroking the beautiful watch that kind woman gave her, dreaming about the homeless hostel she's been saving up for.

I'll be able to afford to stay there for months once I've sold this, she thinks, tummy fluttering with happiness.

Fantasising about the hot meals, heating and laundry at the shelter, she isn't aware of the footsteps approaching where she's hunkered down for her last night on the streets.

Someone squats down, touches her back. Livy jumps, eyes shooting open, body tensed, expecting the worst. She's been pissed on before, a lot of the girls have been. And worse. Drunk bastards.

'Oh, it's you!' She relaxes, smiles. 'You gave me a scare!' Then, 'Sorry, what did you say?'

The dark makes it hard to lip-read. Livy's been deaf since birth. She's never heard the birds sing or anyone say they loved her. Though she knows for a fact, those words never came out of her mother's mouth.

It was bad enough her mum got herself pregnant at sixteen with a baby she never wanted. It was even worse that that baby couldn't hear a damn word she said to it. And perhaps because she was still only a child herself, Livy's mother was as cruel about her daughter's disability as the kids at school were.

'Sorry, can you say that again?' Livy says now, embarrassed.

'You look freezing. I've got hot coffee if you want some.'

They've been warned about what's been going on, not to go off with strange men offering warm drinks. But this is hardly a strange man.

She wriggles out of her sleeping bag, the icy air hitting her body like a mallet.

'Thank you,' she says, with a grateful smile. 'I'm dying for something hot.'

CHAPTER 88

Blomfield Villas, London

I unlocked my front door, the post from downstairs in my hand, Jack behind me filling the hallway with his bulk.

Fingerling had given me the okay to bring him up to speed on Rosie Linger. Given what the arrest team had found at her place and the intel we'd unearthed since, there was a very real chance she was the offender.

And given what we'd already fed to the media about the fan letters, keeping quiet about our lead wasn't an option. By morning, the press would be all over us, demanding a follow-up – especially if another girl died tonight.

I was still sure Char was tied up in the whole wallet debacle but it didn't mean the PRK wasn't somehow involved too. Given how much Sange seemed to know about the killer's activity, it wasn't inconceivable he had two pawns in play.

I couldn't say anything about Char, but I could tell him what we knew about Rosie Linger. The more he knew, the better he could protect himself.

'Fancy a nightcap?'

I added today's mail to the now towering pile on the hall table and marched through to the kitchen without waiting for an answer. There are some problems only wine will sort out.

I cracked open a Stellenbosch Pinotage I'd been saving, the smell of earth and smoke and brambles wafting out as it splashed into the glass.

'Cheers.'

I took a deep sniff and an even bigger sip, rolling it round my mouth, coating the insides of my cheeks with tannins and rich berry flavours.

'So, you really think it's her?'

Another slug, long and deep.

'Profile and circumstantials say it might be.'

'Circumstantials?'

'Her home was in a real mess, apparently. Clothes spilling out of drawers. Books and papers all over the floor. Looks like she left in a hurry. The TV had been left on too. Possibly she'd heard what we put out about the letters and legged it before we could get to her. And her phone's off, which suggests she doesn't want to be found. Tactical response sent us photos of mad scribblings on the walls, including quotes from Ovid, a tangential link to Pygmalion.

'*Be patient and tough; someday this pain will be useful to you.*

'*Beauty is a fragile gift.*

'*The glow of inspiration warms us; it is a holy rapture.*

'All signs of a person in a psychotic break inhabiting a delusion, a fantasy. Rosie didn't turn up to work today either, or give notice that she wasn't coming in.'

Jack leaned against the countertop, cradling his wine.

'I don't know, seems a bit flimsy to me.'

I shrugged. It felt a whole lot less flimsy with her in the wind.

'Like I said, she fits the profile too, more than we realised from the letters. We now know she has an eating disorder and self-harms.

Both are conditions that could make her uncomfortable around others.

'According to the social services files, she had a tough time growing up. Never knew her father. Mother was a drunk, subjected her to horrible emotional abuse. Used to lock her in cupboards and Christ knows what else.

'She ended up in foster care when she was ten. But by then the damage was done. She was often truant from school. Got in fights with the other kids. Wet the bed well into her teens, one of the markers on the homicidal triad. A predictor of violent tendencies.

'No surprise, she suffers from low confidence. But she's bright. You can tell that from the way she writes. She spent her adolescence in Kilburn, not far from the kill sites.

'And no one's seen her since this morning.'

CHAPTER 89

We carried our wine glasses through to the living room. The pile of unopened mail on the hall table seemed to eye me accusingly as I walked past.

I should really make a start on it, I thought with zero enthusiasm.

And maybe I would have done if Jack hadn't distracted me by asking if he could borrow my iPhone charger and where I kept the spare bedding. I came back from the airing cupboard with an armful and we worked together, tucking a sheet into the sofa cushions and shaking out a duvet.

It felt wrong, being home and getting all domestic while the rest of the team was at the Yard, sleeping in shifts, scrabbling for clues to track down Rosie Linger before it was too late.

It was as if the gods were spitting their ambrosia at us. We'd finally got an ident on a viable suspect who fitted the profile and had a clear connection to the Butcher. Only it wasn't worth a damn since we didn't have any idea where she was.

We had a recent photograph, though. At least we could share that with the press. An overweight woman with a double chin and blue eyes so light it looked like the colour had faded out of them in the wash. She was glaring at the camera, her lips thin and tight, her jaw set slightly forward.

'Cheerful lass,' Fingerling had said, the irony bitter in his mouth.

We were all feeling bitter.

'So near and yet so far,' another detective had said helpfully, earning a verbal clip round the ear.

'If you've nothing useful to say, keep it shut, Ginger.'

Right now, the team was monitoring live CCTV feeds, keeping a watch out for Linger. We knew where her hunting ground was, but it was a big place and the camera feeds aren't stitched together.

The odds weren't in our favour.

Fingerling was covering all the bases, though. If Sange was right, the killer was going to attack the next victim tonight. But we didn't have to sit back and wait for it to happen.

Uniformed response units had been dispatched to the abduction zone, pulled in from around the capital to help. With so many cops on the streets, the PRK would have to be invisible to slip past them unnoticed.

And yet, despite everything we were doing and all the precautions we'd taken – warning the homeless community, putting notices up in soup kitchens, encouraging them to use shelters – none of us were feeling particularly hopeful.

I slid a pillow into a case, shook it out, chucked it to Jack.

'You said the killer transported the victims to the crime scenes,' he said. 'Any hits on ANPR?'

Automatic number plate recognition technology.

'We already know where Rosie Linger's vehicle is. It's sitting on the road outside her house with a slow puncture. If she's using a car, it's not hers. Which makes her a hell of a lot harder to trace.'

Jack looked at me.

'Do you think you'll get her in time?'

Same question we were all asking.

I took my phone out of my pocket, checked for updates. Sighed.

'Right now, she's our best lead. But we don't know where she is. Only what she's likely to do next.'

CHAPTER 90

The Artist comes home with a fresh bunch of flowers; pink roses and baby's breath. The tulips bought two days ago are already wilting, their water turned green and sludgy. On the windowsill, the lilies have died part open.

Stillborn, the Artist thinks, filling a jug from the kitchen tap and arranging the new bouquet in it before going to fix Mother's make-up. She's looking pale. The skin on her face seems to sag. The illness is taking its toll.

In her chair, Mother tuts her disapproval.

'Waste of money, all these flowers.'

The Artist blocks her out by quietly singing the opening of Dido's Lament from Purcell's marvellous opera, Dido and Aeneas.

Thy hand, Belinda, darkness shades me.

On thy bosom let me rest.

More I would, but Death invades me.

Death is now a welcome guest.

'You sound like a halfwit warbling to yourself,' Mother mutters.

There's a plate of peanut butter toast on the table in front of her, untouched even though she said she was hungry. The margarine has oozed through the light brown paste. On the surface, a fly tap-taps with a thin black tongue.

'You've got to eat, Mother. The doctor says you need to keep your strength up.'

She narrows her eyes, there's something of Medusa in her stare.

'Think I don't know what you're doing? You're trying to poison me, aren't you? You have everyone else fooled, but I know what you are.'

'I'm not trying to hurt you, I'm looking after you, same as always. Why can't you see that? Those gifts I used to make you when I was a kid, that I'd find later in the bin. The birthday cards you used for shopping lists. It's not me who hates you, Mother. It's you who hates me. I just wish I knew why.'

But these words, like so many others, stay locked in the Artist's head.

And in the face of silence, Mother's lips purse raisin-tight.

CHAPTER 91

Livy is so sleepy. Her muscles have turned to mush, she can't focus. And yet she knows something is very wrong.

She blinks twice, trying to clear her vision, but still she can't see properly. It's like looking through plastic wrap or trying to open your eyes under water. Everything's blurry. Distorted.

Where am I? she thinks. What's happening to me?

It's cold, the air icy against her skin, cutting through her clothes. She's being carried up some steps. As her awareness resurfaces, she realises she got it wrong before. She isn't sure what's happening but she knows she isn't being saved.

They come to a stop. She's set on the ground, the stone hard and cold against her knees. A hand on the base of her skull angles her head down. A metal edge presses against her throat.

Time wades through treacle. She can't move. Only her mind races, jolted awake by the sudden awareness of what's coming and what it means.

Mummy, she thinks at the same moment the knife slices through her carotid.

CHAPTER 92

I was just dozing off when my brain jerked me back. Fingerling might call at any time but I'd gone and left my phone on the arm of the sofa, right where Jack would be snoring. A few months ago, I'd have thought nothing of going to fetch it. But now the idea of him waking up to find me leaning over him in my nightshirt was mortifying.

A part of me wished we could return to that previous uncomplicated state. Easy together, not watching what I said or wondering what he was thinking. Not hesitating to tell him what I thought of whoever he was dating.

Duncan and I watched *When Harry Met Sally* one rainy Sunday afternoon. He was obsessed with it, God knows why. A ditzy blonde faking orgasms in a grotty diner isn't my thing, but it was early on in our relationship. We were still at the stage where we'd try things out to please the other. Though I never did manage to get him to give the shooting range a go.

The movie largely sent me to sleep, but the central premise was borderline interesting enough to discuss afterwards. Can men and women be friends without wanting to sleep with each other?

I've worked with plenty of men, slept with plenty of them too. But I wouldn't have called any of them friends. So, I wasn't in much of a position to make a convincing argument either way.

Duncan was clear, though. Friendship between the sexes works until one of you imagines the other naked. I'd laughed at the time, imagined him naked. Only now did I get what he'd been trying to say.

The moment you consider, even for a second, what someone would be like in bed, a platonic relationship becomes impossible. And I'd most definitely crossed that line with Jack.

I rolled on to my other side, forced myself to empty my mind, let sleep come.

A noise woke me what seemed like moments later. Someone knocking at the door.

'Mac, it's me. Sorry to disturb you. A text's just come through. You better take a look.'

I rubbed my eyes, yawned widely, pushed back the duvet. Last time he'd yanked me out of Dreamland in the middle of the night, I'd thought he was the London Lacerator come to get me. And I'd very nearly got him – in the neck, with my Fairbairn-Sykes fighting knife.

I opened the door. He was standing there, hair mussed, in his boxers and a T-shirt.

First a towel, now this. The gods must be pissing themselves up there.

He handed me the phone.

Pygmalion's been busy. The blonde is at St Luke's. You could have prevented this, Ziba. Shall we try again before the next one?

PS Please send Mr Wolfe my regards. I hope he's enjoying his stay.

SMS 03.17

The message was from Vernon Sange. But how had he sent it? And how did he know Jack was here?

CHAPTER 93

Scotland Yard, London

By the time I made it down to the Yard, it had been confirmed. Despite all our best efforts to prevent it, the PRK had killed again and Vernon Sange had been right on every count.

The victim was blonde. Her lips had been cut off. And she was left on the steps of St Luke's Church in Hampstead; a single pink rose on her corpse, a circle with an arrow sticking out the top chalked on the ground beside her.

But how had he known so much? Was the information in the PRK's code, or was he getting his intel from somewhere else? And how had he managed to text me while on lockdown in a maximum-security prison?

Later analysis of the message revealed it had been sent from a burner in London, not Wakefield. The words were Sange's then, but they hadn't come directly from him.

Had the PRK sent them? It was physically possible but didn't fit with what else we knew. The perp was a braggart but Sange hadn't been mentioned in any of the letters to either the policeman or Jack. It would be highly unlikely to see such a radical behavioural change now.

On top of that, why would an offender hungry for attention want to share the stage with someone else? And why would they want to encourage me to find out more about them?

My fingers danced on my desk as I sifted through the evidence in my head.

Char!

What if she'd sent the message as a part of whatever 'promise' she'd made to Sange?

My heart began to strum.

PS Please send Mr Wolfe my regards. I hope he's enjoying his stay.

I hadn't heard Jack phone her, but he might well have sent her an SMS saying he was crashing at mine. Maybe that's why he needed my charger, to text the bitch.

Or perhaps he called after I'd gone back up to the incident room. He did say he'd 'keep her posted' when he wound up the phone call I walked in on at the Yard.

My brain was spinning round like the revolver cylinder in a game of Russian roulette, only the person with the muzzle pressing into their temple wasn't me, it was Wolfie.

I glanced up at the big clock on the wall. Still zero dark thirty. The canteen would be closed. Vending machine coffee then. Two sips and I binned it. There's a reason I go to Starbucks and it's not because I like seeing my name written on the side of the cup.

Fingerling came over, ran his hands over his hair. It left a shine on his palms.

'Any idea how Sange has your number, MacKenzie?'

'From one of my business cards. Not sure how he got hold of it, though.'

I opened my mouth to tell him about Char then snapped it shut. Duncan's voice was in my ear, as clear as if he were standing next to me.

You could be on to something but he'll think you're off your head if you come to him with this now. Wait till you've got something solid to back it up, hen.

Exhaustion may be playing tricks with me, but the imaginary voice was right. Focus on the facts.

'Jack found my card in his wallet. There was a message from the Butcher written on the back.'

Fingerling squinted.

'What sort of message?'

'The die is cast.'

'I don't get it.'

'I told you. He's into mind games.'

Fingerling grunted.

'How did he get your card? Did you give it to him?'

'Don't be daft.'

'Shit, just when I think we're starting to get a handle on this case, another bloody whack-a-mole pops up.'

If only they were just whack-a-moles.

Fingerling pulled a bee-eating face.

'Things aren't looking good. Rosie Linger has disappeared. Sange appears to have it in for your friend. And unless we catch a break, we're going to have a seventh victim on our hands before long.'

I knew where this was going.

The Butcher was still our best hope of catching the perp. Which meant I needed to go back to Wakefield Prison.

Just what I didn't want to be doing.

CHAPTER 94

Her Majesty's Prison Service, HMP Wakefield

I'd been to Wakefield Prison twice. Both times I'd let Sange get the better of me, forcing me into my least favourite position, defence.

But now he'd involved Jack in his screwed-up games, I was ready to go on the attack.

My previous strategy had blown up in my face. I'd put on a front but all that had achieved was to show where I was weak. There's always a bit of give and take in an interview, you need it to build rapport. But I'd broken the golden rule: never give up details about yourself, never let the subject inside your head.

Doing so had been a calculated move, a bargaining chip. And a massive error. I'd got a name out of Sange, Pygmalion. Though I'd overpaid for it. The Butcher now knew me better than I knew him.

'Just be careful,' Falcon had said before that first interview. 'And for Christ's sake, never forget for a moment what he is.'

I'd been lulled by his easy manner but I hadn't forgotten what he was capable of. I'd just thought I could handle him. I was wrong.

Well, I'll have to handle him better today, that's all, I thought. Rosie Linger could be anywhere, which makes Sange our best chance of finding her before she kills again.

Then after all this is over and the PRK's behind bars, I'm going to book a ticket to Florida, sit behind the glass and cheer as they strap the monster to the gurney.

My self-talk was tough. It didn't reflect how I felt.

The sun was up as I turned down Love Lane, past the high-to-the-sky prison walls and into the parking lot.

Outside, the sky was a dirty blanket; rain was on the way. Or more snow.

Should've brought an umbrella, I thought. And my iPhone charger. Halfway to Wakefield, I realised I'd left it at home juicing up Jack's mobile. When Sange's message about the latest victim had come through, all I could think about was getting to the Yard.

I clicked the phone's home button. The battery was on 54%. Not ideal, but it should just about last.

By the main door, the 'Welcome to HMP Wakefield' sign gave off the smell of a bad joke. Overhead, coils of barbed wire taller than me stood sentry along the roof edge. I was in Sange's house now.

I signed the visitor's log, jotted down my car details and showed my ID card to the guard on the gate.

'Third visit in four days,' he said, smiling inside his beard. 'You must like the Butcher nearly as much as those idiots trying to get him saved.'

'The protesters? Aye, I heard there was another petition doing the rounds.'

'I meant the morons in Parliament. With everything else going on in the world, you'd think they'd have other things to worry

263

about. And now some big shot in the Lords is getting involved, can you believe?'

I really couldn't. Then again, the Sunlight conspiracy I'd recently shone a light on showed just how rotten the Establishment was.

Question is, was Jack's girlfriend, Char, rotten too? I had my theories about her and Sange. Maybe there was a way to corroborate them.

'Vernon Sange has a few buddies, I hear.'

The guard leaned forward over the counter, scenting gossip.

'Politicians, you mean?'

'Journalists.'

'Eh well, there are always a few of them hanging round. Especially now.'

'A woman from the *Telegraph* came up yesterday, I think. Charlotte. You remember her?'

Jack had said she'd been out of London chasing a story. Was this where she'd been? Though if so, why hadn't it flagged up on our system? Given his link to our investigation, we were supposed to be kept informed about who was visiting Sange.

The guard grinned; there was lasciviousness in it.

'Yes, I remember her.'

He flicked through the register, turned it round so I could see.

'Yeah, here we go. Charlotte Fox-Robinson. Came at the beginning of March too.'

The hairs stood up on my forearms. Twice in two weeks?

So why hadn't Barnwell picked up on her name when he'd gone through the logs? Unless her job made him discount her. As the guard had implied, Char wasn't the only journalist to visit Vernon Sange. The magazines are in and out all the time; the Butcher's face sells more copies than Kate Middleton's.

Even so, her trip yesterday was the missing pin in the grenade. It gave her opportunity and me a working theory of how she could have got hold of my business card with the Butcher's writing on it.

He gave it to her, right before she drove back to London to have dinner with Jack.

But that's not the only reason my skin contracted. Beneath Charlotte's signature, written in a hand I recognised, was a second name that hadn't been flagged.

Rosie Linger.

CHAPTER 95

I was taken to the usual meeting room, along the now familiar windowless corridors, through the heavy doors.

Once inside and alone, I texted Fingerling about the Butcher's two visitors yesterday, questioning why the prison hadn't informed us. Ten minutes went by. Then I heard it – the sound of marching boots and a pair of thin-soled shoes on the linoleum floor.

Vernon Sange was on his way in.

I set my phone to record; sat, back straight, hands clasped in front of me, trying to still my knee jiggling under the table.

The footsteps got louder. The door clicked open. Despite myself, I tasted rust at the back of my throat.

'Hello, Ziba. I hope the traffic wasn't too bad.'

He smiled, pleased to see me, relaxed like we were old friends. But I wasn't going to fall for his charm and honeyed accent so easily this time.

Despite the early hour, he was neatly dressed. His hair was combed and he'd recently brushed his teeth. He'd been waiting for me, then, despite this being a spur of the moment visit.

The guards uncuffed him and left. It was just the two of us now.

'How's Mr Wolfe?' he said.

His grin was cheeky, his eyes danced.

Practised, I told myself. A disguise.

'I don't have time for games today, Sange. Where's Rosie Linger?'

He took his time to answer.

'Rosie Linger?'

'The woman who's been writing to you. You encouraged her to cut herself, pick a target. She chose her neighbours' babysitter. But you already know that, don't you? She told you all about it in detail, just like you asked. I know she came to see you yesterday. Where is she now?'

On the table, my hands clasped tighter. I should have played him better, drawn him out. But we were up against the clock. I just needed answers. Too many innocent women had lost their lives already. One on my watch.

Sange looked at me, smiled, the corners of his mouth spreading slowly to his ears.

'You blame yourself, don't you? Didn't you manage to use what I told you?'

I felt a pressure build in my solar plexus. He wasn't just reading me, he was coiled up inside my skull.

'Where is she?'

'Why do you care?'

'You know why. Rosie Linger is the Pink Rose Killer.'

His skin neither blanched nor flushed. His eyelids didn't twitch.

'Dear me, I had no idea Scotland Yard was so full of ignoramuses. Rosie Linger, goodness!' He chuckled softly. '*Stultissimi!* I suppose your team thinks the roses she leaves behind are her way of signing off? Her signature.'

Rosie Linger. Pink roses. We hadn't thought of that, but actually it wasn't such a stupid idea as he was making out. It didn't matter, though. His face told me we'd got it all wrong.

She wasn't the perpetrator. Which lobbed us straight back to square one.

No leads. No suspects. No fucking clue.

CHAPTER 96

If Rosie Linger wasn't our perp, who was the PRK and how were we going to find him?

Sange watched me, slouching in his seat like it was an armchair by the fire and we were here shooting the breeze.

'Did you know my students used to call me "Dominus", a play on the university's motto? Much more interesting than "magister" or "doctor", I always thought. "Manners makyth man", as they say. But the right name can achieve the same effect. I'd imagine you think the same way. The military is, after all, obsessed with rank and title.'

I wanted to punch him. Instead, I tried a more diplomatic tack.

'You've been locked away for three years. There's nothing I can do about that or what's coming, but I can help make your stay here more comfortable. A cell with a view, a window where you can see the sky. Just tell me what I need to know. If Linger's not the killer, then why was she here? And who is the PRK?'

Sange's bright eyes flickered. I leaned forward in my seat.

'You were young when your father died. The two of you were close. Duncan reminded you of him, didn't he? Perhaps it's what attracted you most. And when he was shot, that little incestuous taboo made you live your daddy's death twice.'

I imagined him taking a stroll in a minefield, forced myself to keep my cool.

If bribery wouldn't work, maybe goading him would. From what I heard, he couldn't bear to lose an argument, especially to a female.

A woman thought to be one of his victims, a twenty-two-year-old Oxford rowing Blue set for a double first, challenged him publicly during a lecture in the Exam Schools on Homer's *Iliad*. She dissed his thesis, called his argument pedantic.

A week later she went missing. Her body was never discovered, but her earring was found in his rooms when the warrant was served a whole year later.

'You know what I think? You groomed Rosie Linger because you couldn't murder those women yourself. You needed a girl to help you. I'm curious, at what point did she take over from the master and become the mistress?'

His eyebrows converged. His lips narrowed. Both movements lasted only a fraction of a second, but their meaning was clear. I'd got to him. It felt good.

'*Domina mea!* Rosie Linger is not your killer, Ziba. I assure you she doesn't have the imagination to conceive of these crimes, never mind carry them out. The girl is beyond tedious.'

'How many times did you meet her?'

'Never. We wrote to each other, that's all. It was vaguely amusing for a while – putting ideas into her head, seeing what she did with them. The sport was short-lived, though. She sent a photograph of herself. An unattractive thing. Perhaps if she had been more pleasant to look at, our relationship might have lasted longer. Ugliness is such an affront to the senses.'

'So, if you've never met her, what was she doing up here yesterday, hours before the most recent murder?'

He scratched at his ring finger with the nail on his thumb as though he were strumming a guitar string.

'Word may have reached the brother of one of the girls whose fate they've attributed to me that Miss Linger has been courting my attentions.'

'That word came from you?'

'Perhaps.' He smiled. 'He started threatening her, she said. Following her home from work, lurking around near her house. She got scared. I suggested she come to see me so I could reassure her. She borrowed a neighbour's car, I believe.'

Recent communication then. That's why it wasn't in the mail-bag we'd received from the prison.

'So, you met her for the first time yesterday?'

'No, when I was told she'd arrived, I sent word that I was indisposed. I've already told you, Ziba. The girl bored me.'

The judge at his trial was right. Vernon Sange really was 'the personification of heartless evil'.

But he may still be our best chance of catching the killer.

CHAPTER 97

When you challenge someone, it's rare they don't defend themselves. Maybe I could use that.

'Nothing you've told me proves Rosie Linger isn't the PRK.'

'Your hope is touching,' Sange said. 'Childlike, almost. I'd like to have known you as a girl, before time left its scars.'

A reference to Falcon's daughter? Or the Travelodge attack? Either way, he was reminding me what he was capable of.

'Hope has nothing to do with it, Sange. It's a question of logic.'

'And yet you're still here. What does that tell you? Logically?'

He fixed me with his unblinking eyes. Forget-me-not blue.

'You're a hunter, Ziba. We're not so different really, you and me. I also enjoy stalking my prey.' He smiled, the arch tone was contrived. He was playing a part, enjoying himself. 'You offered to trade before, a window for information. Well, okay, maybe I'll bite. Only I want a different prize. The more you tell me, the more I'll tell you. What do you say?'

Never give up details about yourself, never let the subject inside your head.

But what choice did I have? If Rosie Linger wasn't the PRK, we were shooting in the dark. Without Sange's information, it could take weeks to find the killer. How many more girls would die before that happened?

'This is the last time I'm coming here. If you've got something to say, say it now. And you give me something I can use. Otherwise, when they stick in the needle, I'll make sure the only person watching is the guy who turns on the flow.'

I'd promised myself I'd be behind the glass, cheering on as they buckled him down. But now I saw an audience is what Sange craved the most. It's why he'd gone to so much trouble to get me here in the first place. Putting on a show's no fun without an audience.

Better to let him die unnoticed, like a bug crushed underfoot.

He nodded.

'Very well.'

A deal then.

'Tell me about Duncan,' he said. 'What little pet name did he call you? When he held you, could you feel his heart beating through his chest? When he kissed you, did his stubble graze your lips?'

Last time, the Butcher had made me relive Duncan's death. Now he was making me relive his life.

I'm not sure which was worse.

CHAPTER 98

After Duncan died, Jack packed me off to a therapist. He comes from a big family that talks about its problems and solves them together over his mother's pasta dishes and hot puddings. He was brought up believing a problem shared is a problem halved.

I learned early in life that no one wants to take on someone else's shit.

The therapy sessions didn't do much for me. Week after week, I'd sit in that overheated beige room with its neutral pictures and spartan furnishing. I spent most of the time staring at my feet, waiting for the hour to tick to a close. Even now, my clearest recollections of those appointments are the shoes I wore. Usually ankle boots. Once, slippers that I'd forgotten to switch for outdoor footwear.

'There'll come a time when the memories of your husband will cause you pleasure rather than pain,' the therapist said, in a quiet sing-song voice that made me want to rip out her larynx.

I guess I'd reached the anger stage by then.

More than two years have passed and I still haven't got to the point where I can enjoy dwelling on my time with Duncan. My memories send me hurtling straight to the pit if I wallow too long. What I had is forever tainted by what I lost.

And Vernon Sange was tapping right into that.

I kept my answers brief to begin with, the way we're taught to answer on the witness stand. But it didn't help. I wasn't dealing with a lawyer, I was dealing with a man who understood the human psyche as well as I do.

Though where had he got his intel from? How did he know I'd first met Duncan when I'd been seconded to Scotland Yard after 7/7? That our first kiss had taken place in the Round Table Room? Or that he was addicted to liquorice comfits?

Maybe he really did have a contact at the Yard.

However he'd got hold of his knowledge, he was wielding it like a weapon. Asking question after question to summon up Duncan's ghost till he was living and breathing in front of me. Then when he was just tangible enough for me to reach out and touch, Sange killed him a second time.

'Did he sleep with his mouth open?'

Yes, on his back, his hands crossed over his chest like an Egyptian mummy.

'When he was shot, was his mouth open too?'

Vernon Sange was a genius. And he knew exactly how to play me.

His questions were carefully choreographed, timed to perfection, just like the way he'd been conducting in my dream. When he'd finished, my demons were rising. I was staring into the abyss, my mind turning in on itself.

Sange had to speak twice before I heard him.

And when I looked up, he was smiling.

CHAPTER 99

My black dog was pinning me down, suffocating me. If I'd been less worried about Jack, I might have been less vulnerable. If my trip to Quantico hadn't brought my old feelings to the fore, I might have been stronger. And if another girl's life hadn't been dependent on my squeezing information out of Sange, I may have succumbed completely.

Instead, I inhaled deeply, focusing on my breathing the way I've been taught till I fought the hound off.

'Your turn, Sange. A deal's a deal. Pay up.'

My eyes stung, my throat was tight, but I didn't cry. No way would I give the Butcher that satisfaction.

He leaned back in his chair.

'You are a lioness, Ziba. It's impressive.'

'Who's the PRK?'

'I told you before that I was only interested in the best specimens. Athletes. Often rowers. One was even a ballroom dancer. Sweet little thing. Her skin smelled of toffee.

'He was safe with me, though. I meant no disrespect, I thought he understood that. However, his actions later suggest otherwise. No matter, we have made our peace since. The importance of perfection is clear to him now. He has the vindication he needs.'

He ran the end of his tongue fast across his lips. When it withdrew, they were still dry.

He stood up before I could ask who *he* was.

'Thank you for coming to see me, Ziba. You really are delightful company.'

I thumped the table hard enough for my fist to bounce back up. 'What kind of crap is that? We had a deal.'

'Indeed we did. And you can be sure I always keep my word.'

He slipped behind me and pressed the buzzer.

'Dammit! Who's the killer, Sange?'

The door squealed open. The guards walked in, their gait stiff from standing so long. Sange didn't answer. Instead, he put his hands behind his back to be cuffed and addressed the closest officer.

'Thomas, would you mind reaching into my left trouser pocket? I have something for Mrs MacKenzie. Nothing sharp, don't worry. I know the rules.'

The guard hesitated then did as Sange had asked.

As he was escorted out, the Butcher glanced back over his shoulder and winked.

'Goodbye, Ziba. Best of luck finding your perpetrator. You should have everything you need now.'

I hardly registered what he said, though. I was too busy staring at the wallet that had just been handed to me. The one I'd lost.

This whole time, Sange had had it.

But how?

CHAPTER 100

I sat in the Porsche, turning my wallet over in my hands like I was trying to wring water out of it.

So, that's how Sange had got his filthy paws on my business card. I must have had one left in there. But how had he got hold of the wallet itself?

True, he'd been uncuffed during our interviews, but he'd also been sitting opposite me the whole time. My bag had been hooked over the back of my chair. There's no way he could have reached in without me seeing.

I pressed the flats of my palms into my eyes, hard enough to make red sparks dance. Sange was brilliant, but he wasn't a magician. So how had he done it?

I swept the tips of my fingers down my face, joining them in prayer position against my lips. Thinking hard, forcing myself to recall every detail of our last meetings.

Sange walking into the conference room flanked by guards but managing to look like he was their superior. Me telling them to remove his restraints. Then him brushing past me as he took his seat at the table. How the contact left me cold.

Remembering it, I felt cold again but for a different reason.

The action had been deliberate, the oldest trick in the criminal's playbook.

Vernon Sange had picked my pocket just like Charlotte the Shit had picked Jack's. The two things were connected, the artistry would have appealed to the Butcher. But more than that. When he'd written his message on my card, he wasn't just telling me the game was on. He was also boasting that he'd already got one over on me.

And he'd done the same thing just now.

I'd sacrificed myself for nothing. Coming here today, I was confident I'd finally get the better of Sange and get him to spill about the PRK. Except he'd screwed me over yet again, and I'd come away with nothing.

Fool me once, shame on you. Fool me twice, shame on me. Fool me three times, hand in your gun and leave.

I'd recorded the whole debacle on my phone, my stupidity there to relive at any time I wanted. The masochist in me hit 'play'.

I don't know how long I sat there tormenting myself, Sange's Californian drawl loud in my ears. But suddenly I jerked to attention, heart kicking up a gear.

You should have everything you need now.

Was it possible?

Hands shaking with adrenaline, I went back to the beginning of the recording. Ignoring the slew of missed calls from Jack.

CHAPTER 101

I paused the recording on my phone, jaw hanging loose.

Sweet mother of dog crap! It had been there this whole time, just waiting for me to riddle it out.

When I was in Quantico, I'd told the New Agent Trainees that the best insights into the criminal mind come from criminals themselves. Incarcerated murderers are a treasure trove of information, which is why we interview them. Every nugget we can extract from them about their methods and motivations gives us the intel we need to catch the next one.

Scotland Yard is synonymous with excellence; its detectives are rightly seen as some of the finest in the world. Yet, over four weeks of unending diligence had brought the team no closer to netting the PRK.

Three interviews with Vernon Sange and finally the picture was coming into focus.

'Come on, pick up, dammit!'

'DI Fingerling speaking.'

'Nigel, it's Ziba. I think I've got something.'

'You know where Linger is?'

'She's not the perp. Sange said something, I checked it out after. She was up here yesterday, for all of half an hour. Car she was driving was a Nissan Micra. Registration LA04 RXY. I made a note of it when I was signing in. ANPR should confirm where it was at the time of the murder and hopefully flag up where she is now.'

'So, what exactly have you got then?'

The line was bad, crackling with static. The battery was down to 22%, reduced by half because of the recording.

'We were right, Sange knows the PRK. They have a personal connection from before his arrest.'

'Okay . . .'

That bit was hardly news.

'So how do they know each other?'

I thought about what I'd learned from sitting in a cage with him, and from comforting Falcon three years ago after Janie nearly died. I thought about what the idiots on breakfast TV said about him and how he'd manipulated me. And I thought about how to profile a serial killer already behind bars – not to predict his next move, but to unpick his previous ones.

'Sange draws people in. He makes them feel special, makes them believe no one understands them as well as he does. His attention is intoxicating, his looks and charm cast a spell. He persuades his targets they're kindred spirits, they fall a little in love with him.'

I didn't just have his messages to Falcon's daughter to go on, I had my own reaction too. I hadn't fallen in love with Sange, but in that first interview I had been seduced by him – and he'd seen it. Remembering the way he'd looked at me and told me I was attractive still made my stomach squirm.

Fingerling stuck a knife in without realising.

'I know what happened with Janie Falcon, but she was just a kid, MacKenzie. Naïve. What makes you think the PRK would be the same?'

'Janie wasn't the only one taken in by him. You've seen all those retards on TV. In fact, only the other day the DCI was telling me about one of his students. Apparently, the dickwit called Sange the nicest guy he'd ever known.

'The Pink Rose Killer didn't just know the Butcher,' I said. 'He was taught by him too.'

CHAPTER 102

'The PRK was taught by Sange? I'm not convinced. The Butcher knew a lot of people before he was arrested, not just through the university; benefactors, artists and musicians too. What makes you think it isn't one of them? And if the perp's as unconfident as you said in your profile, doesn't that go against the idea of someone who's been to Oxford? I mean, if he went there, wouldn't you expect him to be full of himself?'

I took a deep breath, shook my head. Forget black and white, this guy saw the world in 'shades of stereotype'.

'They may be super bright, but there are plenty of Oxford students with low self-confidence. A hangover from years of bullying at school for being nerdy. As for the university connection, after I went through the offender's letters to Jack, I profiled him as college educated, remember? The poetic language and literary style made me think he might have read English Lit.'

'All right, I'll give you that. He went to uni, along with God knows how many thousands of other kids ratchetting up debts every year. But English Literature is a far cry from Classics, which is Vernon Sange's area of expertise. So, what makes you think he was taught by the Butcher?'

'Pygmalion.'

'Jesus H Christ, MacKenzie! This is a multiple murder investigation and you're still banging on about Roman fairy tales.'

My fist clenched on instinct. Hundreds of miles away and I still itched to clout him.

'The offender's building a human sculpture and leaving behind sacrificial offerings. A Pygmalion fantasy makes sense.'

'Only because Sange put it into your head.'

My blood temperature dropped five degrees.

'What did you just say?'

'The only reason you think the perp is channelling Pygmalion is because that's what the Butcher told you to think. He's manipulated you, MacKenzie.'

My voice sounded quiet even to me.

'What if I'm not the only person he's been suggesting things to?'

'If this is another of your riddles . . .'

'It's not a riddle, Fingerling. The Butcher did put the idea of Pygmalion into my head. But what if he put it into the PRK's too? What if all this has come from him and that's how he knows so much?'

'Let me get this straight. You're suggesting this bastard's killing on Sange's say-so?'

I thought back to what I'd said to Barnwell in Quantico about Ken Bianchi, The Hillside Strangler, getting his fan, Veronica Compton, to kill for him using his MO to make it look like the cops had got the wrong guy. Then I thought about Rosie Linger being coaxed to cut herself. And Falcon's daughter, Janie.

'Sange has already persuaded one person we know of to try and take her life,' I said. 'Who's to say she was his first puppet?'

CHAPTER 103

Dr Sange tops up the Artist's port glass and leans back in his winged leather armchair, watching his disciple drink.

The bottle is nearly empty. A 1985 vintage, renowned for its exceptional ripe fruit structure and full flavour. Dr Sange has laid down two cases.

'Life's too short to drink inferior wine,' he says.

The Artist agrees quickly, not wanting to come across like a philistine.

Dr Sange's eyes twinkle. He closes them for a moment, conducting with his forefinger as the 'Nessun Dorma' aria reaches its climax on his beautiful antique gramophone.

The Artist watches, mesmerised, and rather drunk; mouth sticky with alcohol, vision out of focus. They've been talking for hours, the strum of voices in the quad gradually fading away as one by one the other students clatter up the stairwells to bed and the porters lock the college gates.

In the distance, the Trinity College clock tower strikes three.

Dr Sange opens his eyes and smiles.

'Your creations sound fascinating,' he says. 'Remarkable. An inspired take on Ancient Egypt. Just think what else you could sculpt.

What the implications could be.' He smiles. 'No more need to imprison imaginary girls until they tell you they love you, eh.'

An old fantasy shared on another wine-soaked evening.

He takes a sip of port; it leaves a dark stain on his lips.

'Tell me, have you ever read the story of Pygmalion?' he says.

CHAPTER 104

Fingerling made a kissing noise down the line; sucking air, processing what I'd told him.

'So, you're saying these murders could all be Sange's doing?'

'The PRK carried them out by himself, but yes, I think Sange put the idea in his head. That's not the only thing, though.'

'There's more?'

I took a breath.

'I think our perp gave the anonymous tip that nailed Sange.'

Over a hundred miles between us and I swore I could hear his face screwing up.

'He dobbed the Butcher in? How the hell did you come up with that?'

'We know that while he was a don at Balliol, Vernon Sange killed his students. He told me he was only interested in what he called the "best specimens". Athletes mainly. Healthy types.

'Meanwhile, according to the profile, our perp has a physical condition that makes him uncomfortable around people. Having something wrong with him would have made him undesirable to Sange. He told me twice that "*he*" was safe.

'If I'm right about him being not only one of Sange's students but also his puppet, it's reasonable to suppose he idolised him. Sange's manipulation wouldn't have worked otherwise.'

Fingerling took a slurp of liquid. Lady Grey tea, probably. He keeps a box of the stuff on his desk next to a packet of stripy lemon bonbons.

As if on cue, I heard the tell-tale rustle of sweet wrappers.

'All right. Let's say the PRK was one of Sange's students and he put the bastard on a pedestal. That doesn't mean he ratted him out. Especially if he idolised him, like you said.'

I put the phone on speaker and hit play. Already the battery had dropped to 19%.

'Listen to this.'

He was safe with me, though. I meant no disrespect, I thought he understood that. However, his actions later suggest otherwise.

'Is that him? Shit, he sounds so normal.'

Been there, done that.

'Hang on. How did you get a phone into the prison? I thought they had rules about contraband.'

'Long story.'

'Can you at least explain what he's saying? Cos from my end it doesn't prove anything.'

I broke it down, Barney-style.

'*He was safe with me though*, means the offender didn't meet Sange's requirements.

'*I meant no disrespect, I thought he understood that*, means Sange didn't think the PRK had felt rejected. It also shows he knew about Sange's proclivities, which is of course how he was able to pass so much information on to us during the trial.'

It occurred to me as I spoke that the PRK might be a hybristophile, turned on by dangerous personalities, just like the fans writing to the Butcher. Though in his case, the reason was darker. He was dangerous too.

I carried on.

'*However, his actions later suggest otherwise,* refers to the anonymous tip. It was an action born out of spite and resentment. Obviously, he wouldn't have wanted to be killed, but he wouldn't have wanted to be seen as "not good enough" either.

'It's likely he experienced rejection during his childhood, probably from both parents and peers, which would account for the way he must have worshipped Sange. Those resultant feelings of low self-esteem would have been reignited and fanned to a fury when it happened again at the hands of someone he trusted and looked up to.'

Fingerling sucked his sweet, the sound of his saliva amplified over the microphone.

'Nice work, MacKenzie.'

This time I thanked him, not just because I learn from my mistakes but because for the first time in the investigation it felt like we were a team. Though the warm feeling that might have created was quickly soured by my next thought.

All this insight came from the Butcher; in many ways he'd handed it to me, which meant he didn't care one bit whether or not we caught the PRK. From the moment he made that first phone call to Falcon, the only thing he'd really been interested in was torturing me.

CHAPTER 105

Vernon Sange had put the PRK into play, flattering his pawn, making him feel loved and understood so he could move him where he wanted around the board. But in reality, he was disposable, the piece you sacrifice to get to the king.

He didn't care a damn about his pupil, what he was feeling, whether we caught him. All he was interested in was using him to get to me.

But that's not all he'd done. Or all I'd let him do.

Back in that interview room, I'd made the fatal error of assuming I knew his game, that he wanted to pry into my relationship with Jack and Duncan to give him power over me.

What he'd actually done was much cleverer. I'd been so busy shielding my heart, I hadn't noticed him slithering into my head. And by constantly trying to second-guess his next move, I'd taken my eyes off the real prize. Solving the case.

Sange didn't want the lowdown on my love life. He wanted to distract me. And he'd succeeded.

My throat constricted; my muscles turned to liquid.

How had I been so stupid? So careless? So predictable?

I allowed myself a moment then took a deep breath – embracing the suck, as my oppos used to say. I'd screwed up, but wallowing was a luxury I couldn't afford, not while there was still a job to do.

Pull it together, MacKenzie. You may be several moves behind, but the game isn't over yet.

I forced myself to concentrate and focus on what Fingerling was saying.

'I'll get the guys to pull up records of Sange's students, speak to the College Bursar. See if there are any hits with the profile.'

First time he'd shown an interest in behavioural analysis. Better late than never.

'You're looking for a male student from north-west London,' I said. 'Likely living in or close to Hampstead, who dropped out of Oxford suddenly around the same time Sange was arrested. There will have been complaints lodged against him by other students relating to fetishistic behaviour.'

'What sort of thing?'

I spoke faster than usual, conscious of my dying battery.

'Peeping Tom accusations, inappropriate behaviour with females. There may also have been incidents involving animal torture and/or arson while he was there. Look out for reports of pets going missing and unexplained fires. Most likely he will have been at Balliol, but you shouldn't rule out the possibility he belonged to one of the other colleges.'

'Okay.'

'And Nigel, let's keep this within the team for the time being. We don't want the media inadvertently warning the killer we're on to him. If we drive him underground, we might not be able to smoke him out.'

'Talking of the media, you might want to check out the news. Your friend Jack Wolfe has shown his true colours. Bloody journalists, they're all the same. Egos the size of buses.'

My stomach clenched.

'What's going on?'

'See for yourself, I've gotta go.'

The internet took an age to load but when it did, the story was front and centre of the BBC website.

What the actual—? Though it explained all the calls I'd missed.

PRK Journalist Suspended Pending Enquiry

Jack Wolfe, crime reporter for the Daily Telegraph newspaper, has been suspended following the online publication of an article in which he thanks the serial murderer, known as the Pink Rose Killer, for giving his career a 'much-needed boost'. He went on to write, 'I'm looking forward to your next letter. Your correspondence has been the highlight of my journalistic experience.'

Mr Wolfe denies writing or publishing the article, which was uploaded in the early hours of this morning, shortly after the discovery of the killer's latest victim. However, it appears his login details were used to access the site and it was sent from his IP address.

He has been suspended from the newspaper pending further investigation.

My body froze, and then I began to seethe. Evil bitch! This was her!

Si vis pacem, para bellum. Sed vis bellum, para pacem.

If you want peace, prepare for war. But if you want war, prepare for peace.

Suddenly I understood the cryptic words she'd written to Sange.

This wasn't professional suicide. It was a character assassination.

Char was killing Jack's name.

How long before she killed the person behind it?

CHAPTER 106

The *Telegraph* may feel the need for a formal investigation into what had happened with Jack but I didn't need to look any further than his psycho girlfriend. What had gone down was as obvious to me as if I'd carried it out myself.

Vernon Sange hated Jack for what he'd written about him during the trial. Psychopaths are often charming and able to remain eerily calm under pressure. But that's not to say they never flip. Push the right buttons and the rage comes gushing out.

For Sange, the button was his reputation. Jack had called him mentally ill. He hadn't been suckered by his schtick like the rest of them. And he wrote a number of articles impugning Sange's sanity in the very paper the Butcher himself used to contribute guest articles to.

Destroying Jack's professional reputation would be the perfect payback, which fitted exactly with the twisted games I knew he liked to play.

Except he couldn't do it himself. He needed help, which is where that bitch 'Char' came in.

Clearly, she had a thing for her old tutor. The letters she'd written certainly implied a deeper relationship than one forged in a question and answer session.

And I knew for sure now that the letters signed by 'Lottie' had been sent by her. When she'd been to visit Sange yesterday, she'd written her name in the visitor log, the guard had shown it to me. Her writing was a match to Lottie's. The same pointy, cramped-together characters I'd analysed only two days ago.

Char and Lottie were one and the same person. Both were obsessed with Sange. And both were out to annihilate Jack.

vis bellum, para pacem.

By asking him on a date, she could cosy up to him and then stick the knife in when he wasn't expecting it. Ask any of my oppos and they'll tell you the same thing; if you want to stab someone, don't let your enemy see your blade. I've used similar tactics, both literally and metaphorically, though never at the behest of a serial killer.

She must have set up that wallet scam, then later logged into his *Telegraph* account to post the phoney article. And from what the BBC piece said about it being sent from his IP address, she probably did so from the computer at his apartment.

His driver's licence had been in the wallet so she'd have known where he lived. And if she could steal and then return his wallet without him noticing, she could just as easily do the same thing with his keys. Once she'd got a spare set cut, she'd have had easy access to his home.

And last night, when the article was uploaded, she could have let herself in without any risk of him catching her there. After all, Sange knew he was staying with me, which likely came from her, meaning she knew the coast was clear.

The whole thing slotted together as neatly as a round of bullets in a magazine, but proving it would be harder. I could demonstrate that Lottie and Char were the same person. But the rest of my theory could be fobbed off as speculation. And no question, Charlotte would have covered her tracks.

To have pulled all this off with such panache, the girl had to be smart; probably wearing gloves so there would be no finger marks on Jack's keyboard or at his flat. And possibly using an element of disguise to avoid detection via CCTV. Certainly a hat, possibly a wig.

I knew what she'd done and could guess how she'd done it. But Jack wouldn't believe me, not least because he wouldn't want to.

Charlotte knew exactly what she was doing. She'd be making all the right noises, playing the part of the perfect girlfriend.

That way Wolfie wouldn't realise he was sleeping with the enemy.

CHAPTER 107

I called Jack as I hit the main road, squeezing the last breaths of life out of my phone battery.

He answered straight away, sounding harassed.

'Thank God, Mac! I've been trying to reach you. I didn't do it. You've got to believe me.'

'Of course you didn't do it! It's bullshit. Someone's set you up.'

'The article was uploaded from my IP address, though. With my login details.'

'So, you're saying it was you?'

I was making a joke – didn't get a laugh, though. Not surprising. He wouldn't be laughing at anything for a while.

'I just don't understand. How could this have happened? It makes no sense.'

I had to pick my words carefully. Say the wrong thing and the barriers would go up. The truth isn't always easy to face, especially if it makes you look a fool.

Jack prides himself on being good at reading people. Not the way I do, but in judging whether or not they're decent. His job requires him to meet unknown sources, often in dodgy places late at night. Gauging whether they're legit isn't just a useful skill, it's a matter of survival.

Showing him he'd got his girlfriend wrong would hit him hard. And coming from me, it would have all sorts of other implications.

I was convinced this Char woman was bad news, one of Vernon Sange's honey traps, but I wasn't exactly unbiased. How could I be completely sure I wasn't the one seeing what I wanted to see? After all, it would suit me quite nicely to get her out of the way so I could steal her place.

I inhaled deeply.

'How are things with you and Char?'

My voice sounded tentative even to me, but Jack didn't pick up on it. Showed how stressed out he was.

'She's been amazing. A real tower of strength.'

Unlike me. How could I not have called him back after seeing all those missed calls? Again.

'There's no way she could have accessed your login details, is there?'

'Ziba! What are you implying? I know you don't think much of the girls I date but you've never even met Char.'

I stuck to my guns. I had to.

'You didn't post that article. Which means someone's trying to frame you. All I'm asking is—'

'That's low, Mac. Even for you.'

'What's that supposed to bloody mean?'

But he'd already hung up, leaving me even more worried than before.

Because if Charlotte was being a 'tower of strength', that could only mean one thing.

She wasn't done with him yet. In which case, nor was Sange.

CHAPTER 108

Rat-a-tat-tat. The sudden knock at the door makes the Artist jump. He's been jumpy ever since last night when the miracle failed to happen.

Are the gods angry with him? Is he out of favour?

Another knock.

Who's there? What do they want?

The Artist puts down the needle. He washes his hands, drying them on a chequered green tea towel as he goes to the door. When he opens it, he is still holding the towel, one corner damp with a rusty-pink stain.

Medusa is outside shifting from one foot to the other, grimacing. Arthritic hag. Making the short journey over here would have hurt. The Artist knows this on a rational level, but it doesn't resonate. Other people's feelings never have, it's one of his strengths.

'Yes?'

The door is only open a crack. Medusa tilts her head forward, sniffs. Her nose crinkles.

'Yes?' the Artist says again, defensive this time. He hasn't showered today.

Medusa is holding a bunch of grapes from the dirty Co-op shop down the road. Two painful journeys then, here and there. Serves her right, if she'd listened to what he'd said last time, she could have saved herself the trouble.

She holds out the fruit sweating in its cellophane. Several of the grapes have wrinkled up like fingers left too long in the bath.

'I brought these. For your mum.'

Bad spirits can only hurt you if you invite them in. The Artist blocks her way, ignores the gift. It's probably cursed.

'Mother's sleeping. She can't be disturbed. Doctor's orders. I'll tell her you stopped by.'

'I've been so worried about her, ever since that first ambulance came. She's my best friend, please let me see her.'

She's a frail little thing really. Stooped back. Bony. Shivering in the cold.

The Artist smiles as he slams the door in her face.

CHAPTER 109

M1 Motorway

There was an accident up ahead, turning the motorway into a giant parking lot. Christ knows when I'd get back to London.

As I sat in the hardly moving traffic, rain turning the view into an underwater scene, my brain raced; flitting between Jack, the PRK and Vernon Sange.

The Butcher clearly knew as much as he did about the perp because he'd taught him at Oxford and put the Pygmalion idea into his head, but that didn't explain how he was able to predict the exact location of the most recent dump site. Either the whole thing had been planned out in precise detail three years ago, before his incarceration, which seemed highly unlikely. Or the details were in the code I still hadn't cracked.

I'd been more than a little distracted, but I should have got somewhere with it by now, given my background. Certainly I should have deciphered it before Sange.

So why had he managed it and I hadn't?

My body agitated as I lined up the shot.

When the thought came, I couldn't believe how it had taken me so long to figure out.

When I'd first arrived at the Yard, I'd wondered why the PRK was writing to Jack rather than to another more senior journalist or editor. Now I knew.

Apart from his frenzied post-mortem attacks, like Sange, everything the perp did was thought out in advance.

The symbolism at the crime scenes. The victimology. The parts he removed from the bodies. They all meant something.

In this case, writing to Wolfie was about atoning for the betrayal of his hero, for ratting him in to the police with that anonymous tip.

In our second interview, Sange told me, 'we have made our peace'.

At last I understood how.

By writing to a newspaper, the PRK had been able to relay the gory details of his crimes to Sange without worrying about his mail being vetted and censored. It would also enable his ex-tutor to experience them vicariously through him and see how far his student had come.

Jack had maligned the Butcher in the *Telegraph* at the time of his trial. Using him and the newspaper as his medium would allow the PRK to pay them both back for doing so and simultaneously appease Sange.

Though it could only work if Sange knew how to unlock the code. Without that, it would be meaningless.

Which meant Vernon Sange must have been given the key.

But was reading the killer's messages all he'd been doing?

CHAPTER 110

Right from the beginning I'd thought there was something off about the third letter from the Pink Rose Killer, though I hadn't been able to pin down what it was. Now, I had an idea.

> *Excellent work, that last job. My next night*
> *approaches, o sun cut short the light that's left to linger.*
> *I'm getting better all the time.*
> *How kind to write and tell you all about it.*

Read a certain way, the last two lines could be read as congratulatory, a disguised pat on the back. The tone was very much like a teacher praising a student. Did Sange write it? Was he telling the PRK how well he was doing and thanking him for relating his exploits?

If he was in on the code, it would fit.

If only I could unlock the cipher. What else might it reveal? Who the next victim was going to be? How we could save her?

It was all very well knowing Sange and the PRK were communicating, but that didn't help us find the killer.

The car in front moved forward an inch then braked again. Up ahead, a long line of red lights snaked the motorway. I was going to be stuck here for ages, hours, going nowhere when I should be at the Yard trying to predict the perp's next move and how to stop him.

I interviewed a serial killer in Germany once, a great hulk of a man with a voice like a child's. A psychopath who believed the only reality that mattered was his own. We were talking about consequences. When threatened with punishment by prison guards, he didn't react. His pulse rate didn't quicken, his body didn't tense. I asked him why.

'No point in getting scared twice,' he said, as if it were the most obvious thing in the world.

Thinking about him now, I wondered if he had a point. Sitting here doing nothing was as frustrating as sitting in an observation room watching an oppo walk into a trap. But there was zip I could do about it. I took a breath, forced myself to relax.

For want of anything more useful to do, I clipped my iPhone into the holder on my dash and replayed the recording of the interview I'd just had with Sange.

His California-warm voice filled the Porsche. Not having to focus on his body language and shield myself from him, I was able to focus more carefully on the words he was using.

'Did you know my students used to call me "Dominus", a play on the university's motto,' he'd said. And later he referred to me as '*domina mea*'.

If I'd been going at any real speed, I may well have skidded off the road. As it was, my foot slipped off the clutch and I nearly lurched into the car in front.

My muscles electrified, my body surged with heat.

> *O D, I must tell you how well my work is going and how much I am enjoying it. That first cut, the release that follows! The smell, the colour, the heat of their blood.*

Finally, the 'O D' from the PRK's letters made sense!

I googled 'dominus' in the unmoving traffic, my iPhone battery lasting just long enough to reveal the final clue.

Dominus (nominative case) = master

Domine (vocative case) used when you address someone directly, e.g. 'oh master'

O D

O domine.

Oh master.

The PRK wasn't trying to avoid swearing as I'd initially thought. He was addressing his one-time tutor, Vernon Sange – his 'dominus'. In some ways, calling him 'magister' (Latin for 'teacher', the other bit of vocab the Butcher mentioned), might have made more sense for an ex-pupil, though referring to him as 'master' fitted with the PRK's idolisation of the Butcher.

So much of what had been obscured was now transparent – the initials, the communication method, the reason he was writing to Jack.

Thing is, Wolfie wasn't the only person the PRK was writing to. He was also sending notes to Felip Dale.

So, what had a softly spoken beat cop done to piss off a serial killer?

CHAPTER 111

The mind is a rifle. If the firing mechanism gets jammed, the weapon won't function. But once you've cleared the breach there's nothing stopping you blasting your target into oblivion.

My bangstick was back in business, in a state of rapid fire.

At a crime scene, posing 'why?' often leads to 'who'. Asking myself now what Felip Dale had done to piss off a serial killer did the same thing.

Though the answer sucker-punched me all the same.

I'd met the guy twice, once when he'd come to the Yard to speak to me shortly after I'd flown in from the States. And then again yesterday when he'd pitched up with another letter from the PRK.

This whole investigation, I'd been operating with an eye over my shoulder. Vernon Sange had busted his way into my head and now Jack was in danger. The jet lag hadn't done me any favours either. I'm not some bitchin' Betty trying to fob my mistakes off on someone else. But by the same token, I needed to understand why I'd done what I had. Or rather, missed the flares that at any other time would have lit up the bloody sky.

Because with hindsight, some of Felip Dale's comments weren't just flares, they were a whole damn firework show.

I realise I'm significant.

One of the first things he said to me, indicative of an inflated sense of his own importance despite the 'I'm so fragile' body language.

And then later, in the same meeting –

What if I were the last person she talked to? If I'd acted differently, she might still be alive.

Another example of Dale giving himself significance.

Ian Huntley had said something very similar in an interview with journalists not long before he was fingered for the Soham murders. Psychopaths have superiority complexes. So much so, they have no regard for other people. They can tell if a person is distressed. They simply don't care.

But it wasn't just those comments that made my brain fire now. Or the way Dale had inserted his way into the investigation, and his contact with the first victim. Actually, as a West End cop, he may well have had prior exposure to all of the victims. And wading into the fray with Ian Heppe would have made him seem like a hero, the sort a vulnerable girl might trust, despite all the warnings not to trust anyone.

No, the bullseye for me was the question I'd posed at the start. Why had a serial killer written to a low-level beat cop?

There was only one answer that made sense.

He *was* the beat cop.

CHAPTER 112

I had to let the team know who Felip Dale really was. A tap on the shoulder and we could finally have our man in bracelets.

But my phone was dead. I was on a dual carriageway, so had nowhere to pull in or make a call. And the traffic had ground to a halt. Again.

I had to do something, though.

I glanced to my left and right, muscles pumped with adrenaline I couldn't use.

Screw it, I thought, leaping out the Porsche and racing over to the Golf in front, the rain pelting down, soaking me in seconds.

'Open up!' I shouted, hammering on the driver-side window. 'Police. It's an emergency. I need to use your phone.'

The guy looked me over. Suspicious.

'Where's your badge, then?'

Ah, that . . .

'Thought so,' he said, accelerating forward as the cars ahead moved, finally picking up speed.

Beep, beep!

'Get out of the road,' one driver screamed, shooting past, making a hand gesture.

'Crazy bitch!'

Beeeeeep!

'Move your fucking car!'

I side-stepped back to the Porsche, pressing myself flat against her as I threw myself in.

Then I shifted her into first and hit the loud pedal.

The way I saw it, I had two options. Take a detour and scrabble about hunting for a payphone or try and persuade someone to let me use theirs without a badge to flash.

Course I could go the long route. Ask someone to call 999 and pass on a message for Nigel Fingerling. But experience has shown that can be easier said than done.

Alternatively, I could get my ass back to Scotland Yard on the hurry up and deliver my news in person.

In the SF, we were taught the only place emotion should have in decision-making is deciding who to share your bed with. Other than that, keep it simple. Weigh up the risk–reward.

I made a mental balance sheet.

My sat nav showed there were no more hold-ups along the route. There wasn't much distance left to cover. And we were days away from the likely next kill, according to the Roman festivals calendar the PRK seemed to be using to set his murder dates. So although the sooner we made an arrest the better, there was no immediate threat.

Risk–reward. Go back to the Yard, I thought.

I wasn't far away now. Thirty minutes tops.

And then we'd nail the clown dick to the wall.

CHAPTER 113

Scotland Yard, London

I burst into the MIR, ready to explode my bomb, but the second I stepped over the threshold, the words dried in my mouth. What was going on?

It was like the air had gone out of everyone apart from DI Fingerling, who was storming about in full drill-sergeant mode, glowering and barking orders.

'Nigel?'

He jerked round.

'MacKenzie, you're back! What's up with your phone? I've been trying to reach you. We know who the PRK is!'

'You know it's Dale?' He gave me a look; there was some hate in it.

'Worked it out, did you? A heads-up would have been nice—'

'My phone died on me. I was stuck on the motorway. I did try. But we know who it is now, that's what matters. So, what aren't you telling me?' I said. 'Cos something ain't right here.'

'All these happy faces give that away, did they?'

The incident room suddenly felt very hot. 'Dale's gone AWOL. He came in again this afternoon. The latest murder was all over the news and social media. The lying bastard made out he was scared, that he'd been having palpitations. Wanted to know how close we were to catching the killer. It was bullshit, we know that now.

'He took some calming down. I left Barnwell with him in one of the soft interview rooms. Biggest mistake of my career. All that Eton education, you'd think he'd have some brains under that yellow hair of his. I mean, I know his mum's death messed him up but even so . . .'

His mum's death? When had that happened? I'd heard him talking to her only four days ago, it hadn't sounded like she was ill. And if she'd just passed away, why hadn't he said anything? We'd spent enough time together, there'd have been plenty of opportunities.

I wanted to ask Fingerling more but some stories you don't interrupt.

'We were digging into the college records at the time. The fool told Dale what our plan was, said he reckoned it wouldn't be long till we had a name.'

My veins froze. We'd lost the advantage. No wonder Dale had gone AWOL. But ripping into Barnwell wasn't going to help anyone.

'Cut him some slack,' I said. 'He was blindsided, same as the victims. Dale may not be a Yarder, but he is one of us. It was a bad move, but an understandable one. Barnwell was extending professional courtesy, that's all.'

'Maybe so, but it gave the bastard a heads-up. By the time we figured out he was the perp and sent a uniformed response team to his address, he'd scarpered without a trace.'

'He cleaned the place out?'

'Not exactly. We did find something. Put most of us off our supper.'

'What?'

'Who, you mean. Come, I'll show you the snaps. You'd better prepare yourself. It's not pretty.'

A minute later he was bringing up an image on the screen on the wall. A woman who looked to be in her early seventies, sitting on a chair at the kitchen table, a blanket over her lap, with the missing body parts from the offender's victims sewn on to her face. Her skin crawling with maggots.

It was Felip Dale's mother. Dead for a month from a stroke. Turned into a human sculpture.

CHAPTER 114

The scalpel's blade isn't big enough for the Artist's next task. In the legend, Perseus used a sword to defeat Medusa. The Artist doesn't have a sword, or the time to acquire one. A kitchen knife will have to do instead.

The carving set is in the drawer under the kettle. The Artist used it last week to make a roast, cutting slits into the skin and posting in fennel seeds. Mother is partial to a bit of pork and crackling but she left her plate untouched.

Medusa must have said something nasty about his cooking.

If it weren't for her, things would have been different with him and Mother. She took advantage of her vulnerability after his father left them, telling her no man would be interested in her with a kid around. That there was something wrong with him.

The Artist can imagine her words as clearly as if he'd actually heard them. No wonder Mother didn't love him. It was all Medusa's fault.

So were the boyfriends.

'It's not good for you to hang around the house on your own with the kid all the time. No wonder you're getting depressed again, Lily. You need to get out more. Have some fun. Take a break from Philip.'

Bitch. Mother wasn't on her own. She had him. And if Medusa hadn't stuck her reptilian face where it wasn't wanted, Mother might have realised he was all she needed.

Deep down, the Artist has known all along what he has to do.

This whole time he's been focused on making Mother beautiful; certain that if she looks perfect on the outside, she'll be perfect on the inside too and say the words he's been waiting his whole life to hear.

But how could that happen with the snake-woman always around, whispering in her ear?

A new energy swells inside him, turning his pale skin pink, making his eyes shine.

The police will be here soon. He doesn't have long.

Decided, he prepares a knapsack with supplies and the book he carries everywhere then kisses Mother on the top of her head, ignoring the strange crawling sensation beneath his lips.

CHAPTER 115

Scotland Yard, London

Felip Dale's mother had recently died. That must have been his pre-kill stressor, the dramatic event precipitating his homicidal spree. And the murders were a coping mechanism, the fulfilment of a fantasy. The date of his first attack was unlikely to be a coincidence. 13th February, the beginning of *Parentalia*, the Roman festival honouring ancestors.

The gruesome photos up on the screen in Fingerling's office showed something else too. Felip Dale wasn't just trying to build the perfect woman. He was trying to recreate his mother in an improved form, one that for the first time in his life he'd be able to control.

Though it might be a long time till we'd be able to control him.

'She'd had a couple of minor strokes before the one that killed her,' Fingerling told me. 'According to the records, ambulances were dispatched to the address on several occasions. Explains why none of her neighbours had thought it suspicious she wasn't out and about.'

I couldn't tear my eyes from the screen, the depravity. And yet despite his obvious psychosis, he was still lucid enough to set up counter measures to throw us off his trail.

'Turns out he'd been going round advising the homeless community to be on the lookout for strange men. Twisted shit,' said Fingerling, as if reading my mind.

Twisted was definitely the word.

'His uniform would have made the victims trust him. They wouldn't have thought the warnings applied to one of us. And none of the officers out there last night would have blinked twice if they'd seen another cop talking to one of the women they were supposed to be protecting. Damn, why didn't I see it sooner?'

'You were right about the rest though,' he said generously. 'Dale was a Classics student at Balliol, taught by the Butcher. Changed his name to Felip in his first year.'

I flashed on a memory from our first meeting:

I changed it from Philip. A friend said it'd make me sound more interesting.

No prizes now for guessing who that friend was.

'He left Oxford after Sange's arrest. And in his first year, he was accused of being a Peeping Tom by another fresher, a Sudanese girl over here on a scholarship. Sange was her "moral tutor", the person responsible for a student's well-being, apparently.'

Fingerling pulled a face, didn't need to say the words. The idea of Vernon Sange being responsible for anyone's personal welfare was hard to swallow.

'He encouraged the girl not to take matters further. A fire broke out in her room shortly afterwards. Nothing to tie it to Dale but fits with everything you said.'

'Not quite everything. I was so sure the perp had a condition he was ashamed of. A stutter or lisp. But Dale's speech is completely normal.'

'Maybe so,' said Fingerling, looking at me archly. 'But he does have a condition that might cause him embarrassment. He was born without a right leg. He wears a prosthetic.'

CHAPTER 116

'So, what are we doing to locate Dale?' I asked.

'I've put out an APW and issued a statement through the press office to turn the public into our eyes and ears, as you're always saying.'

'How about number plate recognition?'

Fingerling shook his head.

'He did a Linger on us. Didn't take his car. Thanks to what you told me, we were able to track her down through the ANPR software. The Nissan she was driving belonged to an old woman from down her road. Linger took it up to Wakefield. Uniforms picked her up a few miles from the prison. She claimed to be too scared to go home, confirmed that the brother of one of Sange's vics had been threatening her.

'Her alibis for the murders checked out. Not that that's an issue now. And Barnwell helped her sort out a restraining order against the brother. I told him to warn her off the Butcher too, not that you can talk sense into a person like that.'

He was right. Some people you just can't help, no amount of reasoning will ever get through to them.

'So now we wait for someone to spot Felip Dale at Burger King or for him to use one of his credit cards. These days you can't get by without leaving a digital footprint.'

I shook my head.

'Not going to happen. Like you said, he's one of us. He knows how we work. And he's smart too.'

'What do you suggest then? Flushing out killers is your speciality, far as I can tell.'

Two compliments in one day. Was he coming down with something?

'We're not dealing with the London Lacerator here,' I said, thinking back to the trap we'd set together last time. 'The PRK is highly intelligent and organised. A fox hiding out for the winter.'

'So what do you suggest? We wait for him to strike again? Try and catch him in the act?'

His tone was sarcastic, aggressive. When I answered I was perfectly calm.

'Everyone knows, to catch a fox, you have to play the fox. And I think I know just how to do it.'

CHAPTER 117

'I'm all ears,' Fingerling said. 'Just tell me this sting doesn't involve dress-up.'

He was thinking about last time too.

I smiled.

'No costumes. All we need is Vernon Sange.' He looked confused. 'Can you pull the perp's letters to Jack Wolfe up on that screen of yours?'

'The other image not doing much for you?'

'Not for my appetite, no.'

He replaced the grotesque picture of Felip Dale's mother with the notes to Wolfie, lining each one up side by side on the screen.

I pointed out the differences in style between them.

'They were written by two different people communicating with each other,' I said. 'The offender. And Sange.'

Fingerling rubbed the back of his neck, pressed his lips tightly together.

'I can see what you're saying about the styles being different. But I don't see how the Butcher would have been able to get a letter out of Wakefield. All his correspondence is closely monitored.'

'It's never been proven but you must have heard the rumours that he has certain politicians and possibly even guys from the Yard in his pocket. I worked his case. It's shocking how many barriers seemed to pop up during the investigation, aside from the lost evidence. If it hadn't been for that anonymous tip, we might have struggled to secure a conviction.'

'Your point being?'

'Who's to say he hasn't managed to insinuate favours on the inside too? Vernon Sange is a bloodhound. He sniffs out people's weaknesses, capitalises on them.'

Just like he did with Falcon's daughter. Is that how he managed to have sway over supposedly upstanding characters too? Did he have something on them, or something they wanted?

I thought about the criminal conspiracy I'd uncovered while working the Hillside Slasher case. I knew it went to the very top of the Establishment; possibly there were even cabinet ministers involved. Was Vernon Sange too? Had he helped the sick bastards get what they wanted? Could he now demand a price? Was that why questions were being raised in the House to halt his extradition? Or was it something else? Another dark web?

Fingerling blew air out of his mouth in three short bursts. It sounded like machine-gun fire. *Pah pah pah.*

'If he could get a letter out of Wakefield, why not just write directly to the perp?'

'Because there'd have been no fun in that. Vernon Sange is all about the game.'

As his revenge on Wolfie showed.

Fingerling dropped into his chair; interlaced his fingers, tapped his thumbs together.

'So, what are you suggesting?'

'We draw Felip Dale out with another letter. Only this time Sange doesn't write it – we do.'

CHAPTER 118

I explained my idea.

'So, you're saying all we have to do is get a letter printed in the *Telegraph* in the same style as Sange's and Dale will come crawling out with his hands up?'

'Not quite.'

He rubbed his hand across his eyes. They were red-rimmed and bloodshot, his skin pale and puffy. I probably looked just as lovely but if this worked, my battles with the Butcher would have been worth it.

Well, almost. I pushed away a mental image of Jack in his towel and him calling shithole 'Char' a tower of strength.

'We've suspected for a while that Sange and the PRK have been communicating through a cipher. It's why he was so insistent that Jack print the letters. He needed to get word to his idol.'

Fingerling started spitting bones about Wolfie. I cut him short, reminded him about that tenet of our judicial system: innocent until proven guilty.

'Felip Dale has never been to visit Sange in prison, Barnwell went through the logs right at the start,' I said, getting us back on track. 'If I'm right about Dale giving us the anonymous tip, it shows he was angry with him at the time of the arrest. So, although

Sange might have planted an idea in his mind, it's unlikely they'd have actually planned anything beforehand. And although he will have had violent fantasies for years, same as all serial killers, the impetus to murder didn't come until his mother's death.'

'Where are you going with this, MacKenzie?'

'The code wasn't developed before the murders started.'

'If they didn't develop a code in advance, and they haven't seen each other since, then how can they have one now?'

It had taken me this long to figure it out, but now I had, it seemed obvious.

'There's only one way. It appeals to both their intellectual snobbery and their obsession with the classical world. They're using a book code. That's what the numbers in the first letter are about.'

Call me up folks. 4.1 10-6.11-7.11 16 20 21

'It's not a standard book cipher, though, which is why I didn't spot it before. Normally you have three numbers each separated with a full stop representing the page, line and number word, starting from the left.'

'You'll have to go back a step. I don't have your spy background.'

'I'm ex-SRR. Not MI5.'

'Close enough.'

Not really. Spooks don't tend to carry Glock 19s and hand grenades in their back pockets.

'A book code is a cipher. The key is in a piece of text. They work by replacing words in a message with the position of words in the book being used. For it to be successful, both parties have to have not only the same book, but also the same edition.

'If we want to draw Dale out with a coded message apparently from Sange, we need to find the book he's been using.'

'What I've heard, the Butcher's cell is stacked to the ceiling with books. How are we going to find the one we need?'

'Dale's already told us. It's in the first line of his first letter. See?'

I pointed to the screen. Fingerling pulled a face, didn't make him look any prettier.

'Suns will set and suns will rise again?'

'Aye. It's from a poem by Catullus, remember? "Let Us Live and Love".

'We start there.'

CHAPTER 119

I'd thought breaking the cipher would be relatively straightforward now I'd worked out the key. I was wrong.

'I don't understand why the Governor of Wakefield's being so bloody difficult,' Falcon said to Fingerling and me two days later. 'All this nonsense I'm getting about prisoners' rights. It's ridiculous.'

Of course, old Goldfish Eyes might have been more willing to let us search Sange's cell if we brought him on board. But we couldn't trust anyone with our plan, given the Butcher's email to me showed someone inside the prison was assisting him.

For a while I wondered if our not being informed about Char and Rosie Linger's visits was part of that, but Barnwell put me straight.

'I checked with my contact at Wakefield and the IT guys here,' he said, rubbing the back of his neck. 'The prison did email us, but it seems there was a virus attached to the message. Our scanners redirected it.' He took a ChapStick out of his pocket, rubbed it over his lips. 'They gave me some jargon but to be honest it went a bit over my head. There's no foul play though, I got that much.'

I stomped out of Falcon's office now and called Jack, determined he shouldn't see 'Char' as his only 'tower of strength' – and still feeling guilty I hadn't been there before when he'd needed me.

'Hello, Jack's phone . . .'

A woman's voice, plummy and self-consciously sultry. The hair on my forearms bristled. I didn't need to ask who it was. And I wasn't going to introduce myself either.

'Can you put him on?'

'Babe,' she called out. 'Someone to speak to you.'

Babe? Made me want to stick my fingers down my throat.

'He's just getting out of the shower. Won't be a minute.'

Fuck's sake.

In the background I heard some chat I'd rather forget, then Wolfie came on the line.

'Hey, Mac.'

He sounded like a tank had rolled over him. Very different from his girlfriend. I took a breath, tried to drown the mental image of the two of them playing naked house.

'I wanted to check in, see how you're doing.'

'I think I'm going mad. Literally.'

'Why, what's wrong?'

'It's little things. You'll say I'm being stupid. Just—'

'Just what?'

He let out a breath. It rattled down the phone.

'It started the day my wallet went missing. There's a homeless girl, has a pitch near the *Telegraph* offices. I always give her a couple of pounds and a coffee. She's so young to be alone on the streets. I think she might have a hearing problem too. I feel bad for her, you know?

'Anyway, as I bent down to drop the coins in her cup the other day, I noticed something on her wrist. A gold watch.'

'A gold watch on a homeless girl? That doesn't make sense.'

'Nor does this. It looked exactly the same as the one my grandpa left me when he died. The spitting image.

'I asked where she got it, and she became all defensive. Said it was hers and to leave her alone. She started shouting, made a scene. A copper came over, told me to stop bothering her, and I had no way of proving it was my grandfather's so that was that.'

'Strange. You'd think he'd have at least questioned her.'

'That's what I thought, but he seemed more concerned about moving me along. I couldn't stop thinking about it. First my wallet and now this. When I got home after staying at your place, I checked the drawer where I keep the watch. Only it wasn't there.'

'You're saying the girl took it?'

'I don't know what I'm saying. There was no sign of a break-in or anything, so as Char says, how could she have taken it?'

Char, of course! What's the bet she stole it then gave it away to the homeless girl? I thought. Certainly fits with the whole wallet MO. And the article scam. That's probably when she pinched it even, when she was up there hacking into Jack's computer.

'Did you try and speak to the girl again?' I asked him.

'Yep. I figured I might offer to buy it off her or something. I didn't want a fuss, I just wanted the watch back. Like I said, it was my grandpa's. The sentimental value's worth more than the monetary one.'

I thought of the items I'd salvaged from my father's possessions. I understood completely where he was coming from.

'What did she say?'

'Nothing. She wasn't there. Every day for a year she's been in that pitch, Mac. So where is she now?'

'Does sound odd, though maybe she just decided to move on after the confrontation. Perhaps she was worried you'd be back on her case and didn't want the aggro.'

'Maybe, though that's not the only weird thing happening.'

'How do you mean?'

'It's what I said before, I think I'm going crazy. Little things. The timer on the oven suddenly going even though I know I haven't set it. All the lights on in the flat when I come home, even though they were off when I left. Things being moved around. The olive oil on the top shelf of the cupboard when I know I left it by the stove. The bread in the fridge even though I always keep it by the toaster. Salt in the pepper pot. It's like I've got a poltergeist or something.'

'Maybe someone's been in, moving your stuff.'

Your psycho girlfriend maybe, trying to screw with your head.

'The only person that's been here is Char.'

'Could she have—?'

'Ziba . . .'

There was a warning note in his voice. He hadn't completely forgiven me since the last time I'd taken a swipe at the bitch. And likely she was standing right next to him. Or sitting on his damn lap.

'I wasn't being funny. She might have moved something. It's hardly a crime.'

Unless you're doing it to send someone round the bend.

'Maybe you should change your locks, Jack. Sounds like some-one's been in there.'

And Char had very possibly made herself a copy of his keys.

'Been in and not taken anything? No, Char thinks it's this business with the article. That it's messing with my head, mak-ing me imagine things, making me see things that aren't there. When I heard the oven timer going off the other day, she said she couldn't hear it. When I thought all the lights were on, she swore it was only the one in the hall. Stress can do strange shit, she says. A similar thing happened to a friend of hers. She's persuaded me to go to the doctor later. Ask if he can prescribe me something.'

Jesus, Wolfie, I thought. Can't you see what she's doing, making you doubt your sanity? It's sophisticated shit and it has a name. Gaslighting.

Charlotte was another of Sange's puppets. My initial fear had been that she'd try and hurt Jack. Only now did I realise that what she was doing was much worse.

Killing him would have been kinder than taking everything away from him. Me. His career.

And now his mind.

CHAPTER 120

I needed to get some air, clear my head. When I got to the lifts, Barnwell was standing right behind me like he'd materialised out of thin air. The idea of Jack's 'ghost' was looming large.

'Everything okay?' he asked, head cocked, appraising.

Again, it struck me he had the makings of an excellent profiler.

I shrugged.

'Had better days.'

He gave a sad smile.

'You and me both. Not sure the DI's going to let me forget how badly I messed up with Felip Dale.'

'He's still giving you a hard time?'

'Between us, I think he's pleased to have something to pin on me besides my accent.'

I pulled a face. Fingerling could be such a dick.

'We're in the same camp,' I said. 'He's not my biggest fan either.' I paused, picking my words. 'By the way, I was so sorry to hear about your mother.'

He looked confused.

'What d'you mean?'

Bit bizarre.

'Nigel mentioned she passed away.'

Barnwell's whole face went pink, right to the tips of his ears. Had I put my boot in it? Maybe the reason he hadn't said anything was because he didn't want to talk about it.

'Look, we don't have to discuss it, but just know I'm here if you want to.'

He mumbled a 'thanks', still looked mortified, though for the life of me I couldn't see why.

'I'm going for a walk,' I said. 'Want to come?'

It wasn't like me to reach out, but I felt sorry for him and frankly I could use a sounding board. With Jack both out of the picture and in the frame, I had no one else to speak to. I hadn't known Barnwell long, though he'd impressed me with his sensitivity and intuitiveness right from the get-go, starting with the way he looked after his mum.

He wasn't Wolfie, but I knew he'd give decent advice, as the last time I confided in him showed.

We walked out on to the Broadway, the frigid air whipping through our clothes, turning our breath to smoke.

For a moment, there was just the rhythm of our feet marching along the pavement in perfect sync. Then I started up.

'I'm worried about my friend, Jack. The *Telegraph* journalist the perp's been writing to.'

Unlike Fingerfuck, Barnwell didn't jump in with vitriolic condemnations of what Wolfie had supposedly done. I liked him for that, knew I'd made the right decision to open up.

'I think the girl he's seeing is behind the article that got uploaded. Also that business with his wallet, which you've probably heard about. And now I think she's screwing with his head. Doing stuff in his flat when he's not there, crap knows what else.'

'What's her motive?'

Another mark in his favour, zeroing in on the 'why', just like a true profiler would.

'I think she's working for Vernon Sange. You've heard the rumours about his sphere of influence?'

He nodded.

'Dr Sange is a very persuasive person. Looks like he might even have some politicians in his corner.'

We clearly thought on the same track.

'The ones raising objections to his extradition? You think they're lackies?'

He shrugged.

'I'm not sure "lackey" is the word I'd use. But, yuh. Maybe.'

He tucked his hands into his armpits, made a *brr* noise.

'So, what are you going to do about this girl?'

I smiled to myself. A bullet straight to the heart of it.

'I'm going to confront her. Deliver a warning in my own inimitable style.'

'Cut off her writing arm?'

He was being flippant but he sounded worried. Poor Barnwell, he was so green.

'Something like that,' I said with a grin, teasing but part serious too.

There were plenty of things I'd like to do to Char, none of them friendly.

'Hmm.'

'What?'

'How do you know you wouldn't be playing right into her hands? If she is doing Dr Sange's bidding, her real focus could well be you rather than your friend. From what I've heard, he's a genius, brilliant at strategising. I mean, just look at how well he handled himself at the trial.'

'What are you saying?'

'That he'd know you'd go on the offensive if someone you cared about was being threatened. So maybe you should do the opposite.'

'Do nothing?'

He shrugged.

'Seems to me the last thing you want to be is predictable.'

CHAPTER 121

'Good news, Mac,' said Falcon the next morning.

I'd had another sleepless night, tossing and turning and agonising about Char. What was she going to do next? And how was I going to stop her if Barnwell was right that my best move was to do nothing?

By the time my alarm went off at zero six hundred, I was still at a loss.

I suppressed a yawn.

'It's time we caught a break,' I said to Falcon now. 'What's up?'

'We've finally got the go-ahead to search Sange's cell,' he said. 'The governor's watched the CCTV tapes. Reckons he can't see any sign of Sange stealing your wallet, which is the line we sold him. But as a gesture of goodwill he's agreed to arrange for the guards to toss his quarters.'

'That won't work. It needs to be me who goes in there.'

'Exactly what I told him, which is why it's taken so long to get his okay. He wasn't thrilled about you doing it.'

'But we've got the nod?'

'Yes, though not for today. Apparently, they have a tight schedule. Interfering with that causes all sorts of problems for the prisoners.'

Toss bucket.

'He says you can go up on Wednesday afternoon.'

So, two more days with little else to do apart from stressing about Char and what she was going to do next to Wolfie.

Back in the MIR –

'I'm going on a Starbucks run. Would you like a coffee, Ziba?'

Barnwell's face had a puppy-dog quality, all warm and open and eager to please.

I asked for a double espresso, dug out some coins.

'I'll get it,' he said, waving my money away. 'By the way, did you have any more thoughts about that girl? The one you were worried about . . .'

Still am.

'I think you're right. Much as I hate the idea, it's probably best to sit tight.'

He smiled.

'Maybe it's not as bad as you think.'

No, it's probably worse.

I watched him as he walked off. There was a bounce in his step. Seemed odd for a guy who'd just lost his mother, though maybe he was just less worn down by life than me.

Later, sipping my coffee, I started thinking I needed to bounce back too. Ever since I arrived back in the UK, I'd been playing other people's games. And I'd been losing, slipping down a snake every time I thought I was about to climb up a ladder.

I was done trying to roll a six. The time had come to change the rules, turn the serpent on the people I needed to beat.

I pulled out my phone and hit a number in my recently dialled list.

'Max,' I said. 'I've got another job for you.'

CHAPTER 122

Clockwork Café, Buckingham Palace Road

'What's going on?' Jack asked the following afternoon, shrugging off his heavy Barbour jacket and pulling up a pew opposite me.

I'd chosen a window table, deliberately in full view of the road and anyone who might be watching.

Wolfie looked like shit; dark circles under his eyes, blotchy skin, a five-day beard. The guy was falling apart. Time to stitch him back together.

'I've got a plan to clear your name.'

'What sort of plan?'

'I need you to call Char before I tell you.'

A shadow passed over his face.

'Jesus, this has got to stop. What is it with you and her?'

'Nothing,' I said, all innocent. 'I just think you should tell her you're here with me, and that I've come up with a way to sort everything out. She's worried about you. You need to keep her in the loop. It's only fair.'

'Hmm.'

'What's "hmm"? Send her a text at least. Say you'll call back in an hour. We'll be done by then.'

He shrugged.

'Fine.'

Once he'd put his phone away, I fed him a load of crap about how I was going to speak to his editor and give him an alibi. That I had a way to prove his computer was hacked. And that knobber Nigel was ready to back him up.

I spun it out as long as I could.

Then finally the SMS I'd been waiting for came through –

All done. Sending it now.

A moment later, Max's email pinged in my inbox. Attached was an MP4 file. I opened it up, smiled.

'Ghost in your flat still playing tricks on you?' I asked Jack.

He looked surprised. It was a bit of a non sequitur, for him at any rate.

'Shorty's gone missing now,' he answered, utterly miserable. His tortoise.

'He got out somehow. I don't understand it. His pen was empty but the door was locked.'

He shook his head, rubbed his bloodshot eyes.

'Char thinks I'm sleepwalking. My GP wants to put me on beta blockers.'

That bitch, she'd really done a number on him.

'You're not sleepwalking. And you don't need happy pills. Take a look at this.'

I passed him my phone, set the video to play and pointed out the time stamp. Five minutes ago.

Jack's mouth dropped open as he watched Charlotte stroll into his lounge, take Shorty out of her bag and put him back in his pen.

CHAPTER 123

Daily Telegraph Building

'Thank you for agreeing to meet with us,' I said to Wolfie's editor, taking my seat at the round table in her office. Jack sat next to me. Charlotte was opposite.

I could see why he'd have been attracted to her, and why he'd have let his guard down too. From an early age, we're conditioned to associate beauty with innocence. Perhaps it'd be different if Disney occasionally created frog-faced princesses. Though to be fair, Walt and Co aren't the only ones to blame. Children's literature is full of big-eyed damsels and ugly villains. We're suckered the moment we learn to read.

Charlotte was a slim brunette with flawless skin. Her nails were manicured and polished pink. Her navy trouser suit was nipped in at the waist and perfectly tailored. She'd done all the right things when she'd seen Jack – touching his arm, kissing his cheek. Made me want to puke.

'Are you okay, babe? What's going on?'

Then she'd clocked me and her expression changed, a sneering dimple appearing in each cheek.

Game on, bitch.

'My name's Ziba MacKenzie,' I told Jack's editor. 'I'm a behavioural analyst working with Scotland Yard.'

Nothing false about that, though I wasn't here on official business. And I was definitely playing up the police card.

Ever since the wallet incident, Charlotte had been using smoke and mirrors. Now it was my turn; Barnwell was right about that.

If I really were a cop, I'd have had to tread much more cautiously. Certainly, I couldn't have fed in misinformation to expose Charlotte. But as in the Gethen interview, I didn't feel bad about bending the rules.

We had Max's video footage clearly showing Charlotte in Jack's flat messing with his pet and then moving his furniture around. It was enough to convince him she was the 'ghost' who'd been screwing with his head and sabotaging his career. But his editor would need more. And in the absence of actual evidence I'd have to fabricate my own. Which is where my profile of Jack's lady friend came in.

The letter from her to Sange and her visits to Wakefield showed she had a deep-seated need for his approval. No way she'd have played her tricks on Jack without bragging to the Butcher about what she'd done.

But calling or texting would have been out. I'd seen first-hand how difficult it is to get a phone into that place. And any calls Sange made would be recorded. Email wasn't an option either, for the same reason, and snail mail would have taken too long.

Sange had friends on the inside, the email he'd sent me after my first visit showed that. But getting a message to him was different. Charlotte couldn't be sure who might intercept it.

Which led to the next point on the profile. She was highly intelligent. And despite craving the Butcher's respect, she had a massive superiority complex, evidenced by her performance over the missing wallet. The girl thought she was invincible.

Not for long.

I hadn't been able to decipher any hidden messages in her recent newspaper articles but inserting coded communication would not only fit with my reading of her, it would also be a brilliant way to get a message to Sange. If they were in cahoots, it's possible she knew about the PRK's code. And given her arrogance, it's likely she'd want to one-up him.

I had no proof. I hadn't found or cracked a code. But she didn't know that and as long as I could make her believe I had, I'd be able to sink her.

I turned to the editor, chose my words carefully.

'I realise you've been conducting your own internal enquiry into the article apparently uploaded by Mr Wolfe. However, given the link to the murder case we're investigating, we thought it necessary to examine the matter for ourselves.'

She looked surprised, but I could tell she was intrigued too.

'I'm afraid I don't quite understand the science,' I smiled, mimicking Barnwell when he'd told me about the email virus from Wakefield.

In this case, though, the reason I didn't understand the science was that there wasn't anything to understand.

'Our tech analysts have found compelling evidence to suggest that although Jack Wolfe's IP address and login details were used to upload the article, he wasn't in fact the person who posted it.'

I paused, looked pointedly at Charlotte, who was still sneering. She picked a stray hair off her jacket and flicked it away. Dismissive and disinterested.

She'd learn.

'We have video footage showing someone at Mr Wolfe's home address earlier today, without his consent or prior knowledge. We believe this same person broke into his premises to upload the article from his computer.'

Charlotte jerked to attention.

'Perhaps you'd like to see?'

The editor put on her glasses and held out a hand. I passed her my phone. She hit 'play'.

I watched, satisfied, as her mouth dropped open. She turned to Charlotte.

'Is that you?'

She was wearing a hat, but no other form of dress-up.

She clasped her hands in front of her on the table. The thumbs disappeared inside her fists. A classic sign of discomfort.

I smiled, enjoying myself. Under the table, Jack nudged my leg with his knee.

'Of course it's not me.'

The editor pursed her lips.

'It looks like you.'

'Why would I be in Jack's flat uninvited?' She glanced at me, smirked. 'If I wanted to go there, all I'd have to do is ask.'

She'd fluffed her lines. Better to have admitted she was there because they were seeing each other.

'And why would I have uploaded that article?'

My turn to smirk.

'Because you were doing a favour for your friend, Vernon Sange.' I opened a folder branded with the Scotland Yard logo and passed across printouts of her most recent articles. 'And you told him how well you were getting on.'

She squinted. Another sign of discomfort. Ha! I knew she wouldn't be able to resist boasting to him.

'That's ridiculous. These are newspaper articles, not letters.'

I sat up straight, lined up the final shot. My last bluff.

'Are you aware we have professional code breakers at Scotland Yard? They were very interested in these so-called articles of yours.

If I were you, I'd be thinking of putting a call in to my lawyer. With everything we've uncovered, you're going to need a good one.'

She sniffed, dabbed at her eyes. Little Miss Crocodile Tears was trying a new tack.

'You don't understand. I had no choice.'

I didn't give a shit about her phoney reasons. All that mattered to me was that I'd just cleared Jack's name. And holed this toe rag below the waterline.

The editor asked the two of them to stay back. As I came round the table to shake her hand, I dropped the card from Sange into Char's open bag.

On it were two new words:

I win.

CHAPTER 124

Her Majesty's Prison Service, HMP Wakefield

I was still smiling about how we'd nailed Charlotte as I arrived at Wakefield prison the next day.

Jack had called after the meeting to fill me in on what had gone down after I'd left.

Charlotte had been sacked and charged with breaking and entering, though the paper hadn't wanted to pursue criminal charges relating to the fake article. I suspect they didn't want any more negative press. Jack's reputation hadn't been the only one hit by her shenanigans.

And now I was about to get up to some shenanigans of my own.

'How nice to see you again, Ms MacKenzie.'

The governor of Wakefield prison stayed seated behind his desk as I entered his office, his goldfish eyes tracking my breasts.

I kept it civil, shook his hand. Resisted wiping my palm on the back of my trousers.

'Thank you for letting me come.'

He smiled; like his desk, it was too wide.

'You've met with Dr Sange, what, three times?' He knew exactly how often we'd met, each time we'd had to get his okay.

'Going in there on your own like that. You've got balls. Impressive for a woman.'

I glowered at him, fantasised about sending my elbow to his jaw.

'Smile, it's supposed to be a compliment.'

No one tells me what to do with my face, but he could make trouble for me if I answered the way I'd have liked. And we really needed that book.

'Is the cell ready for me to inspect? I'm keen to get back to London as soon as possible.'

'Of course. I'll take you down.'

Surely he had better things to do than play escort.

Sange's cage was at the far end of the corridor, well away from the general population. Inside was a low bunk and a table and chair, both bolted to the floor and piled high with books.

The governor unlocked the grills, swung the door open.

'Ladies first.'

Up close, he smelled of cologne and sweat. His nails were long like a woman's.

And he didn't show any sign of leaving.

CHAPTER 125

I knew what I was looking for was in one of Sange's piles of books, all paperbacks. Nothing hard or sharp would be allowed in here. Even the pens were felt-tipped.

I felt the governor's bulging eyes on my back. Hypothyroidism, probably. The guy could do with an iodine boost, I thought. A lesson on interacting with females, too.

Given the story we'd spun to get his okay for this, I couldn't zero straight in on the books without blowing a hole in our cover. The last thing I needed was him asking me to leave before I'd got what I came for.

I made a show of searching under Sange's mattress and bed, inside his pillow and the folds of his blanket. All the while, Governor Gobshite was watching my every move.

I moved to the books. Started flicking through them as though Sange might have concealed something between the pages.

The governor came over, stood very close.

'If you tell me what you're looking for, maybe I can help.'

No chance.

'That's very kind, but it's case sensitive. You know how these things are.'

The muscle by his eyes tensed. He didn't like my answer. And he didn't move away.

I had to sink this rat. Fast.

'Is that my phone buzzing?'

I pulled it out of my bag, turned away from him and pretended to check the screen.

'A message from the boss. Excuse me.'

I typed an SMS to Falcon, no acting this time.

Governor breathing down my neck. Need a decoy.

A minute later, Goldfish Eyes' pager went off.

He screwed up his face, looked concerned.

'Will you be all right here on your own for a minute? I need to deal with something. I'll send a guard along to wait with you.'

I finally gave him the smile he'd been after.

'Quite all right.'

With my shadow gone, I was free to search properly and it didn't take me long to find what I was after. There were three books of Catullus's poetry, but only one had an inscription in the front.

Domino meo, semper gratus

To my master, with gratitude.

It was the key. The next step was unlocking the code.

CHAPTER 126

M1 Motorway

My iPhone rang about an hour after I'd left the prison. Coming through Bluetooth I didn't immediately recognise the number, which put me on the back foot when I heard my mother's shrill voice at the end of the line.

With my head focused on Sange and the book code, she was the very last person I was expecting to hear from.

'I saw your name in the paper this morning. I didn't realise you were referring to the Pink Rose Killer when you called about sacrifices the other week.'

As she rambled on, it occurred to me that it had been seven days since I'd found that letter she'd written to my father and I still hadn't asked her about it. Not because I'd been busy, that was just an excuse. Fact is, I've spent so much of my life stuffing my feelings in the bottom drawer, I'm not very good at airing them.

But if I didn't tough it out now, I may never do it. While I couldn't exactly imagine Emmeline and I ever braiding each other's hair and swapping secrets, talking to her might at least bring us a little closer.

'I found something in one of *Bâbâ*'s books.'

I'd cut right through her monologue. She made a surprised noise, as though she'd forgotten I was there.

'It was a letter you wrote to him. I think you must have just found out you were pregnant. With me,' I added stupidly.

When my mother answered, she sounded embarrassed. She cleared her throat, made little coughing noises.

'Ah well, that was a long time ago. Another life.'

First Jack, now her. Trying to share my feelings wasn't going too well for me.

'It sounded like you wanted me.'

She sounded surprised.

'Of *course* I wanted you! Why would you think otherwise?'

Because you're practically a tundra, you're so damn cold.

'You packed me off to school pretty quick after *Bâbâ* died. I was the only kid who didn't come home during exeats. Your idea, not mine.'

'Ziba, I did that for you. I was a mess after your father passed, and I saw what his family's murder did to him. He was never the same afterwards. A child needs stability. Even I know that. I thought boarding school would give it to you. Living with your friends, midnight feasts.'

'It wasn't bloody Malory Towers, Emmeline.'

And I didn't have any friends. Didn't want any.

'If I didn't care, why would I keep all those clippings?'

'What clippings?'

'From the papers. Every time your name comes up, I cut the article out, put it in my box.'

That stumped me for a moment. But I wasn't letting her off that easy.

'What about after Duncan was killed? You didn't call for weeks. Never once came round to see how I was doing.'

'I didn't think you'd want me to. I thought you'd need your space.'

I sighed.

'I guess I did.'

When she spoke again, her tone was gentler. More motherly, whatever that means.

'Don't make the same mistake I did, Ziba. You're young. You shouldn't be alone.'

'I've got good at being by myself.'

She laughed.

'I used to say that too. You know, we're more alike than you think.'

'Funny, my friend Jack said the exact same thing.'

'Ah, Jack.'

'What's that supposed to mean?'

'Just another thing you do more than you think.'

I felt myself getting irritated.

'What is?'

'Talking about him.'

'Bullshit. I don't—'

'He won't wait for ever, Ziba.'

And that's all I heard in my head the rest of the way back.

CHAPTER 127

Suns will set and suns will rise again.
O D!
She was so young and PURE, just perfect for my purposes; going to the slaughter like a good little lamb. But now she is throat-slit and dead and all used up and I am lying awake thinking about where to shop next.
But O D, how silly of me. The details are what're important . . . how her blood geysered out of her throat.
How her lips twitched as I made the first cut, like she was trying to blow me a kiss. And maybe she was. Ha ha!
Call me up folks. 4.1 10-6.11-7.1116 20 21

Up on the screen in the briefing room were the first two letters from the PRK, as we still thought of him despite now knowing his real name. Next to it, a poem I'd found in the book I'd taken from Sange's cell at Wakefield.

Fourth line down was a line that echoed the perp's: *Suns may set, and suns may rise again.* Felip Dale had been playful when he substituted 'will' for 'may' in his version, showing there was no question about whether he would strike again. And also showing Sange where he needed to look for the key code. Catullus's poem, 'Let Us Live and Love':

> Let us live, my Les**b**ia, let us **love**,
>
> **and** all th**e** words of the old, and so moral,
>
> may they be worth less than nothing to us!
>
> **S**uns may se**t**, and suns may rise again:
>
> but when our brief **l**ight has set,
>
> night is one long everlasting sleep.
>
> Give me a tho**u**sand **k**iss**es**, a hundred more,
>
> another thousand, and another hundred,
>
> and, when we've counted up the many thousands,
>
> confuse them so as not to know them all,
>
> so that no enemy may cast an evil eye,
>
> by knowing that there were so many kisses.

I'd highlighted thirteen letters in bold. The first six spelled *blonde*. The next spelled *St Lukes*, the church where we'd found the most recent victim's body.

Sange had known her hair colour and where to find her because Felip Dale had told him.

'Note the position of each character,' I said. 'And how they relate to the numbers in the perp's letters.

'Take the first number string, for example: 4.1 10-6.11-7.1116 20 21

'The "s" of "St" is in line four, one in from the left. 4.1.

'The "t" is in the same line, ten letters in.

'Whenever the perp wants to indicate a new line, he inserts a dash. So the "L" for "Luke" is in line six, eleven words in. 6.11.'

Barnwell raised a hand.

'Sorry, I—'

Fingerling sneered.

'Did they not teach you code-breaking at Eton?'

A flush climbed up poor Barnwell's neck.

'I'm just a bit confused about something. I understand what you said before this, Ziba, about why the PRK would want to communicate with Dr Sange. How he idolised him and wanted his approval. And by boasting about what he'd done he thought he'd receive that.'

He rubbed his chin.

'What I don't understand is why he'd say anything about St Luke's. And I mean that's *all* he said in code, right? So there's got to be a point. Only I can't see what he'd get out of it.'

I smiled. So many people think profiling is about reading perps and predicting their future behaviour. But most of it is actually about asking questions, trying to put yourself inside an offender's head. Just like Barnwell was doing now. I knew I'd made the right call about him.

'Excellent point,' I said, looking pointedly at Fingerling. 'The conclusion I've come to is that Felip Dale dobbed the Butcher in out of spite. From what Sange has told me, I suspect he felt perversely angry that his idol didn't think he was good enough for his knife.

'However, over time he came to regret what he'd done, especially when he began his own spree, choosing victims because something about them suggested perfection. He started to see things

350

differently, came to realise that he and Sange had more in common than he'd thought.

'Giving his master, as he called him, information about his kills was his way of making up for what he'd done. A peace offering, if you like. Revealing where he was going to strike next was the closest thing they could get to a partnership.

'It did something else too. Unlike Sange's kills, the PRK's crimes have all been bloody and explosive, the manifestation of an unruly mind. I suspect he relies on his old teacher to vindicate and bring a measure of control to his acts.'

'He really said all that?'

I thought back to Vernon Sange's actual words:

No matter, we have made our peace since. The importance of perfection is clear to him now. He has the vindication he needs.

'Close enough,' I said. 'Now, who wants to hear how we're going to get the bastard?'

I pulled Fingerling aside after the briefing. I was through with diplomacy.

'You know, it wouldn't hurt you to ease up on Barnwell. He has just lost his mother.'

He looked at me like I was a moon chicken.

'What are you talking about, MacKenzie? The woman killed herself when he was eighteen. Painkillers in her Merlot, apparently. Any younger and he'd have been put in care.'

I didn't understand. If his mother was dead, why had he been leaving her that voicemail at the airport? And it was definitely her, he'd called her 'Mama'. Unless I'd misheard and jumped to conclusions. Maybe it was some other relative. That would at least explain the spring in his step the other day.

Wouldn't it?

CHAPTER 128

The Artist leans over the sacred hot spring on the site of the Roman temple to Minerva, goddess of wisdom and warfare.

The Great Bath at Aquae Sulis is a rectangular pool enclosed in a pillared courtyard, overlooked by statues of Roman soldiers wearing tunics, capes and *galeas*.

The water is a cloudy green. Steam rises off it in wisps and clouds. Tourists mill around, pointing smartphones and taking selfies. Only the Artist is quiet and contemplative; gazing at the holy waters, stroking the amulet round his neck.

He whispers a prayer, imploring, desperate for the goddess's favour.

The opus is failing, despite the perfect lips he collected from the last model. A deaf girl, someone who'd never heard gossip or cruelty. What came out of her mouth should have been divine, but still Mother hadn't said the words.

It's Medusa's fault. It must be.

'Philip?' she said, opening the front door after his visit to Scotland Yard. Never would call him by his new name.

Her papery palm shot to her mouth, her washed-out eyes watered.

'Oh my God. It's Lily, isn't it?'

'Yes,' the Artist said, drawing out the knife. 'That's right, Gorgon. I'm here about Mother.'

He raised his arm to strike. She whimpered, tried to block him with her liver-spotted hands.

Please—

But the artist stuck her through the neck before she could get the rest out.

He had to shove her out the way with his foot to get the door closed. Her eyes bulged. Blood bubbled out of her mouth. She gasped for air, grasped at his legs. The artist knelt down next to her and calmly began to saw as her airways constricted and failed.

Getting the snake head off her scrawny neck took for ever. He'd only just finished when he saw the police vans tearing down the road, sirens off. Eight officers leapt out, contained the property where he and Mother live. Not one of them thought to look across the street. When they knocked on the door during their house-to-house enquiries, he didn't open up.

There's no CCTV coverage on this part of the road. No witnesses to him coming round to Medusa's. No mobile phone in his pocket to emit a GPS signal.

No reason for them to storm in.

They bashed his front door in, though. He watched through Medusa's upstairs window as the battering ram came out, the 'bosher', and they barged through with their tasers at the ready. The rest of the cavalry arrived shortly afterwards in their Tyvek suits. CSI. CID. Then two men carried out a stretcher supporting a bulk covered with a sheet. The Artist watched from his hidden vantage point as the wind lifted the sheet momentarily, revealing the shape beneath.

They've got Mother!

He howled; a wild animal, the cry coming from deep inside. His whole body trembled, his lungs seemed to burst. He vomited again and again, collapsing to the floor, sweating and shaking. Vision blurred, mouth bilious.

All the signs and all the precautions he'd taken, and still he'd failed. The miracle would never happen now. He'd never hear her say it.

He stayed in the snake woman's lair; eye on the house, checking for updates on her laptop.

Finally, the sign came, the one he'd been waiting for without knowing he was waiting for anything. A coded message in the *Telegraph* online from his master, filling him with red-hot hope.

The miracle could still happen, he said. All the Artist had to do was go to the one Roman temple still intact in Britain. The city of Bath. Aquae Sulis. There he must beg Minerva to help him, just like Pygmalion had implored the goddess to grant him his wish.

He'd been so worried his master wouldn't forgive him for his betrayal all that time ago. The opus he was constructing was for himself, but describing the collections was for Dominus. A sacrifice of sorts. A way of begging forgiveness, of demonstrating he was worthy of his master's admiration.

The message shows it worked. The great man had gone to so much effort to save and protect him.

The Artist knows now he is not only forgiven, but loved too.

Filled with a peace he's never felt before, he approaches the water, closes his eyes, drops in his coin.

Immediately he feels a change in air pressure as the goddess approaches, her hand now on his shoulder, her breath warm on his skin.

He opens his eyes and turns round with a smile that quickly turns to stone as his arm is yanked up behind his back and a pair of metal handcuffs are snapped on to his wrists.

'Felip Dale, you're under arrest.'

DI Fingerling is speaking. Behind him, the profiler, Ziba MacKenzie, looks on and says something too. Though all the Artist hears is Mother. Not 'I love you', the words he's yearned his whole life to hear. But instead the ones she's said to him almost every day:

'What's wrong with you? This is all your fault.'

CHAPTER 129

Elstree Aerodrome, London

'Perfect weather,' said Jack, climbing into his plane, the Grumman Tiger he has a share in and won't ever shut up about. 'Can't believe how long it's been since I've got up. Bloody snow.'

He was flying me down to Le Touquet for lunch to celebrate the end of the case. It's kind of a tradition of ours, though I always have to knock back a travel-sick pill before we go. The ride's never smooth, whatever he says.

He passed me a set of ear defenders, checked they were switched on. Then opened his log book and made some notes.

'It shouldn't take more than fifty minutes to get there. I booked us a table at *Le Jardin*. They do this amazing turbot with pesto and ratatouille, you'll love it. And we can walk over to *Au Chat Bleu* for pâtes de fruits afterwards.'

I smiled. Jack loves his food. I don't know where he puts it, though. There's not an ounce of fat on him.

He reminded me how to open the door in an emergency and how to get to the raft if we needed it. Same spiel as usual. I rolled my eyes at him. He grinned back.

'Right, let's get out of here.'

Cue to fasten seatbelts, only mine had been massively over-extended. Whoever had sat here last clearly liked their food too. I tried to tighten it but the strap wouldn't budge.

'Give me a hand, would you?' I said, frustrated.

'So, you can ask for help!'

'Piss off, Wolfie.'

He laughed and twisted round to face me. The cockpit was small, we were very close.

'It's caught. Give me a second.'

He started messing around with the strap, his arms brushing against me as he did. My mother's words suddenly back in my head. *He won't wait for ever, Ziba.*

'Ha, got it! There we go!'

He pulled the strap tight, straightened up, smiled at me. We were very close.

A current held us together. I spoke without thinking.

'Do you ever think about . . . us?'

He hesitated, then –

'All the time,' he said.

Last time we'd sat like this, we'd been in his car. I'd been the one to turn away. This time I stayed put. Nose to nose. Eyeball to eyeball. Then very slowly lip to lip.

A hot wave crashed through me, my stomach carouselled. It was happening.

His mouth was firm, his face warm and scratchy. He tasted of caramel, smelled like biscuits. I pulled him closer, pressed my lips harder to his, our mouths moving more urgently now. Tongues. Teeth. Hungry.

His hands in my hair, mine in his. No space between us.

I pulled back, lowered my head. Guilty.

'I'm so sorry about everything you went through, Jack. All those calls I missed. I should have been there for you, from the start.'

'You were there for me at the end, that's what counts.'

He kissed me again, more gently this time. Then he started the engine and set the propeller spinning.

Minutes later we were airborne.

CHAPTER 130

'No two killers are the same. Which is why we can't expect to lure them all with the same bait. Only by thinking like them can we ever hope to catch them.'

I surveyed the lecture theatre, standing at the same podium I'd stood at all that time ago when Barnwell had burst into the auditorium, summoning me back to London. A lot had changed since then.

I wasn't fighting off my black dog. My mother and I were speaking to each other more than once in a while. And while Duncan was still large in my thoughts, always would be, for the first time since he died I could imagine being happy with someone else. Really happy.

I glanced at my notes then back up at the crowd.

'When I was here before, I asked "What makes monsters?" Any ideas?'

A jungle of hands shot up. New Agent Trainees are nothing if not keen. No one said what I was thinking, though. That it takes a perfect storm. Personality. Circumstances. Trigger. People aren't born evil, they become it, as the PRK had shown.

I'd interviewed Felip Dale after he was charged.

I understood his signature by then, what had precipitated his spree, Sange's part in it. But as he talked, I learned more about the fantasy world he was inhabiting. I'd already worked out he was trying to recreate an improved version of his mother, one he could control. What I hadn't realised was that what he wanted most of all from this new model was Lily Dale's love.

Or that he hadn't actually taken on board the fact she was dead.

'You're lying,' he said, fists thumping on the table, face tight and angry. 'She's sick, that's all. She talks to me all the time.'

I moved on; there was no need to labour the point. I didn't want Dale clamming up, I wanted to know what had made him rotten.

I didn't have to push hard. Like so many other killers I've interviewed, he wanted to talk, wanted to understand himself as much as I did.

I asked why he'd joined the police.

'Was murder always on your agenda? Did you think a uniform would help you get away with it?'

He shook his head. His voice was flat and expressionless.

'Society needs people like me to impose order.'

So, he killed because he wanted to exert power over an existence he felt helpless in. Same as every other serial killer, despite his need to feel unique.

'Have you always felt out of control, Felip?'

He shot an answer back. He'd obviously thought a lot about it.

'Mother's best friend turned her against me the moment I was born, always gossiping about me, seeing the worst, using the fact Mother's relatives were back in the States and she had no one here. Medusa was an evil Gorgon! Without her around, things would have been different. Mother and I would have had a chance.'

He was talking about the woman from across the street. The true target of his rage. Not a love interest who'd shunned him, as I'd first thought when I presented the initial profile, but a neighbour who'd caused him to be rejected by the only family he had.

'So, you murdered her because she got between you and your mum?'

He shrugged.

'She deserved to die.'

His voice was monotone, his gaze stony.

'Did she?'

A switch flipped. Diffident to belligerent. It didn't take much.

'You're annoying me now.'

'Why's that?'

'Because you're suggesting Medusa didn't deserve what she got.'

'Am I saying that? Or are you?'

His eyes flashed.

'You think you're so clever, don't you?'

'I think it's difficult for you to accept responsibility for the things that happened to you. That it's much easier to blame other people.'

Dale's jaw clenched. He banged his fists on the table.

'Mother locked me in my room every night while she fucked strangers. Did you know that?'

I didn't. But I knew a few other things about him. A picture started to form. Even when a person thinks they're telling you the whole story, they miss bits out. They can't help it. We all have filters, a narrative we tell ourselves.

'Why did she shut you in your room, Felip?'

'To keep me away.'

'Was that because she was frightened of you?'

He smirked.

'Yes.'

'Why was she frightened of you?'

The smirk broadened.

'Because of the way I got rid of her boyfriends.'

'How did you do that?'

'I'd watch her sleeping. Then wake them up by putting a scalpel to their throats.'

A link to his series killings. A direct evolution.

'Why did you do that?'

No judgement, no challenge. The only way to get an honest answer.

He shrugged.

'I didn't like them. They were loud, they got in the way.'

'So that's when she started locking you in your room?'

'I still got rid of them, though.'

He smiled, remembering.

'How?' I said again, working to keep my tone soft.

'I screamed through the walls, loud as I could, *Get away from my mother. I'm going to kill you.*'

'You didn't like the idea of her being with anyone else?'

'Why would I? Medusa was the worst, though.'

'How so?'

'She made Mother think there was something wrong with me, saw malice in everything I did. Like when I wet the bed. She told Mother I did it on purpose but I didn't. It's not nice waking up soaked in urine. I used not to drink anything from lunchtime onwards so my bladder would be empty at night. But it didn't work, nothing did.'

'Did your mother punish you when you wet the bed?'

He answered in his monotone matter-of-fact voice.

'She rubbed my face in the sheets. Medusa said I needed a firm hand. It was all her idea.'

'Did she hit you too?'

He nodded.

'She stopped when I got bigger than her. Maybe she thought I'd hit her back. I wouldn't have, though. It's wrong to hit women, only weak men do that.'

It would have been noble had he not murdered six girls and cut up their faces.

'Nothing I did was ever good enough for Mother. Even getting into Oxford. I thought she'd be proud but she laid into me when I showed her the letter, called me stuck-up. Thought I was trying to make out I was better than her.'

No wonder he was so susceptible to Sange's flattery; his approval would have been intoxicating for a person so isolated and starved of affection. It would never have occurred to him that he was being manipulated.

As a behavioural analyst, I'm always looking for answers. Why does a person do this? What makes them say that?

Lily Dale's behaviour was certainly abusive. But it seemed to me her actions were predicated less on hatred than on fear. She was scared of her child and her response was to try and contain him with harsh discipline.

Waking up in the middle of the night to find him standing over her boyfriends with a knife must have been terrifying. But locking him in his room didn't make him any safer to have around. If anything, it made him more dangerous in the long run.

Much has been written about Beth Thomas, a kid who fantasised about murdering her parents, tortured the family pet and killed a nest of baby birds. But unlike Dale, she wasn't pushed away by her family. Instead, she received professional support to develop empathy. Now an adult, she works as a nurse for children suffering from Reactive Attachment Disorder.

I couldn't help wondering whether Dale might have turned out differently if he'd got the aid he so clearly needed. Might he even have ended up like Beth, helping rather than hurting people?

The human heart is dark and twisted, I know that as well as anyone. But even I have trouble accepting some people just can't be saved.

I also had trouble getting my head round why Dale stayed with his mother all those years. The woman made his life miserable. So why hadn't he left?

When I asked him, he didn't even pause to think.

'My father left because of me. She said he couldn't take my crying all the time. I was the reason she was all alone. So it was my job to look after her. She needed me.'

For a man supposedly devoid of empathy, it was a pretty empathetic thing to say.

CHAPTER 131

I was just about to share the case with the trainees when the door to the auditorium swung open. Detective Barnwell strode in, accompanied by a guy from the Behavioral Analysis Unit. Though this time, instead of a slept-in suit, he was wearing the same FBI polo shirt and khakis as everyone else.

I had a feeling Quantico would bring out the best in him and, unlike Nigel Fingerling, the women here would love his accent. Which is why I'd put in a call to the Director and got him a place on the program.

'I'm sorry to interrupt.'

The same words he'd used before, only now there was a faint smile on his lips, one he was clearly trying to hide. His face wasn't flushed, though; he wasn't embarrassed, then. Rather, he was pleased, but for some reason he didn't want anyone to notice.

'It's about Dr Sange. Something's happened.'

The lecture hall went quiet, a hundred heads swivelled round. Was this to do with Sange's arraignment next week?

I started to smile too, then stopped. Did taking pleasure in the Butcher's inevitable death sentence put me on a par with him? If so, perhaps I'd posed the wrong question before. Instead of asking where evil comes from, maybe I should have asked whether there's potential for it in all of us.

Barnwell continued speaking, his plummy voice carrying across the theatre just like it had the day he flew in to ask for my help profiling the PRK.

It took a moment for the horror of his words to sink in, and the realisation that followed. Nothing else explained that secret smile on his face, so out of place with the appalling news he'd just delivered.

Mother fuck, was *this* what he was so pleased about? All the niggling doubts I'd been suppressing in London came gasping to the surface. The way, unlike the rest of us, he always referred to Sange deferentially as 'Dr'. His failure to pick up on the visit of Butcher's minion, Char, to Wakefield. And that bizarre business with the phone call to his mother.

After I'd finished briefing the team about the PRK's code at Scotland Yard, I'd asked him who he'd been speaking to at the airport, given I now knew his mother had been dead for years. His grandmother, he told me.

Only it didn't make sense.

'But you called her Mama,' I said.

'It's a nickname,' he'd answered quickly enough. Though his eyes had darted to the side and his face flushed.

Not seeing any reason for him to lie, I'd put his physical response down to discomfort, figured his mother was a touchy subject. Now I thought differently. It had been a ruse to get me to like him and he'd been tripped up.

My stomach sickened as I nuked it out.

He lobbied me big time to let him be the one to bring you back from Quantico. Quite the little groupie you've got yourself there.

What if Fingerling had got it wrong too? What if it wasn't me he admired, what if it was Vernon Sange?

I'd thought he was interested in profiling but perhaps he was just interested in profiling me. Was that why he'd pressured

Fingerling to let him collect me from Quantico, so he could establish a relationship between us? And was he somehow passing on the information he learned to the Butcher?

No way of knowing for sure, or how he'd done it, but it would explain why Sange hadn't bought my line about not being into Wolfie.

Standing at the podium, I watched his mouth move as he relayed the details of the episode that had apparently unfolded just an hour ago. And the more I analysed his non-verbals, the clearer the picture became. Unlike everyone else in the audience, whose mouths were part open in shock, Barnwell wasn't reeling over what the Butcher had done. He was glowing with excitement.

He'd been a junior on the Sange investigation. Was he behind the missing evidence too, the reason the monster nearly got off? And if so, what else had he done?

The guy had pulled a hood over my eyes but ultimately I was the reason his plan had worked.

I'd been so focused on my dislike of Nigel Fingerling that I'd gone out of my way to protect and promote the one other person he picked on constantly. It was a massive error.

I'd always known Sange had friends in high places.

What I hadn't known was one of them would ever get this close to me.

Up on the stage, I tried to speak but no words came out, my voice was smothered. Like the Butcher's victims, his hand was over my mouth. And I was rendered mute.

CHAPTER 132

Miami Dade County Pretrial Detention Center, Florida

The corrections officer pulls back the heavy barred door and stands on the threshold of Dr Sange's cell. In his belt is a stick, taser and cuffs. In his hand, a set of keys.

He glances quickly over his shoulder and then back at the inmate in the tangerine jumpsuit.

Dr Sange is writing something on the wall in felt-tip pen. There's a bloodstain of red ink on his long white fingers, a satisfied look on his film-star face.

'We need to hurry,' the corrections officer says, voice quavering. 'Before it's too late.'

He's breathing hard, blinking fast. Not like Dr Sange, whose pulse is ten beats below normal.

As they undress and swap clothes, the officer sneaks a peak at the famous inmate — his chest broad, his muscles well developed despite his incarceration and packaged food diet.

'Thank you, Mathew,' Dr Sange says, in a date-shake voice, putting on the officer's cap and cuffing his wrist to the bunk. 'I won't forget the service you and your friends have done for me.'

The officer simpers but his words are cut off by the hand he didn't see coming. It grips his throat tighter and tighter as he struggles for breath, while the other arm crushes his chest in an iron vice.

What's happening?

A spreading flower of urine soaks his groin. His fingers tingle and numb before he can react and fight back. His muscles weaken, his vision blurs. His eyes bulge and pop. And then his heart stops.

Dr Sange applies three precisely aimed blows to the officer's face with the baton so that his features are turned to meat — torn flesh, a bloody pulp of gristle and sinew. Unrecognisable.

He swallows a yawn, wipes off the stick on the bunk and threads it into his belt beside the taser. His heart rate is 65 bpm.

That should buy some time, he thinks.

As he walks out of the door, he allows himself a last look at his mural.

To my fiercest pupil —

1.3 16 37-2.23 40 51-3.36 50-6.31 55-8.6-9.7 12 17 42-10.43-11.29 34 43-12.2 3-13.6

He smiles. Round three.

CHAPTER 133

Blomfield Villas, London

News of the Butcher's escape set off an explosion in the media. A week on and still nobody understood how he'd done it or where he'd gone.

One of the world's most dangerous men had disappeared without a trace. He could be anywhere.

I dropped my luggage inside my front door and added the mail from downstairs to the skyscraper of post on the hall table.

No more excuses, I thought, scooping it up.

The white envelope was near the bottom of the pile, delivered during my first trip to Quantico, my name printed across the front in impeccable penmanship.

Inside was a handwritten note, just two lines long:

The die is still rolling, Ziba.

And the next move is mine.

ACKNOWLEDGMENTS

Ziba and I have a fantastic team behind us. As she'd say, these guys have our six:

My brilliant agent, Alice Lutyens – Ziba's first and fiercest champion. A force of nature and definitely one of the funniest people I know.

The tireless team at Thomas and Mercer, especially my editor, Jack Butler, whose enthusiasm and razor-sharp insight takes Ziba's adventures to whole new levels. Thank you for believing in me. I can't wait to continue the journey with you!

My developmental editor, Martin Toseland, who helped hone Ziba's character when she was just an ass-kicking figment of my overactive imagination and who continues to work his magic three books in.

The experts. The Special Forces contact I'm not allowed to name but to whom I owe a huge debt of gratitude. My police contact, Graham Bartlett, who keeps my writing on the 'straight and narrow'. If there's any deviation from reality, I take full blame. Anthony Buss for sharing the brilliant anecdotes from his CID days. And Chris Wood for filling in the many gaps in my Latin knowledge.

My family, a long list of awesome people topped by the triumvirate, Tim, Max and Joey, who fill my house with noise and naughtiness. And my mother and father, Martin and Carolyn, they don't make parents more supportive than you!

All my friends who keep me sane, special shout out to my co-hosts on the *Crime Girl Gang* podcast – the seriously fab Niki Mackay and Elle Croft.

And finally YOU – my wonderful readers. I've been awed by your response to Ziba. Seriously, you make everything worth it – thank you!

There are lots of ways to keep in touch. Via:

- **Twitter @VictoriaSelman**
- **My newsletter for previews and giveaways. Sign up at VictoriaSelmanAuthor.com**
- **My Amazon author page**

And if you like true crime podcasts, check out *Crime Girl Gang*, in which my co-hosts and I examine real-life cold cases and then 'solve' them from a fictional perspective.

ABOUT THE AUTHOR

Photo © 2018 Andrew Marshall

After graduating from Oxford University, Victoria Selman studied Creative Writing at the City Lit and wrote for the *Ham & High* and *Daily Express* newspapers. In 2013 she won the Full Stop Short Story Prize and her first novel, *Blood for Blood*, was shortlisted for the 2017 Debut Dagger Award. Victoria lives in London with her husband and two sons.